DOUBLE CROSSED

BARRY LIDSTONE

Tellwell Talent
www.tellwell.ca

ISBN
978-0-2288-2858-7 (Hardcover)
978-0-2288-2857-0 (Paperback)
978-0-2288-2859-4 (eBook)

There are many people who helped me put this novel together, and I thank them all, but first and foremost, I would like to thank my wife Wendy. Although she did not have a say in the content of this novel—she has not read it as of its printing—Wendy was always there to encourage me and give me the time needed to accomplish what I did. Then there was Rob. Always there with a quick stroke of the pen and a quick reply, his input was much appreciated. Then there was Warren, a professional editor who gave me many different insights as to how I should proceed. Thanks Warren.

TABLE OF CONTENTS

PRELUDE

It had only been six weeks, and already I was sick of the place. Well, not really sick, but somewhat depressed.

Galt is an unincorporated community in Kittitas County, Washington, on Interstate 90 about an hour out of Seattle, just west of Galt Lake and the state park, in the Yakima River Valley. It's small, about eight hundred folks, a number of businesses that have been boarded up for years, and the remainder struggling to stay afloat. Not much going on here till I showed up.

In the summer of 2019, it was home to an outlaw motorcycle gang that went by the name of the Horse's Ass. Their patch was a horse's ass strategically placed over the eye of a horse's skull. It seemed a little ridiculous, but what the heck. Some people say stupid things, others do stupid things. I think these clowns were going to do both, and if my hunch was right, we were both in for a lot of trouble.

When I heard the name and had it explained to me, it still didn't make any sense. How could it? Anyone picking a name like the Horse's Ass must have been a little demented. Who knows? The point is, they had been dug in at Galt for just over three years when the DEA approached me, in January of 2019, and offered me a gig where I could maybe do some good and flex some of the skills I couldn't otherwise legally flex.

I'd walked away from the Navy SEALS in October of 2018, four months after my wife passed away from an aggressive cancer, that basically ate her alive and me too. She was a great lady. We had no kids but spent every second we could together. I was no good after that. In fact, I was an obnoxious menace. So, when I say, "I walked away," well, let's just say it was a mutual decision, and leave it at that.

I don't know how they found me, the DEA, or who they talked to, but the guy they sent out after me, an agent by the name of Tony, had my number and knew all the right buttons to press. I was exactly what they were looking for. I wouldn't even have to use an alias. My background was perfect. A big, colored, burnt-out ex-SEAL, with PTSD. Not severe, but severe enough to keep reminding me of my past. A chip on my shoulder and an axe to grind. I was already a biker and mechanic, had no family to speak of, and most of my close friends had been other SEALS, and those relationships were a little strained now. After all, I did leave my team.

Anyway, after a few months of training (if you could call it that), I was installed at the edge of the Cascade Mountains, making myself known in Galt. It didn't take long before I had reason to recognize some of the names, I knew from my DEA briefings, and some of those boys were aware of me too. A badass bunch of guys, or at least that is what I was told. I had a bungalow on Carson Road and was making noise around town about opening a garage somewhere.

The Fourth of July had fallen on Thursday, and Tuesday would be the first anniversary of Ashley's death. It was Saturday morning and I had awoken to a beautiful day except for my obnoxious neighbor two houses down, yelling obscenities at his wife. The coffee, the quietness of my surrounding's—except for Joe's mouth—and the Cascades in the distance were adding up to a great day, until two Harleys roared by. I knew town would be thick with locals gearing up for President Winthrop's rally in Missoula the next day. I was considering joining them for some fun, but my heart wasn't in it. Hadn't been for a couple of weeks now. I was getting cagey for something a little heavier and wondering if undercover was ever going to scratch that itch.

I was about to get up and grab another coffee when my burner went off. The number that came up was unlisted, but I knew who it was. Tony.

Half an hour later I was tearing out of Galt on my way to Boise, where I'd met with Tony and some other DEA boys for a rundown on a potential op in Venezuela; SEAL-type stuff involving a lab in the jungle that was supplying groups like the Horse's Ass with product.

After the Boise meeting, assuming I bit on the op, I'd hit Vegas for a few days, and wait for the DEA to connect any dots that needed connecting.

I hadn't let Tony know over the phone, of course, but I was already sold on the jungle op. I was glad that I would be able to spend Tuesday in Vegas. Maybe an extra drink or two wouldn't hurt either.

Galt and the boys would still be there when I got back.

PART ONE

CHAPTER

July 15, 2019 (02:10) – Venezuelan Waters [8' 37' 05" N, 60' 31' 07" W]

The throaty roar from the engines of the DEA boat that had dropped me off, had all but vanished now, as they headed out into the Atlantic. I was in the water about five miles out, just off the southern edge of the Orinoco Delta where Boca Grande empties into the Atlantic, about halfway between Isla Terceira and Punta Barima. I had already started kicking my way to shore. My exact landing site was to be Estado Delta Amacuro. As the shore got closer, I needed to be certain there were not some bad dudes hiding, just waiting for their opportunity. Even at one mile out, it only took one, sharp eye, to spell disaster. Feeling confident, I slowly started kicking again, dragging my gear bobbing in the surf behind me as I headed for shore.

The surf was high, and the noise was loud. In the distance I could see fairly large rollers pounding on the beach. I hoped it was a sandy beach I was headed for. If rocky, not too rocky, as rocks could be slippery, gathering seaweed and sand, hindering my progress. The noise of the surf and the offshore wind gave me a great advantage, but caution was still in order. I took my M4 from its case and chambered a round with the safety on.

It was a moonless night, and the darkness at this point was to my advantage. I stopped five hundred yards from shore and removed my night vision monocular from one of the waterproof bags. Carefully, not to miss anything, I swept the shoreline and adjoining foliage, back and forth, back and forth, then I laid low bobbing in the water for five minutes, looking, listening and watching. At one point, I thought I saw movement but couldn't detect anything through my monocular, so I decided it was possibly birds or other animals being disturbed by some nocturnal predator.

I cautiously swam forward, and if by magic, as I neared the sandy shore, the rollers subsided giving me an easy release through the waist high water. I silently waded out of the water and was on full alert as I ran the last hundred feet to a grove of trees, which would hopefully give me cover. Next to the grove of trees, there was an overhang of rock with a fairly large stump in front of it—something washed up by a previous surf. This is where I holed up for another few minutes, looking and listening. Once again, senses on high alert, I thought I heard sounds in the distance muffled by the pounding surf. I climbed over the rock, keeping my head low, and made my way into another grove of trees, looking, listening, blending in—not moving at times and watching for the slightest movement. I lay there for ten minutes but even with my night goggles on, nothing sprang out. In the distance, I could see scrub brush for a good half a mile before the lush green jungle started. This I needed to cross before dawn. Under the grove of trees, I removed my dry suit, and buried it with my flippers, in case I needed them on my return, and then I prepared to go. My plan was to head south about fifty miles through the Imataca Forest Reserve crossing into Estado Bolivar near the Venezuela–Guyana border and follow the trails from there.

Compass out, leaving the beach, the trail was good and wide, not some goat trail. I quickly left the scrub and entered the jungle. In some place's overhead, the jungle had escaped to the other side of the trail, causing dark areas that slowed my progress. Good, because they somewhat hid me, and bad because they hid anyone else.

As dawn drew closer, the monkeys became noisy, the birds entertaining, and the snakes plentiful. Coming to a sharp corner in the path, I stopped suddenly. I smelt cigarette smoke, and then I heard them. Gunmen. How many at this point I didn't know and didn't want to find out the hard way. I abruptly and quietly turned around and hurried back down the trail to where I had seen a small indent, I could hide in. Small but adequate. The indent turned into a side trail, and then my plans suddenly changed.

Looking back through gaps in the jungle foliage about forty feet away, I could see a lone gunman meandering down the main trail and walking toward me. Moving cautiously, so as not to make the slightest noise and to give me more maneuverability, I silently removed all my extra gear and laid it on the ground. After the gunman strolled by, I crept out of my hiding spot, and without making a sound, I quickly stepped up behind him. With one swift move his neck was broken. I dragged him into my hiding spot and removed his grimy shirt, pants, and headgear. I noticed his shirt had a special patch on it, which might make it easier for me to pass through the troops sleeping on the trail. The best time to walk through a camp would be just before sunrise, and it appeared, I was going to be right on time. I had to get down the trail and get down it now.

I donned the gunman's clothes and started down the path. As I neared the men sleeping on the path, I could see this was a good choice their leader had made. The path was significantly wider here and allowed for his men to stretch fully out.

It looked like fifteen well-armed gunmen were lying here, most were asleep. As I approached, my senses were on high alert. Weaving and stepping over sleeping bodies I was almost upon the last guy when someone from behind whispered something. I almost tripped over him but kept my composure, and with a slight backward wave kept walking. Around the first bend and out of sight, I started running, then slowed to a jog. I needed distance. It was not in the book to run down a trail, but I figured that there would not be any more gunmen for some time, or at least that was what I was hoping. The trail wasn't too bad—narrow in some places with growth that needed to be pushed out of the way to enable a person to pass through, and wider in other spots, with a high, dense canopy that looked like it was trying to reach the heavens above.

I could see that too much haste could be disastrous with the many twists and bends in the narrow trail not allowing a person, in some places, to see very far ahead. I slowed down. Twice I heard or smelled smoke from a group of gunmen coming, and both times I was able to quickly backtrack and find a spot that let me blend into my surroundings. At three in the afternoon, I started running into what looked like booby traps, but found out they were only dummies to scare off any unsuspecting intruders. Sleeping in the jungle is not one of the most pleasant experiences with bugs and snakes galore; however, with my exhaustive previous training, a night hideout that would all but conceal me from the enemy was not difficult. I chose to sleep on the ground. This would be one of many nights.

Knowing I was nearing the lab, I needed some sleep to put my senses on high alert for the task ahead. I forced my way into the jungle again, where I found a space big enough to accept my large body. Taping my pant legs to my boots, sleeves to my wrists, shirt to my neck, gloves on my hands, and a breathable cover over my head, I was ready for sleep. Hopefully this would keep all intruders away from my bare sensitive skin. Waking up at 05:00 with what appeared to be sunrise, I took my facial cover off, removed my gloves, removed the tape from my arms, legs, and the shirt to my neck and started looking for spiders or other creatures that may have tried for a warm spot to spend the evening. Finding none, I rolled up my bedroll and stowed it away.

The sound of monkeys swinging from branch to branch, birds squawking, and the sound of a dog barking off in the distance warned me that the lab was near. After checking my compass, I quietly crept out of my hiding place and onto the path, where I walked very cautiously, looking and listening for any different sounds or movements not normal to the jungle. Once again, I stopped and listened, then checked all my gear to make sure everything was in its correct place with easy access.

Off in the distance I could hear different sounds piercing the quietude of the jungle, which were normal; it was the dog that worried me. I was not in a rush as I knew lookouts would be posted at regular intervals along the way, hidden in the jungle barely off the trodden path and hopefully smoking a cigarette.

The path at this point was close to four feet wide with branches and foliage jutting out from the jungle looking for freedom from the dense growth that surrounded everything.

I was walking very slowly listening and trying to get a feel of my surroundings when, without warning, not thirty feet in front of me, appeared two gunmen meandering down the trail. Luckily headed in the same direction that I was. I decided to hang back and follow the two gunmen to the compound, as they would be greeted by other sentries giving their hidden positions away. As luck would have it, the first two gunmen were met by other sentries, and quite a contingent had gathered and was entering the compound. I hung back, waiting to see if there would be any guards leaving the compound before I started formalizing my plan to enter.

Off in the distance were two very large structures. Both were made out of rough sawn planks with pitched thatched roofs. No windows or doors visible. What looked like a smaller open sided building built on stilts, with many antennas protruding from the roof was standing in the middle of the compound. There was a dirt path meandering through the compound with heavily armed guards walking in pairs along the paths talking and paying attention to no one or anything in particular. The building on stilts was obviously the command post, and at the moment housing two guards, smoking and occasionally glancing at a bay of computer screens. My plan was to try to ignite two of the buildings hoping that those two buildings would ignite the others.

I saw what looked like a small clearing off the main path. Crawling into it, I dropped my gear and took out my binoculars.

It was very quiet with no movement or sound coming from the compound, almost eerie. I opened my small, black, three-pound briefcase and very carefully extracted my other set of eyes. Carefully setting it on the ground, I fixed in place the four sets of rotors, connected the required wiring, and tested the battery. All looked good.

The KOP-5000 drone was one-of-a-kind. This was going to be its first jungle test. Weighing less than a pound and a half it was capable of carrying an extremely high definition camera and all the electronics required to operate the drone, the camera, and other information it was programmed to gather. It came with a small touchscreen, and once airborne it was super quiet, could reach heights of four thousand feet, could not readily be detected, and could hover or do slow circles around its programmed GPS coordinate. The battery had a running time of 35 minutes and upon running low, it would automatically return to its takeoff location or any other location programmed into it. The camera would send down colored pictures to my screen and also to the satellites overhead, that it was connected to. It was equipped with heat sensors and gathered other electronic information I was not involved with. It relayed this to the satellites overhead also.

Programming completed, I turned on the KOP-5000, and it was airborne. Hovering just under the canopy I flipped the camera to its night vision, and it showed that the building in front of me and its twin had sloped roofs with no access points except from the path where they each had a single door. There was another large building some distance away which I could not see from my location, and this must be the lab and storage facilities. As I turned the camera around, I saw the command hut and counted a total of eight guards walking the property with no sense of urgency or discipline. I needed to take a closer look at the command hut, so I brought the drone down under the jungle canopy.

As it came below the canopy, I could see the guards. They seemed to be very busy smoking and meandering down the paths paying attention to no one in particular. One hundred and sixty feet up, the drone was almost silent and virtually impossible to see especially on a dark night like tonight. I zoomed the camera in on the command hut and saw two guards dressed in fatigues. One was sitting looking at a set of monitors and the other doing paperwork. They were armed and looked like two very mean commandos.

I swung the camera around and saw the door I needed to enter on the first building. A few hundred feet down I could see the river that was on my map as well as the actual factory. There were many people coming and going and heading towards the river, loading many small boats tied to a makeshift wharf. I positioned the drone at a higher altitude for a further overall view until I had a good sense of the layout. Then it was time to bring the drone home. With the drone stowed, it was time to take out the lab's security cameras. I had noticed three on the adjoining buildings, but there might still be more. I needed all of them taken care of. I could've programmed the drone to do this job as it flew past the cameras, but it would take minutes away from its flying time, which I figured I might need later.

Taking out a remote-controlled deactivation device, I turned it on and waited for the green light to start blinking, signaling that it had located the camera database. Programming the cameras to cancel their feedback for forty minutes, but to still run the previous forty minutes of film, was not going to be a problem. Part of my university education before becoming a Navy SEAL was two years of electrical engineering. My specialty was in research and development where I became a proficient expert in the latest state-of-the-art electronics.

It was time to get to work. I slid through the jungle like a snake, head low, crawling slithering and twisting my body towards the first building, keeping in the shadows where possible, and staying out of the range of the high beam searchlights. There were no windows or doors on this end or the sides of either building. The sides were covered with overlapping wooden planks designed to keep the monsoons out.

Normally a lab would hire three or four manufacturing workers who could produce over four tons of cocaine a week. The others would be guards, loaders, mules, and stackers. This lab, my report said, was one of the highest producing labs in the region.

Crawling to the building closest to the edge of the jungle, I eased myself along the back wall listening for any unusual sounds or smells. When I reached the corner, I cautiously peered around for a quick glance to investigate a glimmer I had seen from the drone.

My heart skipped a few beats. The two buildings were not sixty feet apart as first thought, but only forty-five feet and the adjoining building was positioned about fifteen feet forward. Between the two buildings was what looked like a stagnant pond. That's why they had no security guards watching between the buildings, no one in their right mind would go near that water.

As I drew closer, I could see and smell that it was indeed a cesspool. The drone had shown me that there was no other possible way to enter the compound except the way the guards had entered, but that was definitely an unlikely choice. I had seen sleeping accommodations just inside the compound near the entrance point. On the far side of the pond was a slight raised section of ground growing scrub bush. If I made it that far it would give me some cover.

I squatted, watching the guards, and decided this might be harder than I thought. The guards sauntered by paying no attention to the cesspool I was hiding behind, but I would be in the open while crossing it.

Returning to the shadows, I laid out my gear remembering the crap I had to crawl through. One item I was thankful for was a waterproof outfit which should keep me dry and clean. I made sure all the gear was firmly attached to my belt with my throwing knife in my left hand and gun in the right. It really didn't matter which hand held which, for I was ambidextrous and thus equally good throwing a knife, shooting—or just writing—with either hand.

Peering around the corner and looking at the pond, not thirty feet away, I wished it were closer. Something about the guards was bothering me. They seem too relaxed and never looking my way. Were they urging me forward?

Crawling to the edge of the pond at a pace that would not draw attention, I peered in. Scum and other nonjungle items were floating in the water. This was a cesspool and definitely smelled like it. I quickly found what was apparently the lip of the pool, and, trying to avoid falling in, spread the sparse jungle foliage so that I could sit on the edge. Swinging my feet in first, I was as pleased—pleased as one can be entering a cesspool—that it was only three feet deep.

Eyes watering, stomach churning, Glock at the ready, I crossed the pond as quickly as I thought advisable. I crawled out in an interval between guards passing. I carefully removed my smelly coveralls and stashed them in the nearby bush. Rechecking my Glock, I flicked the safety off, then put my knife in my right hand and started to crawl through the low scrub, slowly slithering like a snake toward the path.

It was dark in the low scrub. The searchlights would flash across the top of the scrub and onto the pond. Nerves on edge, I hugged the ground as close as possible only moving amongst the scrub when I was sure there were no guards on the path or lights shining my way. I hadn't gone twenty feet when I abruptly stopped, then backed up. This shouldn't be here. I had touched something warm, furry and it moved.

CHAPTER

Oh shit!

I withdrew my hand and lay perfectly still.

What the hell was that? Many thoughts raced through my mind. Heart pounding, I lay there wondering if I should retreat.

There was no way around whatever it was, and it appeared very substantial. Shooting was out of the question, the best thing to do was to shine my flashlight on it for a split second. It was more than likely some dead animal that the guards had shot and thrown in the bushes, but I had to make sure. I waited till the guards had passed and the searchlights were shining in my direction, then, I crawled forward, aimed the flashlight and putting my fingers over the lens leaving a tiny gap, I did a quick on and off. A quick flash no one would think anything of and hopefully not see.

It was as I thought, and I didn't like it.

Shit

This was not good. Two red eyes, that were surrounded by yellow fur, closed and reopened with the flash of the light. They were looking directly at me, but thankfully there were no growling or aggressive moves from the animal.

I thought the eyes must have belonged to one of their guard dogs—but why wasn't he attacking or giving my location away? Was he stationed here waiting for the command to attack? Was he injured or was he hiding from someone, or is this where he came to hide away from all humanity? Or did he not recognize me as an enemy? I had to get past the dog and quickly, as time was not on my side. My best option was to use my knife as it was quick, silent and effective.

Once again, I waited till the guards had passed and the search lights were shining elsewhere. I shone my flashlight on the dog for a split second to make sure he hadn't moved. Cautiously, I crawled forward to where the dog lay, and slowly raising my knife to bury it in the dog's neck. He let out a quiet moan and started crawling closer to me. I stayed my blow.

As the tension grew, I held my knife at the ready as the dog crawled closer, then he lay beside me. I gingerly put my hand over the dog's back keeping the blade against his neck, not sure what to do. I was having second thoughts and starting to have a feeling of closeness towards this animal, when he let out another quiet moan, then rolled over on his side.

What the heck is he doing?

This was not a puppy, but a full-grown dog, that looked somewhere between a Labrador and German Shepherd.

Now what?

I was still feeling very nervous about this animal. "What the heck do you want?" I whispered.

Holding my knife at the ready, I very slowly put my other hand on the dog and started rubbing his fur. In the darkness, with the dog's head close to mine, when the search lights flashed over us, I could see sadness as his eyes looked into mine. This dog was trying to tell me something but what?

All I needed was for him to bolt and give my hiding position away. I couldn't chance it, I had to use my knife. The dog felt the tension return to my body as he gave another quiet moan and rubbed his snout against me. Was he really trying to communicate with me, or was he trained to do this? I decided to crawl around the dog leaving him where he was and get my charges set before the cameras came back on.

I gave the dog a scratch behind the ear, and he let out another moan.

"Sorry, buddy, but I got to go!" I whispered.

I no longer feared he was going to attack, and so, leaving the dog behind, I very slowly started crawling toward the corner of the building where there were more shadows. I no sooner got started than the dog was in front of me blocking my path.

What the heck? Once again, I had my knife at the ready. Head down and out of sight, the dog abruptly turned around and headed for the opposite corner of the building where the light was much brighter. He stopped and let out another moan and thankfully not a bark. It took me a few moments to figure why he was heading toward the brighter spotlight. Then I saw why. One of the lights had fallen down, lighting the ground to a greater extent, but it was also shining directly in the guard's eyes as they walked by. I crawled to the dog and gave him a little pat and with his head down, he started crawling away with me in tow.

Even though he seemed friendly, I still wasn't sure about this dog, so I kept an extra watch thinking he might be leading me into a trap. Every so often the dog would stop, and even though I couldn't hear them, the guards would appear sauntering down the path doing their rounds.

When I had gone as far as I thought I should, I stopped, and looking around, was wondering how I was going to get into the front of the building to lay my charges without being seen. Thanks to the drone, I knew there was an entrance door around the corner, but it would leave me exposed to the guards, especially if it was locked.

I was listening for the guards, when the dog abruptly jumped up and disappeared around the corner. No sooner had he left, than he came running back coming to a four-paw halt beside me. I was thinking either the dog's time was up or mine was when he let out another small sound and started running the way he had just returned from. Still on high alert I stood up against my better judgment and went running around the corner after the dog expecting to come face to face with the guards at any moment. When he heard I was following he ran faster and so did I, petrified.

What the hell am I doing, following the enemy's dog?

Around the corner, I could see the entrance door in the distance and no guards. My heart and I both ran faster.

Reaching the door, I looked down at the dog but couldn't read anything in his expression, as he looked up at the door, then back at me. I quietly opened the door and we stepped into a small vestibule. I had no sooner shut the door behind us when I heard the guards walk by. The dog went and sat in front of the second door and looked up at the door handle. Heart still pounding, I quietly leaned over and put my ear to the door and listened.

I could hear muffled screams from a panic-stricken female and equally loud shouting coming from a male. I looked down at the dog, checked my gun and knife.

"Are you ready, boy?" I whispered.

As quietly as possible, I pulled the door towards me, releasing pressure on the latch, and turned the knob. Before the door was open an inch, the dog hit it without warning, pulling it from my grip and raced in toward the screaming girl. Through the small shaft of light from an adjoining door, I could make out the form of someone on the bed and the dog attacking a struggling form on the floor.

I stood in a shadow just inside a large room. Letting my eyes adjust to the dim light, I figured there were only two in the room, the girl and the guy. As I cautiously crept toward the girl keeping in the shadows, I could see a female with the utter look of shock on her face. She was tied to the bed and desperately in need of clothes. Any clothes. She glared at me dumbstruck for words. I instantly put my fingers to my lips telling her to keep quiet. The dog had knocked the guy off the girl. "Rider, you're right on time," a deep voice said. "We had no wait at all, and I couldn't have done it better. Glad you made it safely, now we can take care of business."

I tore my eyes off the girl and looked to where the voice was coming from. Two figures emerged out of the darkness. One with his gun pointed at my chest the other with a complete look of authority about him. I recognized him from the pictures the drone had sent back from the command post.

That dog had tricked me all the way! Smart dog, very smart dog.

As they neared the girl, the commander looked down at her. "Fine looking specimen, isn't she? We prettied her up just for you."

I could see that the pock-faced guard was an old hand at handling his weapon, very steady with neither gun nor eyes wavering. Gun pointing at my chest where its point of entry would be instant death, if the trigger was pulled and eyes staring into mine looking for any sign of hostility.

The girl, by this time, was having a fit. Fighting against her restraints, I could see her wrists and ankles starting to bruise. The light was not that good, but I could see that she was a nice-looking gal, with what looked like red hair and fine features.

The dog was sitting next to the guard he had just knocked over waiting for further instructions and following my every move with a look of bewilderment in his eyes. It was obvious that this dog was very well trained and would attack on command.

There were no sounds coming from inside the building except for the girl struggling and from outside the steady drone of the diesel generators straining to keep up with their high electrical demand.

"We've been waiting for you, Rider," the commander said, again looking up from the girl.

I looked at both of them with astonishment on my face as I lowered both my knife and Glock to my side. All this time, the girl, to gain some privacy, was still thrashing on the bed trying to break her bonds, so she could cover herself.

"We've been following you as best we could since your landing," the commander said, as the guard held his gun steady on my chest with a non-flinching gaze.

I figured at the moment there was no chance of an escape, what with the dog watching and the gun pointed at my chest.

"We were notified about your order. When you landed, we lost you? You were good, actually, very good! We had guards positioned all along the trail, but you eluded them all."

"Thanks, nice that I could elude you at least this far," I said, smiling. "I tried my best. Who's the mole?" I asked, fuming inside and trying to think of the few who knew of my orders.

"At the moment I can't tell you that, but perhaps I will before you leave us." he said, with a smile on his face. "However, I will tell you that it's someone you know, and you're going to be very surprised and upset, so we'll just leave it at that."

The girl had stopped thrashing on the bed and was looking up at us with a deep frown on her face, trying to figure what was going on.

Four men, had brought her to this room, stripped her naked, and kicking and thrashing, tied her to the four corners of the bed. Three of the men had hid in the shadows in the corner, and the fourth was told to stand looking at the girl. This new guy, dressed in fatigues and acting like he was trying to save the world, and looked like he could, bursts into the room with a dog of all things, and is now, or in a short period of time, going to be killed. What a fool!

I couldn't take my eyes off her. She was beautiful and ruining my train of thought.

"What are you staring at?" She pulled at her restraints again.

The more she pulled the better she looked.

"You've never seen a woman without clothes on, moron?" She hissed.

I ignored the girl and glanced over at the commander, then the gun trained on my chest, then slowly looked at the dog. "You train him?" I asked. "He seems rather bright to be hanging around here."

The girl looked at me with astonishment on her face.

"Good sense of humor my friend, but it's a she, and she is my pride and joy. She's the smartest dog I know of. Easy to train and faithful. When we heard you were coming, we had only a few days to train her to do what she did. I wasn't sure if she would attack you in the scrub, but she followed orders to a 'T'. By the way, her name is Chance."

Appropriate, I thought. I could give her a second chance.

"Chance," he said, clicking his finger and pointing to his side. The dog, not too happy, sauntered over and sat by her master's side. Chance was obviously not a happy dog and showed more affection to me in the short time I had known her than she was showing to her master—perhaps she would not do as he commanded.

"Sorry, Chance," I said, in a loud voice to see what her reaction would be. Her ears picked up and her tail wagged once. That was promising, I thought. Maybe she was bilingual or liked the tone of my voice?

"What about the gunman she just injured," I said, glancing down at the guard on the floor then looking back at the gunman with the steady hand and his weapon still pointed at my chest. His eyes never wavered from mine. I winked at him, still no reaction.

"Lots of those around," the commander said. "It's a bloody shame you know, now take Pedro here. He would never stoop as low as this guy did because he wants to go up the friggin' ladder, and he knows if I offer him a weak job like that idiot and he takes it he'll go nowhere. In fact, I'm thinking of training him to handle Chance here. This dog is one of a kind. She will take commands just by looking at my eyes. In fact, in two seconds, if commanded she would run around this bed and have you down on the floor before you even knew what happened."

"No kidding," I said, still stalling for time. "Looks like she could do that alright."

"And a few seconds later, she could sit on the floor with a child and share his little bottle of milk!" the commander said, with a look of pride on his face.

Don't look so smug, I thought. *Given the chance I could wipe that look off your face, dog or no dog.*

"What's with the girl?" I asked, looking at her prone body lying on the bed.

The commander followed my gaze, but Pedro kept a steady hand and steady gaze on my eyes.

Damn! This guy's good, I thought.

"Her name's Angela," he said, still gazing at her body. "She was kidnapped out of Singapore. We brought her here and cleaned her up just for this special occasion. We're waiting for the ransom. A portion of the ransom, a very small portion I might add, will be given to the troops and that way we know they won't hurt the girls. Beautiful specimen, isn't she?"

"Can't argue with you there," I said, still looking at Angela. Pedro stood stock still, neither gun nor eyes moved.

"How large is your lab?" I was stalling, trying to figure out some form of escape.

"You know *exactly* how large this lab is, and as you know it is one of the largest in the country. We produce over four tons of coke a week. It's stored in these buildings till we can ship it, then it gets delivered all over the world."

"So how do you ship it out?" I kept Pedro in my peripheral vision.

The commander also seemed to be stalling for time—or was he just testing to see how long Pedro could keep his gun and gaze on me.

"Normally, I wouldn't be talking to anyone from the outside about this, but seeing as you won't be leaving here, what's the difference?" He shrugged, with a smirk on his face.

"And why would you think that?"

"Well I think the odds are pretty much stacked against you, wouldn't you agree, Rider?"

"Yeah, I guess they are, but I've gotten out of worse situations, but then, you do have the dog."

"It's not the dog that would stop you. I could take the dog away and you still wouldn't leave this room alive."

"I'm not too sure about that."

The commander, by this time, was getting a little exasperated—his shooter never moved.

Angela, hearing all this, tried to sit up letting out a painful moan as her bindings tightened around her wrists and ankles, she lay back down looking at the ceiling trying to figure what was happening.

"We have mule trains" the commander said, "human transport, high powered watercraft, seventy-foot subs capable of carrying nine tons each but the newest and best are drones. We fly them over the Mexican and American borders or across the Gulf dropping coke wrapped in high impact plastic bags at designated sites, where people are waiting to pick them up. The drones are refueled over unpopulated areas by a mother drone, so landing is not an issue, and nobody is the wiser."

"What do you want with me?" I asked, still stalling and keeping my eye on Pedro. I was looking for any weakness I could spot, and I could spot none. He was really good. Steady eyes, steady gun. Damn! He was one good soldier, at least at pointing a gun.

As the commander opened his mouth to speak, his phone rang. He stepped back into the shadows touching the phone's screen.

I didn't have a plan, but I had to do something.

"Angela," I said, smiling at her and still watching the guard, "are you ready to run?"

Angela started struggling, cursing and stared at me with a look of hatred in her eyes. The guard's eyes didn't budge, neither did his gun, I don't think he spoke English.

"What kind of a dumb lightheaded fool are you?" She hissed. "You've got a gun pointed at your chest by a gunman who looks like he knows more than you do, a dog watching you and waiting for the command to attack, a commander who also has a gun and phone and there you stand asking ridiculously stupid questions. It's very obvious were not getting out of here alive, but there you stand still asking stupid questions. None of this will help us—you're still holding your gun in your hand" she said, getting more agitated. "Get real! Do you even know how to use that stupid thing?"

I smiled at her again.

"It's pointed down Angela. If I were to raise my gun a fraction of an inch, I'd be dead. This guard is that good, but you're absolutely correct, except I do know how to use a gun and so does he, and he's the one in control at the moment with his gun pointing at me. Right now, there is not too much that I can do, but I'll think of something."

"You could at least untie my feet."

"Yes, I could, and in doing so I would be shot instantly!"

It was obvious the guard didn't speak English. There was no recognition of any words that were spoken, not even of my gun pointing down.

"Hang on," I whispered. "I have a plan."

"Well, keep me out of your damn plan. What I've seen so far does not impress me at all, and I want nothing to do with you or it." She said looking away.

"Let's just give this one try, okay? You have nothing to lose. Look at the guard and say something to him."

"Like what? What do you think would be appropriate at a time like this?"

"Um, untie me, sounds good doesn't it?" I said, smiling at her and still watching Pedro out of the corner of my eye.

"Okay," she mumbled, looking at the guard with a frown on her face.

"Hey, how about untying me?" Angela said, in a seductive voice.

There was not a flicker from his eye, nor a movement of his gun towards Angela. They both stayed on me. I winked again. Still no show of expression.

"Well that didn't work, did it?" I said, smiling at her.

"What were you expecting?" she asked, getting more frustrated. "Think he'd put his gun down and untie me. You're a real moron, aren't you?"

"Here comes the commander," I whispered. "We never talked."

Walking back into the light, he looked me in the eye. "That was the boss, and he will be here in ten minutes to talk to you. In the meantime, Pedro and Chance will keep a watch on you two, I have an errand to run. Make sure Angela doesn't get up and run away," he mumbled with a smirk on his face. Looking down at the dude on the floor he signaled for him to get up and leave.

Turning, he told Pedro in Spanish—which I totally understood—to be very careful with me as I supposedly was one of the best, then he gave Chance the command to watch, looked at me again with a smile on his face and I thought I saw a slight wink.

What was that all about, I thought? Maybe he was daring me to escape.

"Oh, and Rider, I think, before I leave, you should place your gun very carefully on the bed, very carefully Rider, we don't want to upset Pedro now do we? Besides, it's not much use to you here as Pedro is my top marksman, and as instructed, he has his finger lightly depressing the trigger. Ready to put a bullet through your heart if you make one false move. I'd hate to see you do that when I have so much in store for you."

I looked at Pedro. I then told Pedro in Spanish what I was going to do. I realized my one shot at this moment if I could get it off, would only get me killed.

With two fingers, and looking Pedro in the eyes, I carefully laid the gun on the bed, safety off, bullet chambered, grip towards me, then slowly and carefully put my hand down against my side. I then did the same with my knife. There was still no reaction from Pedro. Steady hand, steady gaze. The commander turned to face me one last time and, as he did, I thought I saw a slight flicker of light from the corner he and Pedro had come from. *Secondary backup*, I thought. This was going to be very difficult.

"Before my phone rang, Rider, you asked me what I had in store for you."

"Well, first we're going to question you extensively about this job and the others you are doing in America, and then we'll see what happens from there. Could be that you somehow found your way into our supply of coke and overdosed, you never know, these things happen, don't they, Rider? We have ways of extracting information, some pleasant some not. After all, this is a drug lab."

One slight nod and he was out the door leaving me to look at Pedro and his gun, pointed at my chest.

CHAPTER

I was processing all the escape options open to me when Angela blurted out, "Okay, smart-ass, you still have a gun pointed at your chest with his top marksman holding it, a dog who on command could severely injure you, a woman tied up on the bed and who knows what else, so what are you going to do now? Thought of any great plans?"

I was on one side of the bed, and then came the girl, Pedro, the dog and then the corner where the flicker of light had come from. I gazed down at Angela and noticed she had a small colorful tattoo on the inside of her left breast, just below her tan line.

"Cute," I mumbled. I didn't know if Angela spoke Spanish or not, but I said, with a big smile on my face staring at her breast, but keeping the guard's eyes in focus, in Spanish first then in English, "nice tattoo."

"You bloody pervert," she yelled. "Get your eyes off of me."

Out of the corner of my eye, for a fleeting second, I saw the guard glance at Angela's tattoo and in doing so—ever so slightly—moved the barrel of his gun. It was the fraction of an inch I needed. In that split second, I grabbed my knife and executed a perfect underhand throw, burying it deep into the guard's throat. I heard the knife hitting bone and the air rushing out of him. He hit the floor with a thud. As he went down, and using him as a shield, I grabbed my gun and fired two shots into the corner where I had previously seen the flash. I heard another thump and knew my shots had hit home. Now I had the dog to contend with.

Upon hearing the two shots, and before I could get a bead on her, Chance was up and charging around the bed full tilt with feet searching for traction, headed in my direction.

There was a moan from the bed, distracting me momentarily.

"Kill the dog, or she'll kill you!" She shrieked, trying to sit up to see what was going to happen.

I was expecting Chance to jump up, hitting me in the chest knocking me down then go for my throat, but she fooled me. My guess was wrong. She came to an abrupt stop and looked up at me her tail wagging. With my heart pounding, I bent down and gave her a scratch behind the ear.

"Well girl, you certainly fooled me," I said, patting her head as she rubbed her face against my hand.

I slid into the shadows and checked on the unknown shooter in the corner. He was dead. Then, coming back I ran to the door, followed by Chance, and was reaching for the doorknob when Chance let out a moan then ran back to the girl.

I headed for the bed and saw a look of utter astonishment on Angela's face. I retrieved my knife from the guard's throat, laid it on the bed then turned to Angela. I stood next to the bed looking down at her. "Listen to me and listen closely, Angela."

"Untie me first, you idiot," she yelled. "Before he comes back."

"No. first, you listen to me" I said, knowing I was going to have my hands full with this temper ridden redhead. "Time is not on our side. I need some questions answered and answered fast, then I'll see about getting you out of here." I knew this was going to be a tough interrogation.

I told her what I was going to do and, with defiance in her eyes, she said, "Untie me first. Just untie me, *please*." She was pleading now.

The change of tone and the please got to me. I cut the ropes on her ankles first, then her wrists.

"Thanks," she said, swinging her feet over the side of the bed then reaching down to rub them.

"Where are your clothes?" I asked, looking around.

"They took them somewhere after they had stripped them off of me. I don't know where they are, and you wouldn't want to see them anyways."

I had my back to her when she grabbed my knife, jumped me from behind and thrust the knife against my throat.

"Now, you answer my questions," she said, in a hissing voice.

"Angela, listen to me, I'm a trained SEAL. I've been trained to get out of situations like this."

"Try it mister! I'm holding the knife."

I must admit she was a very spunky girl, but this was not working, time was not on our side. I didn't want to hurt her. I felt her grip around my neck lessen and then both hands dropped to her side.

"I'm sorry," she said. "I guess you're right." She handed me the knife.

"Look, we have got to get going." I glanced at the door. "If someone comes in here, we're dead meat and I think you know that. You have to do as I ask and do it right away. Understand?" She gave a slight nod. "First, let's get you dressed. You're sticking out like a sore thumb with no clothes on."

"There is no hope for me anyways," she blurted. "Neither of us will be walking out of here alive, there are too many of them."

"There is hope," I said, pulling her up from the bed. "You've got me, what else could you ask for?"

"You are a real smart-ass, aren't you?" she said, smiling for the first time.

She helped me get the uniform off the gunman in the corner then I instructed her to put it on. With a look of dismay, she started to get dressed.

All this time, Chance was sitting by the door turning her head from side to side as if listening for something. For what I wasn't sure—hell, I wasn't even entirely sure she was on our side.

"Angela," I said, "my name's Rider. I'm sorry if I acted stupid to you a few minutes ago, but I was trying to get you agitated to see if our guard would glance at you. I needed a split second to react, and he gave me that. I was using you as a prop."

"I understand," she said. "Sometimes these things work out for the best."

"I'm going to set charges to go off in thirty minutes, and I have others to place. Do you know what's in the building next door?"

"I don't know," she said, trying to make a diaper out of the sheet. "They blindfolded me when they dragged me in here, sorry, but I didn't see a thing."

I grabbed the sheet from her and folded a diaper the way my sister had taught me. "There," I said, handing it to her, "lots of good protection."

"Thanks," she said very modestly. "Are you married with kids?"

"Four little toddlers and three wives." I hurriedly said, looking away from her trying to suppress a smile.

For a split-second Angela looked downtrodden then she recovered.

"Only three wives?" She replied, with a big smile on her face.

"No, at the moment I'm single. Now get the boots on and let's go. Take this gun." I said, handing it to her.

It looked like a cannon in her small hand.

"If you need to shoot, this is the safety; flip it this way. Hold it like this with two hands. That's very important because if you don't, the kick could break your wrist. Use two hands to point, and then pull the trigger slowly. Don't jerk it or you will miss your target."

I thought I heard the sound of a pistol being fired. I looked at Chance, and she let out a small growl. I took this as a signal that all was clear, but maybe not.

Cautiously, opening the door and peering through the crack, Chance and I stepped into the vestibule, I signaled Angela to follow.

"Angela," I whispered. "You know that I'm better alive than dead, so please point the gun down and not at me, it will just make me feel a lot better."

"Dream on, Rider," she replied, with another big smile on her face. "I didn't have my finger on the trigger, but I'll remember to keep it pointed down."

I was starting to like this lady, which in my profession was not a good thing. The trick now was for us to get across the sidewalk and into the jungle. There we could regroup, then I would come back and lay the rest of the charges. But what about Chance? I still wasn't sure.

CHAPTER

Commander Ricardo, who had left Rider standing by the bed, had actually returned to the command post to check on his monitors with Carlos, his boss. Looking at the monitor and shaking his head, Ricardo pounded his fist on the table.

"Sure, enough, Carlos," he yelled, "Rider hit José down the trail. I recognize all the troops and we're minus one, José. Pedro and the dog have good control of him now, but we should act fairly quickly before something else happens. We were warned about him."

"You sure about José?" Carlos said. "Did you get a backup report?"

"It was Juan who sent the report in, and he's pretty reliable. He doesn't know how Rider did it as José is pretty careful, but he stripped him and took off with his clothes. That asshole. No, he's not going anywhere for a long while. Pedro is holding a steady bead on him, and Luis is standing in the shadows, with his gun at the ready, and Chance is there, although I noticed a change in her. She seemed happier standing near Rider than me."

"That's expected," Carlos said, with a smirk on his face. "No woman likes you; your dick's too small."

There was a small commotion from up the trail. Both men looked at the screen but noticed nothing out of the ordinary.

"I don't like this," Carlos said, scratching his private parts from a sexual germ he picked up last night. "If he's that good, we have to be really careful with him."

"What about the bitch? Is she going to follow her orders?"

Ricardo was feeling pretty cocky with himself. "We have promised her a safe passage home which she won't get even when we receive her ransom. If she screws up, I told her she'll be given to the troops. She'll cooperate. Besides, she has nothing to do unless he escapes, and he won't."

"Ricardo," Carlos said with panic in his voice. "Have you been looking at these monitors or reading those skin magazines? This monitor is repeating itself. Did you see that? That's how the asshole got in here so easily."

"No, I didn't see anything," Ricardo said. "I was busy! I thought you were watching them!"

"That's your job, Ricardo, what else has he done we don't know about? You better get back in there and bring the son of a bitch back here now. Tie him like I've never seen you tie anyone before and don't let me down this time. Get Julius in here to monitor the screens, I'm coming with you," he said, giving himself another good scratch.

"Julius," Ricardo yelled through the open walls of the command hut, "get your ass in here and quick!"

Walking out of the command post, both Carlos and Ricardo pulled their guns not wanting any surprises and not knowing what to expect.

"Stop!" Ricardo yelled, picking up his phone again, "I want a backup, I think we're going to need it."

"What," Carlos said, his face going red with anger and his pecker getting itchier by the minute.

"I don't like opening a door to the unknown, and besides, if *you* get shot, I'd be in command and you wouldn't like that."

Two troops came running down the trail past the door Rider was behind.

CHAPTER

"Something's up, Angela," I said. "Chance looks agitated and wants out, and I think we should trust her." Chance was standing by the closed door to the vestibule shaking and looking up at the handle.

Angela nodded with a look of wariness on her face, still not sure about Chance or me.

I ran to the door and turned out the light. I patted Chance and turned the doorknob. Chance walked to the outside door and moaned again. All we needed was to have Chance dart out and give us away.

"Rider, *Rider!*" Angela said again, in a louder voice. "Do you think we should trust Chance? I've seen her patrolling around here and she can turn on you. For practice they had her turn on unarmed gunmen and the next moment she was as friendly as ever. She may still be doing what she was trained to do and turn on us at any moment or lead us the wrong way. I'm worried about her."

"You may be right," I said, hesitating and looking down at Chance, "however, she has shown signs that she likes us, or at least me. You saw them back there; I think we should trust her."

"Okay, but if I see her being aggressive against you, I'm going to try to shoot her. Only in the worst of situations, okay?"

"Just make sure you don't shoot me!" I said, with a smile on my face. "Remember, I'm your ticket out of here."

I opened the door a crack, looked outside and it looked clear.

"Good girl!" I said to Chance.

Turning to Angela, I took her free hand. It seemed so small in mine. "I want you to be careful, but you need to trust me. Keep your head up and eyes open. Look for anything unusual or different as we're running down the trail. I'm still not sure about Chance, but she has saved our bacon a couple of times. We're looking for a side trail off the main trail, and it may be overgrown, then, we're looking for an even smaller trail a hundred feet in and to the left off that trail! Okay?"

"Okay, Rider, but I'm scared. Will we get through this?"

"You'll be okay. Let's go."

I opened the door fully and was faced with an empty path. To the left, out of sight, was the command post, but we were taking the path to the right. Chance ran ahead and soon found the path we were looking for. How, I don't know, but this was the path I had seen from above. We ran after Chance for another short distance then I saw the trail I was looking for which would lead us to the area where the drone had sensed all the heat. There were no sounds coming from behind us, so it looked like we were in the clear. Stopping and calling Chance back, I turned to Angela.

"Are you okay?"

"Yes," she said bending over and gasping for breath. "I'm fine. I haven't had any exercise for some time, but I'll be okay. Let's go. I don't want to hold you back."

Running down the trail dragging Angela and pushing branches out of the way, I found a spot that looked suitable for her to hide in.

"Okay," I said. "I want you to make yourself comfortable here, I need to go back and set the rest of the charges. That's what I'm here for, to demolish this site."

"No," she said, standing up grabbing my hand with a tear running down her cheek. "You can't leave me. I'm too scared, you can't, I'm too scared! What if you don't come back, what would I do? They would torture me in unheard of ways; you're the only one around here that has treated me like a human. Please," she begged, "take me with you."

I looked at my watch. "Here's the thing, before I walked into the building you were in, I foiled their security cameras and our time is running out. Before the cameras become active again, every second counts, and I have to get going or neither of us will survive this ordeal. If I don't return in fifteen minutes head down that trail to the first large clearing you find. Hide there and eventually an American helicopter will come to pick you up. Don't worry though! I'll be back and don't even think about leaving till you feel sure that I won't return, but I will, one way or the other!" I said, giving her hand a squeeze. Standing up, I adjusted my gear, making sure everything was easily accessible.

"Rider," Angela whispered, stepping closer to me. "Be careful and please come back."

"Come on Chance, let's go." Nearing the junction, I had Chance run ahead of me to check the way. We hadn't run very far when I could see the building Angela had been in. I clicked my fingers calling Chance back as I wanted to see the main control center, but I thought it would be better to approach it from the back. I found an animal trail leading behind the control shack that was slow going but passable.

Every time I saw Chance's ears go up, I'd stop, and a guard would pass by not thirty feet away.

We were nearing the control hut when Chance again suddenly stopped. One of the guards was walking directly toward us with his rifle raised and pointed in our direction. I looked down at Chance hoping she wouldn't move. I then slowly eased my gun out of its holster and with safety off and a bullet chambered, watched as the guard came closer. I was hoping the noise the guard had heard was a bird or monkey behind us. Without warning, Chance darted out of the jungle with the point of the guard's rifle following her nose. I couldn't yell or make any noise, but realized Chance was giving up her life for me. There was a loud crack as the guard's rifle sent its deadly bullet flying through the air headed for Chance. Then there was another shot equally as loud and with my heart stopped, I looked away, as I couldn't bear to look at the dead form of Chance laying on the ground after all she had done for us. But I had to look to give my final respects, and turning, I almost let out a yell, as I saw Chance running up the stairs of the control shack. Running past her master, he gave her a good whack on the snout. Chance let out a yelp and retreated to the furthest corner. There was a command yelled from the control shack and two guards appeared, picked up their dead comrade and vanished.

CHAPTER

The shack was built on stilts not three feet off the ground. There were no walls but a railing that was twelve inches off the floor and three feet high. This allowed for air circulation and also allowed for me to see in. Built on a ramshackle foundation of posts, with a railing and roof weather-beaten from the drenching monsoons that frequented the area, the shack looked like it had seen better days—it wouldn't see many more. Antennas protruded through the roof, feeding data to numerous electronic devices inside. Heavy armaments were leaning against the railing, betrayed its real purpose.

Carlos, who I'd seen earlier was there. His eyes were darting from one screen to another as he studied the monitors, with great concern. Unsure whether the girl and I were missing or not, he had the look of a beaten man. Every so often he would kick at the chair, cursing wildly and sending Chance cowering further into her corner.

I had crawled further along the trail till I was at the back of the hut. To get to the hut to set my explosives was a near impossibility as it was thirty feet away through open ground.

I couldn't do it. I clicked my fingers in desperation hoping Chance would hear me and respond.

With two guards in the hut looking the other way, no gunmen on the path, explosive in my hand and ready to place, the coast looked clear. I had no choice. Run in and out as fast as possible. I started crawling through the jungle heading toward the hut, moving slowly, wary that a guard might come along the path at any time. I had made it to the edge of the jungle when I saw Chance coming down the stairs. The commander was engrossed in his monitors and didn't see Chance pass.

In no hurry, Chance turned and headed toward me, keeping close to the edge of the hut and out of sight of her former master. I retreated back into the jungle waiting to see what would happen. I waited. Chance walked into the jungle as if she were on a personal mission, sniffing here and there. Soon she was by my side. "Good girl, Chance!" I whispered, scratching her ear and giving her a pat. She looked up at me with those sad eyes.

Chance sat down looking at me waiting for a command. I put the charge in her mouth and pointed toward the shack. She looked up at me with a question in her eyes. I pointed to the shack again and Chance looked then turned and walked through the clearing to the edge of the hut. She was standing close enough that the commander could not see her but anyone coming down the path could. As she turned around looking to where I was hidden, I clicked my finger. Chance wagged her tail, turned around again, crawled under the shack, dropped the charge, and moseyed back into the jungle. I spread the foliage and looked further down the path. I could see another building. The one I'd seen from the drone. This was the manufacturing building, and next to it was the river and what looked like boats, that were being loaded with drugs.

"Now we'll see how smart you are, Chance!" I whispered, giving her another explosive. Chance took the explosive in her mouth and looked at me. I pointed down the trail toward the manufacturing house. Checking to make sure the path was clear, and the commander was not looking this way, I let Chance go while I pointed to the manufacturing hut once again.

Chance hurried unseen past the command post and down the path toward the manufacturing house. Through the foliage, I could see two gunmen on high alert, rifles pointing at Chance walking towards her, as she walked beside the building. One of the guards struck out with his boot just missing Chance by inches but in doing so Chance jumped and dropped the explosive. The guards stood frozen for a moment, then, without hesitation, started running in different directions, yelling to alert others.

Ricardo, inside the hut, hearing the yelling, grabbed his phone. Not getting an answer, he started feverously scanning all his monitors looking for any sign of unwanted activity.

With Chance at my side, I set the first detonator off. Debris flew everywhere. The manufacturing hut went up in a cloud of white dust, the two gunmen were blown into the river, and anyone in the vicinity was either killed or severely stunned. Chance and I headed back to the main trail where I detonated the remainder then the command hut. Nothing was left. With Chance in the lead, we ran back down the trail. Nearing where I left Angela, I started to slow down, I sensed something was not right. I had a funny feeling in my gut. I stopped and listened then looked at Chance who showed no sign of fright, her tail was wagging.

But she was wrong.

We carried on, and nearing Angela, Chance stopped suddenly. I called her back as a gunman came running towards us at full speed. We had been seen. Hitting the ground, he let go a spray of bullets. My return shot was a direct hit. Chance looked at me and then Angela. I ran over to Angela who was convulsing as I held her hand. She was trying to put her arm around my neck but didn't have the strength. I could feel the warmth and vitality draining out of her body. I was devastated. The gunman for some reason had shot her.

"Angela, talk to me, talk to me, what's your last name?" I pleaded. I had to find out something about Angela before she left me. I put my ear close to her mouth and through gurgling heard what sounded like Fletcher. Still holding her close and feeling a great loss, I asked where she lived. Her mouth was moving saying nothing, while her enchanted eyes were becoming more distant.

"Angela, what town!" I cried. Her mouth started twitching and moving again. I listened. "Say it again, Angela." I couldn't believe my ears! There was a twinkle in her eyes as she closed them and mouthed.

"Thank you, Rider. Goodbye."

"Shit!" I said, as a feeling of total and utter despair, enfolded me. I liked this girl very much and maybe liked her too much, and I was looking forward to getting to know her better. Thoughts were running through my head faster than I could process them. Why would the gunman shoot Angela. I picked up Angela and carried her into the jungle out of sight of the path and laid her on the ground. I returned to the site, cleaned up the mess as best I could. I was drained, spent, double-crossed, lonely and utterly pissed off.

CHAPTER

7

"Looks like it's just you and me, girl," I said, with sadness in my voice as I bent down and gave Chance a scratch behind her ear. Chance looked at me as if she knew what had happened.

"It's okay, girl. I liked her too." I wasn't fond of dogs licking my hand but gave Chance this moment to show her affection. I owed it to her.

I pointed down the path, and again, with Chance in the lead, we cautiously headed down the trail to where I thought the drone had sensed heat. The path grew very narrow and overgrown, almost to point that it was getting difficult to traverse. Chance stopped suddenly, listening and twisting her head. I knelt down putting my arm around her, trying to hear what she was hearing. Standing, we slowly moved forward, listening, taking another step then listening again. I could hear a murmur of voices, hushed voices, strained voices. Female voices.

We were struggling through the jungle as quietly as possible. The dense bush gave no release to the strangle hold it had on us, and Chance had to leap or stumble over every obstacle. In the bush, I could see a small clearing not ten feet in front of us and whistled for Chance to come back. I could hear the voices clearly now, and they were definitely female. I couldn't see any danger nor was Chance looking nervous. A few steps further, and I saw what looked like a door hidden by jungle bush and barely visible, well camouflaged, never used, but leaking cries for help.

From where I was standing, I could not see if there were cracks or openings in the door but getting closer, I saw where a door handle had once been installed and now a root was growing through the hole. I grabbed the root and gave it a gentle pull, hoping not to alert anyone inside. The root moved, and the talking stopped. Pulling it out would not work, but pushing it in would. I started cutting it with my knife, not too worried about being heard anymore as there was quite the discussion going on inside. With the root cut, I pushed it in a little, leaving enough room to slide a small pencil camera beside it. Hooking the other end of the camera cable to my monitor, I was able to make out at least twelve people, all woman, and all dressed in rags, and all in need of a bath and food by the looks of it—and they were all looking at the camera with fear on their faces.

Their talking had stopped, and other than the birds and other jungle creatures around me, all was quiet and motionless. Not knowing exactly what was on the other side of the door, I quickly moved to the side and had Chance follow. A stray bullet if one was to come through would not be welcome. I looked down at Chance, who was lying on the ground with her head on her paws.

I tapped three times on the door and watched as everyone looked at each other in bewilderment and fear. I tapped again. I was too busy concentrating on the captives and didn't see Chance jump up. I heard her a second later, almost a second too late as she let out a warning moan. I pulled the camera out and headed for the bush with Chance on my heels.

We concealed ourselves as well as we could, standing still, not breathing—or at least *I* was not breathing.

Four gunmen came crashing and stumbling through the jungle. They didn't stop or look in the direction of the door but continued struggling on their march down the trail. They were on a mission and in a hurry.

I returned to the door and pushed the root through to the inside. My note that followed was pulled through immediately and no doubt read quickly. Chance and I cautiously headed down the trail following the guards. Chance stopped so suddenly that I almost tripped over her, narrowly avoiding disaster as the guards had stopped no more than two hundred feet ahead.

The guards were digging up and loading into sacks what appeared to be a huge amount of currency obviously stolen from the lab. With Chance and the help of another man, it would be easy to take the four men out, however I wasn't sure that's what I wanted to do, and I didn't *have* another man. I signaled Chance to follow, and reluctantly she did, looking constantly back down the trail to where the action was. She wanted a part of it. We walked back to where Angela was lying, and I instructed Chance very sternly to stay. She lay down next to Angela and put her head on her paws like she always did and looked up at me with those forlorn eyes again.

"Now stay!" I said, pointing my finger at her.

The officer and his gunmen came stumbling down the trail, partly because of the explosion that would have rung their bells and partly because of the weight they were carrying. I followed them down the trail a good way wanting to know which way they were going. They were halfway to the main trail when Chance came flying by me like a bullet. She passed the gunmen in two bounds and with a mighty leap knocked the leading officer to the ground, winding him and scattering his money.

Everyone was in a state of shock, and confusion, as Chance attacked one of her previous handlers, digging her teeth in deeper with every curse the officer let out.

"Chance," he was yelling, "you stupid bitch! Get off me or I'll kill you! Get off me now!" He was rolling around having trouble defending himself as blood trickled from different wounds.

The commander had managed somehow to find his gun despite the tumbling and turmoil Chance was causing, but he was a second too late as Chance dug her teeth in deeper severing an artery draining the last drops of blood the commander had.

I had my gun out and, making sure Chance was not in the line of fire, shot the three guards as they were bringing their weapons around to shoot me. I stepped over the prone bodies of the gunmen and called Chance off the officer with no luck.

"Chance!" I yelled again. "Come here, girl!" But Chance would not obey my command. "Chance!" I yelled again, with more authority in my voice, "come *here*!"

Chance came running back to me, tail wagging as if to say, *it's over and he'll not bother either of us again*. I walked over to the officer and looked down. Chance was right! It was over for him at least.

Finding a spot just off the trail, I dragged the bodies and laid them one on top of the other, well hidden from sight. After gathering up the money and making many trips to deposit it just off the trail where Angela was, I needed a rest. I went further into the bush where Angela lay and with

Chance at my side, started to doze off. Slumber was just arriving when I was thrown wide awake and alerted to the sounds of someone running down the trail. Chance was up and alert also!

"Chance," I whispered, "come here, girl."

Chance looked at me then the trail, and then me again and then obeyed my command.

"Who is it, Chance?" I whispered.

Chance looked at me then towards the bunker door then she took off leaving me scrambling to catch up.

I could see the bunker door in the distance still closed and grown over. Past the door and further down the trail where the money was dug up, was a lone gunman looking lost as if he expected to find his buddies here. I needed to talk to him. I needed information and quick. I motioned for Chance to stay and I crept up to within fifteen feet and said in English then Spanish, "Do not move. Do not move a muscle. A dog and I have you covered. Hands in the air and turn around slowly, very slowly."

As he slowly turned around a look of fear then astonishment came across his face as he saw Chance looking at him and me with my colored skin. I kept my gun leveled at his chest and then ordered Chance to guard. He looked like he was only a kid of twelve or thirteen, and on seeing Chance move closer, he started to tremble with fear in his eyes.

He apparently knew this dog. "That's Chance!" he stammered.

"Yes," I said, "and she's switched sides. Who are you?" I asked. Unarmed the kid looked scared and lost, and I felt a little more relaxed. "Keep your hands in the air!" I said, as I slowly walked around him keeping my distance. "What's your name?"

"Reynaldo," he replied.

"Reynaldo what?"

"Reynaldo Alego."

"Okay, Reynaldo Alego, what are you doing here?" If others were coming, he knew that stalling worked in his favor—and it looked like he was stalling.

"I was told that if I helped move something to safety, I would be given a bonus."

"What were you going to move to safety?"

"I wasn't told, but he was going to give us something."

"You weren't told what you were going to move?"

He hesitated. "Yes, I was, one of the other guards told me."

"And what was it?"

"Money! Cash!"

"So, he was stealing cash from one of the drug lords, and you expected him to give you some—even as a witness you expected some?"

"I never thought of that, but we all like money!"

"How many gunmen are left at the plant?"

"Two," he said, still shaking and looking at Chance, "but more are coming from another village down the trail."

"How long before they arrive?"

"I'm not sure which village they would be coming from, but not before late this afternoon."

I walked slowly around Reynaldo, watching his every move very closely.

"Why did the explosions not injure you?"

"I was inside one of the speeding boats packing packages of drugs, when it went off."

"Packages of coke?"

"Yes coke, and all those who were outside were killed. I was lucky."

"Do you do drugs?"

He slowly looked up at me wondering if he should tell the truth. "I have, but not this stuff. I did once but it was too strong."

"You work here?"

"Yes."

"How long have you been working here?"

"One year ago, they came to my village and took me saying they would not bother my parents if I was good and worked hard for them."

"And good you have been!"

"I've been good and loyal! But I do not like these men. Some do drugs, and they're not allowed to. There are no kids for me to hang out with. I can't go home to see my parents as they're dead, so are my sisters, and they have ladies hidden here and they do not feed them. The only friend I have is Chance. We would chase each other through the jungle and her tail would wag. When I got tired, she would come and lay beside me putting her head on my lap, and I would scratch her ear. Why do dogs like their ears scratched, do you know why?"

"Well, amongst other things it's a sign of affection and bonding." (Where is a mom when you need one?)

"Do you know how many ladies are here?"

"There are fourteen. Twelve back there" he said, pointing through the jungle to the bunker, and two others were taken out some time ago."

"Why do you speak such good English, Reynaldo?"

"My parents were doing drug runs to America, but they needed to learn English first. My parents, every evening, taught my sisters and me, English. They said with English we would get jobs. The guards thought my parents were traitors, but they couldn't prove it. Later they weren't nice to them."

"Are you armed?" I said. "Any weapons?"

"No," he said. "I have nothing."

"Want to change your answer?" I said, looking at Chance.

"No, I have only a pocketknife."

"Okay, empty your pockets slowly and drop everything on the ground."

Out fell a piece of string, a piece of tinfoil, a coin, and his small pocketknife.

"Okay, put your hands down. But if you try anything you know what Chance will do?"

"Yes, I know, she's been trained and abused, and she's my only friend. But I know she is loyal."

Chance perked up her ears but still stood guard.

"What do you know about the girls that are housed in the bunker?"

He looked back down at his feet. "They are holding them here for money, and that's all I know. I would sneak them food when no one was looking because they were not feeding them. Once, I got caught and was hit lots of times, too many, it hurt. It just made me be more careful. They kept them in there with no clothes, no food, and nowhere to shit."

"How did they get the girls here?"

"Some they brought back in the speeding boats and the others, tied hand to hand, they marched them through the jungle. I don't like it here. I would like to leave, but they would kill me or treat me like the ladies if I tried to run. They have not told anyone that the girls are still alive or who has them. This is bad. I'm glad this happened."

"Anything else you think I should know, Reynaldo?"

Reynaldo looked down then over at Chance. "I can tell you how the drugs are getting out."

"Okay, let's hear it."

"Well," he said, looking down and kicking dirt with his foot. "The drugs are made here then packaged. The packages are then taken down to the river where I was and stacked in many speeding boats."

"How many boats?"

"Oh, maybe fourteen. I have a friend who I don't see very often, and he drives one of the speeding boats."

"How old is your friend, and let's call them speedboats?"

"Okay. My friend is around eighteen. The boats leave in groups at the same time and go together down the river in case one breaks down, he can be towed. They go very fast and scare other people on the river. Everyone knows when they hear the noise to get out of the way, they are coming. There are two drivers in each boat, and they don't stop. They take food for the two-and-a-half-day trip. There are many dangerous turns in the river, but my friend likes it. Near the mouth of the river, they tie up under plastic and unload. My friend said he would ask if I could come one day, but I don't think so. I think they think I would run away, but I wouldn't because my friend would be in trouble. The drugs are stacked in a submarine that is also under a plastic cover. The submarine takes the drug out into the ocean where many big speedboats with lots of engines come to it. The speedboats leave like *this…*" he said, splaying his fingers.

"You mean they go in different directions?"

"Yes, and very, very fast. The speeding boats, I mean speedboats are filled up with gas then containers of gas and diesel are put back in the speedboats as well as food for the plant and the return trip. They left not very long ago. When they return, they unload here then my friend has a short rest when I can talk to him. The boats are reloaded with drugs and this time taken upriver where they are loaded into drones, then they come back and do it all over again."

"That's it, nothing more?"

"If I think of more, I will tell you, okay?"

"Chance, guard!" I said again.

Reynaldo jumped so high I thought he was going to pee in his pants.

I looked at him with sadness in my eyes, knowing that a kid like this could cause great harm given the chance, but something was telling me he was different. I had a good feeling about him.

"You know that one false move and the dog will rip you apart?" I said.

"Yes, I know, I've seen her hurt others before. Sometimes in training he would use someone he didn't like. I couldn't watch but they made me. They said it would make me stronger. I would shut my eyes."

"How did *you* make friends with Chance?" Reynaldo asked, with still a fear of the dog in his eyes. "They had trained her to kill you or lead you somewhere where you would be killed," he said, sheepishly looking at his feet.

"We'll discuss later how I befriended her. What do you think I should do with you?" I asked, pondering what my options were. First the dog, then Angela, twelve ladies and now a kid.

"You're what, fourteen? Can't be much help to me and just a skinny little runt." I said, trying to provoke him and make him think.

Choking and trying to hold back tears, he answered. "I'm thirteen, no parents or sisters as of two months ago. I follow orders, I won't get in your way, I can show you the way around here, I'll do whatever you say and for all this you can feed me. Okay?" And for the first time he looked up, smiling.

I considered him for a moment. "Okay, that sounds fair, but Chance and I will be watching you."

I liked the kid and I thought I could trust him.

"Now listen and listen closely. I have a good feeling about you, and I hope and think I can trust you, so I'm going to give you a chance and the benefit of the doubt."

"What's that mean?" he asked. "Benefit of the doubt."

"Well, it means I'm going to wait and see what happens. So, if you disobey my orders, or if I see you doing something that would put any of us in danger, I will have Chance pay you a visit, and we both know what that means. And if you obey my orders, I will give you some of the money that was buried here."

Reynaldo looked at me with a look of disbelief on his face, then he looked at Chance, then he looked down the trail and nodded, yes, sticking out a clenched fist for me to hit.

"I want to hear it," I said.

"Yes, captain," he said, with what looked like a sign of relief on his face.

"Forget the *captain* stuff," I said. "Just follow orders."

"Yes, I will," he said, with a big smile on his face, "but what can I call you?"

"Rider." I said, "just Rider."

"Rider," he said smiling. "Okay, I'll call you that. Can I pat Chance? She was the only friend I had. We would go for walks and she was happy when she was away from here."

"Chance," I said. Chance jumped over to Reynaldo almost knocking him down. I had to put a stop to this although it was good for both participants. We had problems to solve, serious problems to solve, and we had to start solving them now.

"Rider," said Reynaldo. "I can get you in the other end of the bunker which is easier than here if you want."

"Thanks," I said, "but at the other end there will be little or no cover for the girls once they are out. Using this end, they are still hidden in the jungle, and we don't have to walk through the camp until we're ready to leave."

CHAPTER

"Reynaldo," I said, still watching him closely, "we need food and water for the ladies. Now that everything is blown up, do you think you can find some?"

"I think I can," he said, jumping from foot to foot, excited to having been given something important and meaningful to do. "I'll go look behind the kitchen and see what there is."

"Okay, pick up your belongings, but I keep your knife to make sure you come back. Now go find us some food and if you see any water bring that also. Don't get caught, don't let anyone see you return here, and hurry so we can feed these ladies. Got it? Oh, and see if you can find a machete or something."

"Yes sir!" he said, with a big smile on his face. "I'll be careful."

Running back past me, he tore down the trail so fast I didn't think he'd ever return. It looked like he was running for his life.

"Come on, Chance." I said, running down the trail to where the money had been dug up. I stuffed enough in my pocket to buy a new car. I was going to pay Reynaldo in advance so he could see that I meant what I said. Hopefully, thinking he would get more at the end would keep him on my side. I looked around then bent down and gave Chance's ear a pull.

There didn't seem to be any threat in the area, but of course, the kid could come back with gunmen—I didn't think he would though. I knocked lightly on the door, there was a knock in reply. I inserted my camera again and counted twelve with no one hiding although they all seemed to be wary. I slid another note through the door. Chance and I went down the trail out of sight of the door and ignited the small charge. There was a muffled whoop, not too loud but loud enough. We returned to see the door hanging by one hinge. I ripped the door off and, gun in hand, signaled the girls to come out.

No one moved. I stuck my head in, and then retreated instantly. The stench was unbelievable.

"Let's go, time is wasting," I yelled rubbing my watering eyes. "Let's move it ladies!"

"Put the gun away," a weak voice from inside croaked.

I holstered my gun and held my hands reverse to palms up facing the door as I backed away. I ordered Chance down the trail to guard and whether this was good or not we'd find out when the boy returned.

The girls staggered out, covering their eyes. Some were semi-clothed—some completely naked—and they all smelled as though one bath would not be enough to cleanse them of their filth. Their hair was tangled knots, and their sunken eyes squinted against the bright sun as they slowly filed out. They were holding hands for moral as well as physical support, as they came into the bright sunlight, forming a rough circle around me.

"My name's Rider," I said, turning around and acknowledging them all. "I'm an American citizen, and I didn't know you were here, but I'm going to do my best to get you out and back to the States. I've just blown up the compound and most of the gunmen are dead. I have befriended a dog and a kid named Reynaldo."

"Reynaldo," one of the girls yelled! "You mean the young boy?"

"Yes, Reynaldo. Is there a problem with him," I asked questionably?

"He's been keeping us alive by bringing us food and water," another said. "You can trust him, he's a good kid."

"We'll see," I said, looking around at the motley group. "Reynaldo's gone to get you food and water. We are very short on time ladies. I need for you to do as I ask when I ask you to do it or we'll be in more of a pickle than we are now. I need one lady who I will deal with, one you all trust and respect?"

There was a moment of mumbling before the name Melissa was agreed upon.

"I'm Melissa," she said, holding out her hand.

"Pleased to meet you, Melissa."

"Not as glad as we are to meet you," she said. "We've had a grueling time in there."

I handed Melissa a pen and paper. "I want you to print everyone's name, address, phone number, and city down in legible printing, then on the back write all the info you know about and Angela Fletcher."

I pointed to three girls and instructed Melissa to get their information first and then when done to send them over to see me. "Tell the other girls to keep quiet and stay here, with no wandering. I don't know how Chance will react when she comes back and sees you all, I need to introduce her to you for safety sake."

The three girls were not sure they wanted to be separated from their friends. There was a huddle and whispering.

"What do you want them for, Rider?" asked Melissa.

I gave Melissa the info and headed over to the trio.

"Follow me down the trail," I said, "no talking, and if you see a blond dog running toward you stop instantly, I need to introduce her to you. One girl in front and two behind, let's go!"

Their hesitation was only a split second too long. If the girls had a plan, utter defeat showed on their faces. When we reached the area where I had stashed the troops, they looked at me with shock and horror on their faces. I could see they were on the brink of attacking me, and I had to set their minds at ease.

"These troops were coming down the trail," I said, "and if Chance and I had not stopped them you may very well have been left in the bunker to die."

Their unease did not diminish.

"It's okay," I said, "concentrate on what you're doing not what you see, and it'll be much easier. Strip the clothes off the four troops. Do not touch Angela, leave her clothes on. Don't forget the boots. When you're done, return to Melissa and have her distribute the clothes."

One of the girls was choking back tears. "Angela was the nicest of us all."

The girls did not look like happy campers.

"You're all okay doing this?" I asked, not knowing what I'd do if they refused.

"We're okay," one girl answered, screwing up her nose. We can do it."

"Let's get moving then ladies, it won't take long."

I returned to the bunker where I found the remaining girls and was handed the list of their names.

"Thanks," I said. "First, I'm going send your names by satellite back to America. The authorities will contact your parents or whoever the phone number is on this paper. I'm then going to have a good look over our surroundings and make some decisions. Then I'm going to try to get you ladies out of here, but I'm going to need your help. I hope Reynaldo returns with food for you, and I hope this all falls into place."

Some of the women now had hope in their eyes.

One girl asked, "How did you find us?"

"That you'll see in a moment. Any other questions?"

"One question," Melissa said, "but first we want to thank you for what you have done so far. We'll try our best to help you as much as possible. We have two very sick gals with us. Do you have any medical supplies?"

I gave Melissa what I had and proceeded to unpack the drone. They all gathered around intrigued with what I was doing. I quickly assembled the drone and had it airborne hovering and taking pictures of all the names on the paper.

"This is how I found you. The drone picked up your heat. I came to take a look, and here we are. I'm going to be busy with this," I said to Melissa, "so I want you to watch the trail for Chance, Reynaldo, and your three girls."

I was just about ready to take the drone up when I heard footsteps coming down the trail. I put it down and signaled the girls to spread way out giving me room to maneuver.

I raised my gun as Reynaldo came stumbling around the corner at full speed. He was out of breath.

"This is all I could find," he stammered. "I did my best, Rider."

In his arms he was holding a big armload of grub wrapped in a blanket.

"You did a good job. Everyone here is thankful. Where did you find all this?"

"At the back of the manufacturing plant was the kitchen, so I grabbed whatever food I could find, looked around and found some sacks and then hurried back. I saw two guards stumbling around, but no one followed me!"

"That's awesome, Reynaldo, come over here."

He approached, thinking he was going to be reprimanded. Reaching into my pockets I pulled out all the money I had stashed in there and handed it to him. "This is for you?"

He just looked at the money then held out a shaking hand. Taking it, he was having trouble stuffing it all in his pockets.

"Reynaldo, how about giving me some to keep for you," I said. "I'll give it back to you when you find more room." Hesitating, he stuffed more in his pockets to the limit and reluctantly handed me the rest.

"How's the dog?" I asked

"She came at me growling then realized who I was. I patted her, but she wouldn't take any food. I tried but she just wouldn't take any."

"Well trained, isn't she?"

Even though Reynaldo's back was turned to them, the girls would walk around us without any inhibitions. They must have looked a very pitiful sight to him.

"Were you able to find a machete?"

"Yes, it's in the bottom of the bag."

"Grab it and come with me."

I called Melissa over. "We have a quick job to do, we will only be gone for a few minutes."

"Where are we going, boss?" Reynaldo asked, as we hustled down the trail.

I didn't answer but stopped where Angela was lying.

I asked Reynaldo to cut green foliage so I could cover Angela. He was thrilled to be able to help. With Reynaldo chopping away, I soon had enough foliage to conceal Angela.

"Thanks, Reynaldo, I have enough now. Go down the trail and see if Chance will come back with you? Don't try to force her though, if she won't come that's okay."

I went back and sat next to Angela. I picked up her hand and, even though her fingers were cold, they felt warm in mine. I sat there saying nothing for what seemed like a long time just reminiscing of the few hours we had known each other. I told her how much I liked her, I would always remember her and was sorry the way things had turned out. I also told her that I would phone her parents and tell them what had happened. I kissed her hand goodbye and tucked it under the green foliage.

Returning, I asked Reynaldo if he had seen any guards around.

"Just the same two I saw before, but I think others are on their way from the village down the trail."

I gave Reynaldo the receiver I had taken from Angela.

"Take this device down the trail to the jungle path. Climb a tree and make sure you stay hidden. If you see anyone coming push this button and I'll know! Then stay hidden till I come for you. You may see three more ladies on the trail, there with these ladies." I picked up some rice out of the sheet and rolled it in my hands to get my scent on it. "Give this to Chance, she'll eat it and you grab some for yourself."

He walked over to the blanket and leaning down picked up some rice, had a few hushed words with the ladies, then got up and ran down the trail. I started the drone up again while the ladies gathered around looking at my screen.

"Nothing secret about this, ladies. It sends the pictures you can see on the screen up to a satellite then back to earth!"

Hovering over the plant it looked like a war zone with no activity. I hovered over the river, looking at the boats. What I hadn't noticed before was a newer speedboat pulled up on the shore under some branches. I carefully lifted the drone up through the canopy, keeping the plant in focus. I could now see the river snaking through the jungle towards my pickup site some four miles away.

"That's our pickup site, ladies," I said, pointing at the screen. They all gathered for a closer look. "And this is the river I'm hoping will take us up to it."

The boat would be a godsend if we could find gas. Some of the girls were in pretty bad shape. I increased the drone's altitude, following the trail that the approaching guards would be on.

"Look here, ladies." I said, as I pointed to the screen and zoomed in on eight guards, in full gear about eight miles out. One of the ladies was looking over my shoulder and let out a loud moan, sending a shiver down everyone's spine.

"What are we going to do?" Another gasped. I took one more look around then called the drone home.

"I think our best plan would be to ambush them. We will have rifles and guns when the other ladies return. I will position you around the trail so you don't shoot each other, then we can hopefully catch a plane home."

I could hear the drone returning and had the ladies stand back. Bingo, right on my palm.

The three ladies arrived, hauling all the clothes they could get, ammo and guns. I had Melissa dole out the food and clothes, while I busied myself packing up the drone.

"Okay ladies," I said, glancing around and wondering if they would be capable of pulling this off. "We need to get out of here and in position and work as a team. Anyone who needs to pee do it now. Once we're in position there is no leaving. The two ladies who are ill can make themselves comfortable, and we'll come back and pick them up after the coast is clear. Keep your eye on Reynaldo just in case. The dog should be okay. I'll introduce her to you when she arrives. There are eight gunmen down the trail coming this way, so we need to go now. If you left anything in the bunker, you should go and get it, you won't be coming back."

No one moved, and I didn't blame them. Just opening the door almost killed me.

"I need one girl to act as your jungle leader, someone who's a good shot, so pick one now."

The girls had a quick huddle and one girl came forward. "My name's Linda."

"Melissa, send two of the girls who just returned, back down the trail to get Reynaldo and the dog. Reynaldo's hiding in the jungle near the main trail up a tree. Have them show Reynaldo where the guards are stashed. I want him to get all the ammo he can find then return here."

The two girls went scrambling down the trail. I packed the drone and stowed my gear. I beckoned to Melissa. "You know we're going to be in a gunfight, and things could get nasty."

"Yes, we all figured so," she said, with a big smile on her face. "We were hoping we would be given the chance to get even."

"I have no concrete plan for your extraction, now that there are fourteen of us plus a dog, but I'm hoping to find a boat or two to take us partway up the river."

"We'll do everything we can to help," Melissa said again, "it's going to be tough with twelve of us but we're strong-hearted."

"Good." I said. "We'll talk later."

I activated my phone, hoping there was a satellite overhead. I phoned in that I had a payload of twelve ladies, a dog and possibly a young boy. Then I heard scuffling coming towards us from down the trail. "Hide the girls, Melissa." I whispered, putting my phone away.

She led the girls to a far corner and concealed them in the jungle while I found a good hiding spot. Into the small compound ran the two girls loaded with weapons and ammo but no kid or dog.

"Where is the dog and Reynaldo?" I demanded

Melissa had a quick chat with the two girls. "The dog wouldn't come, and Reynaldo took a machine gun from the girls and said he's going to stay guarding the trail."

"Shit," I said, getting more frustrated by the moment.

I quickly checked the remaining weapons with Linda and had her hand them out with a short explanation on how they worked. Linda said she was a firearms instructor and could give them a quick lesson freeing me up. I called Melissa over and explained that I had to go down the trail and get the kid and dog, and now that he was armed, he was dangerous—sending the girls alone would not work.

"Also, I'm going take one of the girls with me and seeing her, he may come out if he thinks she is alone. I'm not worried about him hurting her, as I believe he likes all of you."

I went over to one of the girls. "What is your name?" I asked.

"Margo."

"Okay, Margo," I said, taking her by the arm and leading her away from the group signaling Melissa to follow. "This is what I want you to do."

Margo looked at me, and I'm sure her stomach was churning, and I could see in her eyes that she thought I was crazy.

"Okay, let me get this straight," she said, then repeated her instructions back to me.

"You got it, are you going to be okay?" I asked, not sure she would be able to carry out our plan.

"I will be okay when this is over," she said, with a worried look on her face.

"You'll do fine," I whispered, patting her back.

We made our way down the trail. I held back while Margo, with a trembling voice, went forward softly calling Reynaldo.

"Reynaldo, Reynaldo, we need to talk," Margo yelled. "Reynaldo…" Further down the trail, she heard the bushes rustling and saw Reynaldo cautiously come out of the jungle with his rifle pointed at her chest.

"It's important that you come back now," Margo yelled, "Rider has something he wants you to do."

He kept his rifle still pointed at her chest. "Well, then why didn't he come?"

"He did," Margo said, and she fell to the ground. At the same instant Margo fell, the kid looked up the trail to see my rifle pointed at his chest.

"Drop it, Reynaldo!" I yelled, walking toward him. "You don't want to get hurt or hurt anyone do you?"

"Okay! I'm putting it down," he yelled, but he was not quick enough. Chance, who was stationed up the path, heard my voice and came to investigate. Seeing Reynaldo with a rifle and Margo laying on the trail and me with my rifle, her training was to attack Reynaldo. Down the path Chance came at full speed, lunging into the air to knock Reynaldo down.

"Drop, Reynaldo," I yelled, and as Reynaldo dropped, Chance flew over his head. The kid and Margo looked at each other laying on the trail with fear in their eyes. "Stay down, Reynaldo!" I instructed, as I took Margo's hand and helped her up. I picked up the rifle, and said to Margo, "Good work." I handed her the rifle. "Hold it like *this*," I instructed. Chance looked at Margo, and Margo looked at Chance—neither was pleased. Margo had the rifle and Chance didn't like that. I called Chance over. "Friend," I said.

"Is she okay now?" Margo asked.

"You can even pat her if you like."

"You're sure she won't bite me?"

"Nope! Go ahead, she likes you."

"Stand up, Reynaldo!" I demanded.

The kid stood up on shaking legs. Looking at me, he wondered what had happened.

"That was a silly move you made. Chance saw you with a rifle and was protecting us. Good thing I was here. Don't touch a weapon again till I have introduced you to Chance while holding a weapon. Do you understand?"

"Sorry," Reynaldo said, still shaking, "I thought I could protect us better with a rifle. I've had lots of training."

"Let's get back up the trail you two," I said, shaking my head.

Arriving back at the bunker, I could see Melissa looking down at two of the ladies who were lying on the ground, and she looked worried.

"What's wrong, Melissa, you look like you just lost your best friend?" I said, walking up to her.

She looked at me without speaking for a moment. "Ann and Mary are too sick to even move," she said. "Internal problems. We'll need to carry them or at least *you* will. I don't think any of us are strong enough to even help!"

"We're all leaving here together, one way or the other," I said, looking at the two sick girls. "I'll carry them one at a time."

"Reynaldo, come here," I said, pointing to the ground in front of me. "I have an important job for you to do. I want you to go down to the river and check on a boat for us. There is one hidden under some brushes which I saw with the drone. It looks fairly new. See what you think."

"I know that boat. That's the boat that I was in when the blast went off. It's a good boat, but I'll check it out."

"We need two boats, but we can tow one if needed. We'll need fuel for both boats if they are running and check for keys. Then turn them around so they are facing upriver. If you see any guards push the signal, I gave you, and I'll come. We also need any plastic or canvas bags you can find. See what you can locate, and don't be followed back here. Got it?"

"Yes, Captain," he said, then, "Sorry. I thought I was doing the right thing back there with the rifle."

"That's okay," I said, giving him a slap on the back and almost knocking him over. "You're out of here."

I then picked two different ladies who had eaten. "Names?"

"I'm Claudia, and this is Naomi," Claudia said, with a wary look on her face, not looking forward to what she thought was coming.

"I want you to go down the trail to where it meets the main trail and hide. If anyone comes, including the kid, push this button," I said, handing them another device. "Do not come out till I come to get you. It's very important to stay there hidden."

"Okay," they said. "We can do that." They both scurried off a little worried, looking back at their friends.

I introduced Chance to each of the healthy girls then went over to the two sick ladies and did the same. Chance lay down between Mary and Ann, wagging her tail and nuzzling her nose against each of them. She knew the two ladies were not feeling well.

"I want you two to make yourself as comfortable as possible," I said, kneeling down beside them. "Linda will give you a rifle just for your own peace of mind. Don't shoot anyone coming down the trail before you make sure who it is, and don't worry about going anywhere as I will come back and carry you out. We won't leave you here. You may hear some shooting, but don't worry, it's only the girls and I taking care of business." I gave them a smile. "Okay, ladies?"

"Were fine with that, Rider," Ann said in a weak voice. "Anything from here on in can't be as bad as that chamber. It was deplorable."

I walked over to Melissa. "I want to do one last thing before we leave. I'm going to put the drone up for one final check; I want to see how close the gunmen are before you girls get into place." I unpacked the drone and prepared it for flight, as eight ladies craned to look at the screen. "There's Reynaldo checking for a boat," I said, pointing to the small figure on the screen. "Over here are the remains of the lab, and here the control shack."

"Wow," one of the girls mumbled, "The site has been obliterated, there is nothing left. Good work."

I raised the drone higher and followed the trail. "Over here are the troops, and it looks like they're three miles out and having a rest."

Turning the drone around, we could see the plant, or what was left of it in the distance. "There's Reynaldo turning the boats around. Does anyone see any other troops?"

Craning to see, they all said, "no." Then lights started flashing on the screen.

"Time to bring it home," I said. "Batteries are running down."

"This is our predicament," I said, looking at them one at a time. "Now listen close. Three miles away, as you saw, are the eight very well-trained gunmen. We have no option but to ambush them which means we have to take them by surprise. If anyone is squeamish about firing a firearm and killing someone who would first like to kill you, let me know now. It's not a problem, but I can give the firearm to someone who will shoot." Everyone stood still and looked like they could and would shoot.

"Okay, let's go get you ladies settled in the jungle so as not to shoot each other, or me and don't forget that Reynaldo and Chance may come running up the trail at any time," I said, turning and waving goodbye to the two ladies who would be left behind. I yelled back. "Each of you, with rifles, hand them to Linda, and she'll load them for you with a bullet chambered and with the safety on."

One by one the ladies went through the check. We picked up the two ladies hidden at the end of the trail and armed them also. I explained what my plan was and hid the ladies along the trail so shooting me or each other wasn't an option. *Very important at a time like this*, I thought, laughing to myself.

"Chance, smell this!" I said, holding it under her nose. "Again, girl." I said, then pointed down the trail. Chance took off in a cloud of dust on a mission, I hoped, to protect Reynaldo.

"Okay girls," I said, keeping my voice low. "Listen up, they're on their way. Let's be quiet, ready. Safety off before you shoot and aim before pulling the trigger. These handguns and rifles have a kick, so be ready for that. Two hands on the guns and press the rifles hard against your shoulders. There are eight of them and eleven of us. We will be okay."

I walked further up the trail till I found a spot that would conceal me. It was out of the ladies' line of fire and it would allow me to see the troops as they came down the trail. I had given Linda one of the receivers and said I would activate mine as soon as I saw any enemy movement. The problem was that the troops were coming one way and Chance and Reynaldo would be coming the other. I hoped Reynaldo would arrive before the troops or he could be caught in a crossfire. I heard what sounded like muffled talking and, sure enough, saw movement as the troops grew closer. Unfortunately, they were not close together but staggered. In the distance, I heard Chance bark in excitement, and then all was quiet. *Great*, I thought, *now they're in my line of fire and there was nothing I can do!*

Chance noticed the troops, and in a blink of an eye made a left turn and headed down the trail towards the bunker with Reynaldo on her heels. It was time. I pushed the detonator and the explosion resulted in five dead gunmen. Those who were not killed were wandering around in a state of confusion. Before the dust had settled the ladies opened fire using far more ammo than needed—but in doing so released all their tensions.

One by one the remaining troops died. I had not fired one shot. I signaled Linda again to get the ladies to point their rifles towards the sky. I was coming down the trail. I had passed all the troops heading towards the ladies when Reynaldo came storming up the trail followed by Chance.

"What happened?" Reynaldo yelled, puffing from all his running. "I heard this big bang then rifle fire and wasn't sure what it was. "Oh," he said, looking around with a smile on his face. "Good work, Chief!"

I had to laugh to myself; at least he had a sense of humor.

"These were the troops you said were coming, so I let the ladies take care of them. Tell Melissa I need two fit ladies. Then find Linda and have her collect all the firearms. Tell her to make sure all the safeties are on and to keep only four of the best rifles with plenty of ammo and stash the rest in the jungle."

Returning, Reynaldo had a big smile on his face. "It's all done, boss."

Reynaldo had two empty coke bags. I took him plus the two ladies and Chance down the trail to retrieve the cash that I had stashed. Then I returned to have a talk with Melissa.

When I was done, she called each of the girls by name into a tight circle. "I have information from Rider. We're not sure if this will pan out, but in theory it sounds good, and he thinks it will work. We're going to go down through the plant to the two boats where we will divide ourselves up.

Mary will go in one boat with Rider and Ann in the other with Reynaldo. We will make the girls as comfortable as possible as they're not looking too good. There will be two armed girls in each boat with Linda choosing who. Keep your eyes and ears open for any hostiles. Linda will bring up the rear and sprinkle her shooters amongst us. Rider will carry Mary down first then he will return for Ann. While he is gone, Reynaldo will stand guard and we ladies may have that time to bathe."

There were big smiles and light clapping from all the ladies.

I called Reynaldo over. "Are you ready?" I asked, giving him a big smile. He looked at me with sadness on his face. "What's wrong, Reynaldo, what are you looking so down about?"

He looked at the torn and tattered thongs on his feet and kicked at nothing. "You'll be gone soon, and I'll have nowhere to go. My parents were killed, I have no friends, and I want to go home with you. I like you, and I'd be really good if you'd take me."

"I know you would be good. You have already shown that to me; however, till the helicopters arrive, I don't know for sure what's going to happen."

Melissa had heard us talking and approached. "Excuse me, Rider."

"What's up?"

"I heard what you were talking about with Reynaldo, and I know my father would be willing to look after the arrangements for him if you can arrange passage home. We're all very grateful for what you and Reynaldo are doing, and without Reynaldo and his food, we would almost certainly be dead by now."

DOUBLE CROSSED

I didn't want to commit myself just then. "If there is room for Reynaldo on one of the helicopters, which at this moment I can't promise, but if there is, he will be coming with us and then we can talk." Reynaldo jumped in the air, scaring Chance, then he ran over and gave me a hug around the waist then did the same to Melissa. It was an emotional moment for all of us as our stress of the last few hours and commitment to each other was released.

"Reynaldo," I said, "don't get your hopes too high. I don't know what's coming in to pick us up yet. The original plan was only for me, now there are twelve women, a dog, and you as well. That's a lot of weight for two helicopters!"

"You'll find a way, Mr. Rider. I know you will." Reynaldo blurted, dancing around.

"Melissa, you and Linda get the ladies ready to go. Have the stronger gals carry the money; I'll go back and get Mary. Wait here for me, and we'll walk down together with Reynaldo in the lead.

"Reynaldo, get a rifle from Linda. You're going to point the way to the boats. Stay alert."

The two ladies didn't look very good. *Infections,* I thought, *and bad.*

"Don't worry, Ann, I'll be back shortly to get you," I said, handing her the rifle.

"I'm not worried," she said, in a weak voice. "I know you will. You're a good guy."

I picked Mary up—she was like a rag doll in and out of consciousness with arms and head lolling around. Finally having her tucked close to my chest, I was ready to leave.

CHAPTER

10

The walk to the boats was a real eye opener for the ladies. Devastation was everywhere, but when they saw the water, all was forgotten for the time being.

There was no hesitation; the ladies ran for the river jumped in and had water splashing everywhere. The ladies were in their glory frolicking in the muddy water they had stirred up.

"Hang on, Mary." I whispered in her ear. "We're taking you for a boat ride."

I signaled to Reynaldo to stand guard then ran back through the jungle and found Ann lying where I had left her, looking worse than ever.

"Okay Ann, are you ready?"

"Rider," Ann said in a weak voice, "I need to pee really bad. I need you to hold me; I don't have the strength to even move."

Ann was much lighter and just had the strength to put her arm around my neck. I held her while she did her business and then carried her to the river where the girls were still splashing and jumping in the water, all of them washing the filth out of their hair.

"Melissa," I called, "round up the troops, get the ladies ready, let's go now! No time to waste."

"Reynaldo, swim across the river and pole the boat back here," I said. "I need to put Ann in it. Chop, chop."

"Yes, Captain."

I shook my finger at him, and with a smile he swam across to retrieve the boat. He was one excited youngster. Hopefully I could arrange a new life, friends, security, and parents for him. Reynaldo was halfway across when Chance let out a growl. I put Ann down gently, grabbed my rifle, and signaled Reynaldo to stop. Two guards were going through the rubble, guns at the ready, and headed our way. I signaled for Melissa to keep the girls quiet. Pointing at the manufacturing site, I held up two fingers, then sliced them across my throat. Reynaldo started pushing his boat under nearby foliage. I held a finger to my lips then backed into the foliage myself, leaving Ann hidden in the scrub grass.

Reynaldo was about two hundred feet from me and entering an area where the guards could see him, if he wasn't careful. The guards had moved out of my sight, so I quickly ran over and picked Ann up and put her in the boat along with all the other girls. I had the girls row the boat under the jungle overhang and out of sight. I held my rifle up and pointed to it and shook my head, no, so Linda and her shooters would not fire.

I signaled Linda to come over and whispered instructions in her ear. She smelled and looked much better as all the other girls also did, after their short time in the water. Reynaldo was doing well keeping out of sight, but not well enough. I heard one of the troops yell at him. Reynaldo stood up with his arms in the air and pointed back at the boat he had been dragging. I couldn't hear what he said to them, but after a few words Reynaldo continued in our direction. The guards must have had other things on their minds as Reynaldo slowly kept approaching us without a care in the world, or at least that's what it looked like.

I waited for Reynaldo just out of sight of the guards, and as he approached, he gave a slight nod for me to head back to the boat. As I was about to turn, I saw a ripple in the water, then a large poisonous snake slithering toward Reynaldo. Not now, not now, I whispered to myself.

"Psssst…" Reynaldo looked up at me, and I wiggled my finger, then pointed to the snake. Reynaldo knew what I meant but kept coming, not wanting to draw attention to himself by putting the others in danger.

The snake was getting closer. I unsheathed my knife and with only one chance did what I did best. A few more steps and Reynaldo was hugging me shaking and mumbling.

"Reynaldo, go back and get my knife." I whispered.

With the girls loaded, poles out, guards positioned, and lines undone, we started pushing up the river and around the bend to where it was safe to start the motors. The trip on the river was uneventful. As we neared the pickup zone, we shut the motors off and drifted toward the bank.

"Out of the boats ladies," I whispered. "Linda, get your ladies positioned, and use Reynaldo as one of your guards. He knows how to use a rifle. Melissa, let's talk!"

I picked up Ann, then Mary, and made them comfortable in the grass. Mary looked a little better after I gave her a drink of water. I then took my phone out and sent a coded message that we were in position and a few seconds later a reply came back ETA forty minutes.

"Okay Melissa. This is what I hope is going to happen. There are three helicopters coming in with one medic on board. Ann and Mary will be put on the first helicopter as the medic is on that machine. I will carry both ladies to the bird. You put your girls into two groups boarding the last two. Reynaldo, the dog, and I will go with the sick ladies on the first machine. Do not waste any time getting on board. If the gunner or the pilots see any danger, they're gone, with or without us, so make it snappy and quick."

"When I give the signal, run to your machine and remember to keep your heads down, the rotors swing low on these machines. The three helicopters will all be landing in a clearing and very close to each other. We have a ten-minute walk to get there. No talking. And watch where you step. We don't know who's around. The gunners on the helicopters have a bird's eye view before landing, and they will cover our backs if needed."

"Any questions?"

There weren't.

"Okay, get the ladies saddled up, inform them what is going to happen, then ask Reynaldo to come here."

Reynaldo came running over, excited.

"Are you ready Reynaldo?"

"I'm really excited boss, really excited!"

I told Reynaldo what was happening.

"Now, you're going to stay here with Ann while I carry Mary to the landing site. I'll be back in about fifteen minutes. Don't shoot me on my return. I'll whistle when I'm near."

"Okay, I can look after her, and I'll be listening for your whistle."

Picking up Mary, I started walking, signaling Melissa and the ladies to follow. The going was fairly easy, and Mary handled it well in her bad state. When we were near the landing site, I picked the best spot I could find, and made Mary as comfortable as I could. I had Melissa position the ladies around Mary in the groups she had designated for the helicopters. Rifles at the ready and with strict instructions not to talk, or walk around, I headed back for Ann.

I gave a whistle for Reynaldo as I neared their position so he wouldn't shoot me, but there was no response. I listened, not moving a muscle. Standing stationary with only my eyes moving and ears listening, holding my breath, I neither heard nor saw anything unusual. Had Reynaldo not heard me? Then I heard it, a twig snapping very faintly but a bad mistake on his part. Had he seen me?

I loosened a knife.

It seemed the jungle had become silent for the moment. Listening and watching, I saw in the distance what looked like a solid mass, it was something out of place. I slowly crept forward quietly putting one foot in front of the other, not making a sound, and getting as close as I could to where the dead trooper lay. The small clearing had allowed me a clean throw. I retrieved my knife then silently crept forward again, stopping and listening and being careful where I placed my feet. The trail wasn't wide but widened some, then opened up where it met the river and that's where I had left Reynaldo and Ann. I stopped and listened again, nothing. The jungle had gone quiet. I had the feeling something was not right. I stood still and listened again. Still nothing, and then another sound, a click. It came from somewhere in front of me. But where? Another bad sign!

Slowly and quietly creeping forward again, looking and listening, watching for any movement, I saw him standing in front of me, well camouflaged, but I saw him, gun raised and pointed in my direction. My throw was silent and accurate, burying itself deep into his neck, where the spine meets the skull. He fell silently to the ground, dead without knowing what hit him. I crept forward and retrieved my knife then crept back into the jungle and whistled again. Still no answer. *Shit*. This wasn't looking good! The choppers would be arriving soon.

With a knife in either hand, I stood perfectly still, listening again, only my eyes moving. The jungle seemed to have gone to sleep. Quiet, dead quiet. Then I heard it again, another twig snapping as it caught on his jungle outfit. I turned around ever so slowly watching as my eyes swept the jungle in front of me, knives at the ready. Instinct took over—I threw.

I crept forward ten steps and retrieved my knife buried deep through his eye, stopping in his brain. Another blow and he was out. I whistled again. Still no reply. Shit. This was really not looking good now! Three birds arriving and three passengers absent.

I carefully took my sender out and pushed the button three times. Blink, blink, blink—one blink came back, still more hiding somewhere nearby.

I listened again. Nothing. I stepped over the first guard and could see the river some sixty feet ahead. I listened again. Still nothing. I moved closer to the river but keeping in the jungle, making sure I was not seen or heard. Nothing! I slowly bent down without making a sound and picked up a rock. I threw the rock high so it would land in the river. *Splash*

Nothing. Then I saw a faint flicker of light. It was a reflection but from what? I stood still not moving but listening. I carefully picked up another rock threw it in the river and watched again. Nothing! Time was ticking by—the three choppers were nearing our landing zone. We should have left by now. We should be there, all of us. I watched. I waited. I listened. I hoped and I prayed. Then I saw him. Not too far and not too close.

With both knives out, one in each hand I crept forward again. He was looking at the water where the rock had landed but he could turn at any moment. He did turn and my knife buried itself in a tree behind him. He turned around to see what the noise was and with his back to me the second throw was all it took. Cautiously I crept up to him keeping low and retrieved my knives, one from the tree the other from him. I wiped the blood off and stepped back into the jungle. I signaled four beeps.

Now what? I thought. Four beeps. I waited. No reply. I whistled. I listened. I looked.

Nothing. Damn! I heard a bird squeal behind me. I turned around in a blur burying my knife in his chest and the second in his neck. Five beeps. I waited, still no reply. I whistled, giving five distinct sounds. I listened, looking around. Nothing! Then I heard a noise and it was coming closer. Knives at the ready I waited.

Reynaldo.

"There were five?" I mouthed.

"Five," he whispered in my ear. "How did you get them all? I thought we were goners."

"I got five, how close is Ann?" I whispered.

Reynaldo pointed to a spot about sixty feet away.

"Stay here and cover me," I whispered again.

I silently crept the sixty feet over to where Ann was lying and put my finger to my lips. "Quiet," I mouthed. Looking around to make sure the area was clear I knelt down positioned one knife in my right hand and with both hands I carefully picked up Ann. She was in great pain; she gritted her teeth but didn't say a word. I couldn't see Reynaldo, but I knew that he was near. Cautiously, one slow careful step after another, carrying Ann, I started heading to where I had left Reynaldo. The going was easy, and then good. I was making time. I came to a sudden stop. There standing in front of me about twenty feet away and pointing his rifle in the direction of Reynaldo, was a lone soldier. *Dammit!* I didn't like this one little bit. Ann moaned as I swung her onto my left hip causing the gunman to turn our way. As I threw my knife Ann moved causing my throw to whistle past the soldier's ear. In doing so he ducked, I dropped Ann with a thud and was able to get a second throw away with my left hand before he had time to reposition his rifle. I retrieved my knives then bent down to where Ann lay on the ground writhing in great pain. "Sorry about that," I whispered. "At least were both still alive even though at this moment, you may wish differently. I'm really sorry, but I'm going to have to run all out with you, as were running late for our ride. It's going to be uncomfortable, but I have no choice."

"I can stand it," Ann croaked, gritting her teeth.

I picked Ann up as carefully as I could and headed for Reynaldo once again.

CHAPTER

"You okay, Reynaldo?" I whispered.

"Yeah fine," he said. "I didn't see that one. Let's hope you got them all. I was lucky. He must have walked within thirty feet of me."

"Let's go," I whispered again. "We can't waste any time, it's too dangerous here."

With Reynaldo in the lead, we started down the trail.

"Faster Reynaldo, hurry up," I said, running on his heels. "We're going to be late for our ride."

Reynaldo picked up the pace, now I was struggling to keep up with his scampering little feet.

Chance was the first to greet me, tail wagging, eyes aglow, she could hardly contain herself.

I laid an exhausted Ann next to Mary and turned to Melissa. "Anything?"

"No," she whispered. "All seems clear."

Chance's ears twitched, then I heard the rotors, and then I saw the helicopters.

I felt sick. There were only two. Someone was going to be left behind.

I turned to Melissa with two fingers pointing up. I looked at Reynaldo, he was beaming all over. If kids only knew the turmoil adults go through for them. The choppers were coming in fast, and they were obviously in a hurry. Reynaldo still had that look of sheer boyish delight on his face, but I could immediately see a problem. Weight.

As the choppers landed with a thump, in a cloud of dust, I picked up Mary and ran for the first machine giving Melissa the signal for her gang to follow. I carefully laid Mary at the medic's feet and held up three fingers. The gunner replied with two fingers then spun them in the air: *Hurry! was his signal, let's go, we got to get out of here.* I pointed to Melissa then held up five fingers and pointed to the two machines.

Returning and picking up Ann, I headed for the first machine again.

"Rider, I don't know how to thank you and Reynaldo," Ann said, struggling to get her words out as she was lifted on board. "You've risked your life many times for us, and we would still be in the bunker were not for you. I sincerely hope I see you again down the road."

As I laid Ann on the bird's floor, she sat up and gave me a peck on the cheek.

"Thanks again," she said, in an exhausted voice slumping back down.

"There is only room for one more!" the gunner yelled. "Hurry, we have to get up, gunmen are a mile out and headed this way, and they're running."

I ran back to Reynaldo who was helping the girls on board.

"Leave the guns and sacks of money here, let's go!" I yelled, literally throwing the ladies on board. Reynaldo

81

started to climb on the platform of the second bird, when I pulled him off.

"Reynaldo!" I yelled as the first helicopter lifted off. "There is no room for you, you need to stay here." A look of utter dismay crossed Reynaldo's face. All his hopes and dreams of the last few hours were shattered. No parents, no kids to play with, no friends and now no Rider or Chance. I knew he was going to cry.

"Now get these sacks and get them into the jungle as well as the better firearms."

Reynaldo obeyed his orders as I had a quick conversation with the pilot, said goodbye to his passengers, slapped the gunner on the back and jumped out of the chopper grabbing the last bag of money, and running for the jungle stopping halfway and giving everyone the thumbs up. Turning around, I saw the biggest smile on Reynaldo's face that I have ever seen on anyone's.

"I thought you were going to leave me behind?" He said, running and wrapping his little arms around me.

"Never, Reynaldo, never," I said, as the bird lifted off leaving us standing in the middle of the landing site, with a cloud of dust swirling around us.

I'm sure there was not a dry eye on board the helicopter. We both ran into the jungle where Reynaldo had placed the money and firearms. Once hidden, I turned to Reynaldo.

"Helicopters are gone, we have money, rifles, I have you and the dog, plenty of jungle and no doubt troops looking for us. Not much to work with except you and the dog," I said. "Here is my plan. We need to get out of here and quick! There are troops headed this way! They were a mile down the trail when the choppers landed, and no doubt the noise of the helicopters has alerted them. We have a six-day hike to the coast, and when we're nearer, I'll code for a pickup.

At the moment I don't know where that will be or when it will be. Do you know where the river flows to?"

Clearing a small patch in the dirt Reynaldo nodded. "Yes," he said, and drew me a map using his finger.

"After the river leaves here, it goes slightly this way then cuts back that way." Thinking he said, "It's fairly wide and navigable by boat all the way."

"That's good," I said. "I think we should wait just to make sure there is no one lurking to foil our plans. We have about four hours fuel in the speedboat so I think we should run it till the fuel runs out. I'll take the first watch."

Reynaldo lay back and got comfortable as I took the first watch looking and listening with Chance by my side.

Chance's ears perked up. I shook Reynaldo and pointed to where the choppers had landed. Three gunmen were carefully approaching the arsenal we had left on the ground and at the same time pointing their rifles at the perimeter as they looked around. My phone vibrated and the coded message.

third chopper five minutes out

I messaged them back.

abort. we're walking out

"Reynaldo," I whispered, "can you take me to where they are flying the drugs out of here? Can you get me there?"

"I know. I know, I've seen them doing it, I've worked there," he said, excited. "They are delivering them by large drones. I can take you there."

"How far away is it?" I asked, getting excited myself.

"It's about a two-hour walk. A large field, surrounded by many huts and a few guards."

"Reynaldo," I said, very concerned, "we have to get out of here! There are over fifteen gunmen in the field snooping around."

"Okay," Reynaldo said. "It looks bad doesn't it? Follow me." Crouching down and heading away from the troops he started leading us out of danger.

I patted Chance and pointed to Reynaldo.

"Reynaldo," I said in a quiet voice.

"Yeah?" he whispered

"Take Chance, go slow, and don't take any chances."

"Okay," he mouthed. We were on a narrow jungle trail, and when it rained it would become a stream. The going was tough as the trail was overgrown and full of snags. Even Chance was finding it tough. She stopped suddenly and started shaking. I whispered quietly and Reynaldo turned around. I pointed to Chance and Reynaldo had a look of concern on his face.

Reynaldo whispered. "I have seen her do this before and it usually means there is a snake nearby. She doesn't like them."

I looked around, and as I glanced back, I saw it strike. In a flash I had my knife out, but not quick enough. It looked like the snake had buried its fangs in Reynaldo's upper arm. A look of sheer despair came on his face.

Pushing Chance out of the way, I slashed at the snake cutting it in half. I grabbed the snake just behind its head and as I yanked it away from Reynaldo's shirt it released its lethal injection. I was hoping the venom I saw was its first shot. Crushing the snake's head, I turned to my first aid kit.

"Bare your arm, Reynaldo!" I whispered. He looked at me with fear in his eyes. "No," I said, with a concerned look on my face. "I'm not going to cut you."

I didn't see any fang marks, which was a relief. "This won't hurt, and it may save your life," I said, fitting a needle into the tube of serum.

"It looks like it just grazed your skin." I removed the needle and told him to sit still. Chance had stopped shaking, and I gave her a god pat. I didn't want Reynaldo to move till I felt the serum had taken effect, so while we waited, I took the tail section of the snake and skinned it.

Still writhing from nerves that had not yet received the death sentence, I cut the snake into small pieces and gave Chance a good meal. I put the remainder into one of the money bags we were carrying as this would serve Chance many days.

"How are you feeling, Reynaldo?" I asked.

"I'm okay but that stuff makes me feel woozy. I think you got him just before he broke my skin."

"I think your right. I didn't see any marks."

"We've got to go, Reynaldo. Let's move out slowly. No rush." After ten minutes of struggling through the jungle, I asked Reynaldo again how he was feeling?

"I feel a little dizzy but otherwise good. I'm okay to go."

"The dizziness is from the serum," I whispered. "Not to worry." The going was long and laborious. Reynaldo had to make frequent stops to rest, but we arrived at the drone site in two and a half hours. Just as Reynaldo had said, it was a large field with many buildings and few troops. The security was very lackadaisical, and we were able to get to the edge of the jungle without incident. Obviously, they hadn't heard about the plant yet. There were three very large drones, one being loaded and the other two were being fueled.

"Reynaldo," I whispered. "Hold Chance and don't let her go. I want to concentrate on the drones and not Chance. How often do they fly?"

"I have seen four here at once, sometimes taking off within a half hour of each other, depending how fast we could load them. There is a man inside that drone over there stacking the plastic bags as the other two guys throw them in. That was my first of two jobs here till I moved down to the plant as a guard. The other two drones, they are fueling now and will be refueled in midair at least twice by another drone so they don't have to land. They don't land to unload, but a field has been picked somewhere in the states. I don't know where, but I heard sometimes over Indian land. They will fly low over the field; the bay doors will open, and the bags will tumble out. The bags are made of heavy plastic and damage is little when they hit the ground. When the coast is clear a group of men who were previously hidden, will gather up the packages and take them away. My other job here was taping the bags up after someone else filled and weighed them."

They were loading these drones from the top, and I could see drop doors on the bottom. Looking around, including the gunman in the drone, I counted eight men. I signaled Reynaldo to keep low and quiet and to keep holding on to Chance. I had a thought.

The loaded drone was now sitting at the end of the runway, twin props turning, engines warming up. It slowly picked up speed and following its programmed instructions floated up into the silent afternoon. I waited till the drone had picked up cruising speed then using the controls I used for my drone, I was able to jam and override the drone's preprogrammed instructions. I turned my GPS override on and watched as I was able to turn the drone around in a lazy circle and direct it back, lining it up with the runway for a landing. Everyone on the ground was looking up in amazement, as the drone lined up doing a full power on landing. My plan was to hit the two grounded drones at full speed causing a fire. Reynaldo was watching in amazement at what was unfolding in front of him. With a perfect touchdown landing, it had landed three hundred feet from the stationary drones and, in a few seconds, would hit both of them. Four troops started running away but were caught in the explosion that ensued. White powder, red flames, empty plastic bags, rubber, fiberglass and metal were thrown high into the air as the fuel tanks ignited.

I watched the four remaining workers run in all directions dodging explosive debris. Flying objects killed two outright, and those remaining with severe wounds, were wishing they had died in the blast.

There were twelve huts sprinkled around the end of the runway. I sent coordinates up to the satellite with a note about the drones.

"Still feel okay?" I whispered to Reynaldo.

"I'm good now!" he said, smiling and watching as the drones exploded and went up in flames.

Even with all the damage already done I still wanted to look inside one of the huts. It didn't look like there was too much of a threat. I turned to Reynaldo. "I need to look in one of the huts. Wait here. I'll take Chance."

"Be careful," Reynaldo said.

As I left, creeping closer to the hut, staying in the shadows of the jungle, I could see that maybe entering the hut was going to be easy. The huts were on the edge of the jungle so anyone looking from above, satellite or plane, would have to have a very good trained eye to spot them. As I neared the hut, I looked at Chance, but there was no change in her stance. I pointed to the first hut and gave Chance the signal to crawl. I watched with rifle at the ready as she made her way around the first hut. She showed no signs of a threat.

I was about to call Chance back when she stood up and started wagging her tail. I took the safety off my rifle and undid the clasp of my knife and gun. I slowly crawled forward slithering through the grass not wanting to give my position away by scaring a flock of birds or anything else that might be alarmed by me.

Chance was holding her own, with her wagging tail toward me causing quite a dust cloud I couldn't figure out what her problem was. Maybe it was the snake she had eaten that was having this effect on her, but I didn't think so. She was trying to tell me something as her whole body was shaking as if really pleased to see someone. I crept back into the jungle and crawled over to the other side of the building where, spreading a large bush aside, I could see what was exciting her.

"Shit!" There was no way I could have seen this. In front of the hut were four well-armed guards facing Chance and two with their rifles pointed at her. I was so involved in watching Chance lay down on her side, with her tail flapping on the ground asking for a pat, that I didn't at first hear the sound behind me. Then I did. It was the sound of a branch cracking that put my nerves on edge. I laid flat on the ground with my rifle pointed toward the sound. I felt a slight vibration at my side and when it didn't stop, I carefully did a quick glance down and saw that it was a response from the device I had given Reynaldo.

Had Reynaldo left his position? Was he crawling toward me and warning me so as not to get shot? Or were there troops guarding the airport, spread in the jungle hidden around the site? I hadn't told Reynaldo that by prying the back off the device you could send text data. I texted him.

is that you?

I waited and tried again, not knowing if he could read or write English.

No answer.

>pry the back off! push the text button.

Then a reply.

>they almost found me.

I texted back.

>four with chance. someone behind me.
>keep low.

I didn't have the heart to tell him things didn't look too good. I was sure this was the end for Chance. With four guards in front and someone behind there wasn't too much I could do. I shut my eyes and said a silent prayer. Then I heard it! Not a rifle shot but the sound of a drone arriving back from its mission! There was rustling of the jungle as two guards burst out, not thirty feet behind me, and raced for the landing drone. I texted Reynaldo:

>come here.

A moment later:

>okay.

He arrived at my side as quiet as a snake slithering through the jungle. All six troops went running for the drone, leaving Chance lying there, wondering what had happened.

I whistled for Chance, and she came running back. I was never so happy to see her, even Reynaldo was getting in on the act!

"I need to disable that drone as well as the remaining troops. I'm going to put two shots in the gas tank, and hopefully it will explode and set the drone on fire. Get ready and shoot anyone who is able to escape. I will take those on the right, you aim for the outside left and then work your way in!"

"Okay," he whispered, with a nod of his head.

I chambered a special bullet that would explode on impact. I lined up my shot and was holding my finger lightly on the trigger, ready to pull, when Reynaldo crawled up next to me.

Touching me on the shoulder, then touching his lips, Reynaldo held up four fingers and pointed behind us. Then whispered, "far back."

I aimed my shot. It was perfect. The explosion was immediate. For quite some time white dust obliterated the remains of the drone.

"Do you think you can get us out of here," I whispered again.

"I can do it, boss." he said, as quietly as possible, with a look of pride on his face. We skirted where he thought the troops were. It was slow going, but it was important that we get away unscathed. Chance was on a leash and was acting like she thought she should be leading the way. Two hours later, nearing the site where we had left the boats, we stopped and listened. Neither he nor I could hear anything, and Chance's ears were not twitching. I had Reynaldo go ahead with Chance still on her leash, and scout it out. I checked all my gear and reloaded my gun. "Boss," he whispered, returning silently. "The boat is as we left it, and there is a little more gas than we thought. One boat is nearly empty. I dumped the gas into the boat that had the most gas and it's ready to go."

"Good work!" I was amazed at how mature he was for his age. "Let's gather everything up and get started. You can drive, and I'll stand watch. Bring it up to full speed then drop it back to three quarters. That will leave us some power in reserve and should move us along at a fair clip, keeping you well occupied."

He handled the boat admirably, going around sharp turns and shallow water. "How much experience do you have driving a boat Reynaldo?" I yelled.

"Not much, but a bit with this one," he replied, smiling. "It's fun, more fun than standing watch."

"When we're near the factory," I yelled, "give her full throttle. We don't want to be dancing around there in case someone hears a boat coming." Chance and I lay low out of sight as we screamed past. He reported no activity.

The river was a mass of twists and turns, taking most of Reynaldo's attention. At one point where the river widened, we found a spot that we could stop and hide the boat for a few minutes to let Chance relieve herself.

"Can I ask you a question?" he asked, looking up to me.

"Sure, we have a few minutes, fire away."

"Well, I was just wondering what your job is?"

That was a tricky question. How much could I tell him without tweaking his imagination too much?

"Here is the short version," I said. "After finishing school, I did two years in law. It wasn't too interesting so switched to electrical engineering. It's a four-year stint. After completing two years, the Navy saw how good I was, and we made an agreement that, if they paid for me to finish my electrical degree, I would become a Navy SEAL."

"You're a Navy SEAL?" he said, with a huge smile on his face. "I knew that there was something different about you. You always knew what to do. I want to be a Navy SEAL when I grow up. I wanted to be a race car driver, but I've changed my mind. I want to be like you."

"No, I'm not a Navy SEAL anymore. Now let me finish. I became a SEAL then an Elite Navy SEAL which I was for many years."

"What happened to your SEAL friends?"

"Oh, they just swam away. No, once a SEAL friend, always a SEAL friend. Now no more interruptions, okay?"

"On my last mission, I returned home to find out that my wife had cancer."

"You were married?"

I shot him a warning look.

"Sorry."

"My wife died a number of months later, and I quit the SEAL team."

"Why did—" Then he caught himself. "When you're a Navy SEAL there is a very close bond between you, and your partners. Your life depends on each other. I felt that after my wife's death I couldn't protect my fellow team members to my fullest, so I resigned. The fellows that I worked with will always be like close brothers to me."

I looked around to see how Chance was doing in the hopes that Reynaldo realized I had finished.

"Well, who do you work for now?" he asked, with a frown on his face.

"I'm on a special contract with the DEA. Do you know what that is?"

He nodded. "Is that why you're so good at what you do?" He asked, looking up at me with awe on his face.

"I was very well-trained, now whistle for Chance. We should be moving."

"One more question? You're not white. How come you're so good?"

"One more answer. You don't have to be white to be good. There is good in both colors. The boat ran for four hours till the gas petered out. We drifted to a sandy bank and secured the boat to a large branch that was overhanging the river.

"Where do you want me to stash the boat?"

"We won't stash it. Let's leave it in plain sight so someone will see it and perhaps be able to use it."

I jumped out with the extra rifle and had Reynaldo leave the key in the boat, "grab the money and follow me." I looked at my map.

"We need to make some distance in case someone heard the boat and comes to look."

At this point the jungle had thinned out with slight rolling hills, which enabled us to see what lay ahead. Reynaldo was good at finding trails, and we were soon on our way. The going was easy, but because I had an extra person sharing my rations, we were going to run out of food soon. I would, under different circumstances, sneak into a village early in the morning and take whatever I needed to sustain me for the day, leave some local cash and vanish.

"The next village we come to, I need you to go in and get us some food. Steal it, buy it, whatever. But if you do steal it leave some money for the farmers." It was three in the morning, Reynaldo had left to find food, and Chance and I were holed up in a small clump of bushes. Dawn was approaching when I heard a sound and turned around to see Reynaldo crawling toward me. He was good! I only saw him twice on his return.

"I stole some food and was given some." he said, "and I left money for both."

"We'll eat later. Let's hit the trail in case someone is trying to follow us." As I did one last check of the surroundings, I spotted a slight movement in the far distance. Someone *was* following us.

"Look down there," I said, pointing toward the village he had come from. It looks like there are three of them."

"Sorry, I was sure no one was following me."

"That's okay. We'll shake them. We're going to backtrack and hole up in those rocks up there. That will give us better coverage than here. It's not going to be the most comfortable hiding spot, but we will get a panoramic view. Let's go."

When we found a good location, I assembled the drone with its rotors exposed to the sun to charge the batteries. I figured the coordinates on the beach where I wanted our helicopter to pick us up and worked out the time to travel there. Then I retrieved my phone and coded the message.

two men, one dog

After a moment I got my reply.

roger that

The wait wasn't long. Coming out of the village Reynaldo had previously left, were three gunmen on high alert with a dog. I figured that if their dog was trained anything like Chance had been trained, we could be in big trouble.

The gunmen were moving slowly, following their dog, who was tracking our scent. As they neared our former hiding spot, the dog went down on her belly, and the gunmen scattered for better cover. The dog, with its tail wagging, circled around our previous hiding spot sniffing where Chance had been.

From half of a mile away, we watched as the dog went into a small depression, and we lost sight of it, then it suddenly appeared, abruptly turned, and headed crawling toward one of the hidden men.

"It looks like it's our guy, plus the kid and they have a dog," the leader said, looking through his binoculars. "The tunnel goes directly under them and up the hill with an exit by that clump of trees just to their left. We'll enter the tunnel come out behind them, and boom, they're gone!" He had a smile on his face.

He turned to his underling.

"Go back to the hut where you'll find the keys for this lock. Bring flashlights and a shovel—and hurry it up. I want you back here in no more than fifteen minutes. Tack, see if you can find a better hiding spot, and make yourself comfortable, but stay out of sight! I'll keep Jaco here with me."

"*Here*, Jaco," he said, calling the dog and looking up the hill—but the words were no sooner out of his mouth than Jaco was gone, charging up the incline to where he heard a distant barking.

"Shit," said the leader, "it's like I thought, that's got to be Chance's bark. Jaco recognized it or he wouldn't have run off." He looked at his underling returning with the key. "Those dogs were trained together. We may be confronted with a serious problem if he takes a liking to her. But on the other hand, he may just return here with her. Okay, let's forget the dogs for now and head up the tunnel. He will know where we've gone and come charging up the tunnel after us when he returns. Let's go!"

—

"There are three gunmen and a dog," I said. "With your training, what would you do, and what do you think they're going to do?"

Reynaldo looked pleased to have been asked. "The other dog might be Jaco. If he is, they were often together. Let me think for a minute. We could pick them off from here, but that would alert the village and possibly more troops. We could crawl back to where they are and take them out by hand, but they have a dog, which creates a problem. We could send the drone over to eliminate at least two of them by dropping a grenade amongst them or we could leave now and track around them."

I smiled. "Or we could stay here and let them come to us. Jaco may be friendly when he sees Chance, which would be an advantage to us."

I could tell he liked this last suggestion.

"Wait here with Chance," I said. "I'm going to scout up above us."

He looked at me as if I had gone batty. "Don't worry, I'll be back in a few minutes. Keep low. I have a plan. *Here,*" I said, handing him the binoculars. "See if you recognize anyone."

He studied the troops and dog for some time with a look of concern on his face. "One of them, the one who was handling the dog, was associated with the boss at the plant, Chance's handler, and he was a real mean dude," he said frowning and "Jaco was almost as good as Chance."

I crawled up the incline some distance above Reynaldo till I found what I was looking for. The opening was covered with bush, but I knew how to recognize it from previous missions. Exposing the opening, I was glad to see that I did not need to crawl into the tunnel, it was high enough to walk through stooped. Flashlight in hand, I slowly started down the incline which at this point was not too steep, but steep enough to be wary. I couldn't hear any noises so figured the gunmen hadn't started up the tunnel from the lower end yet.

The tunnel had been dug out through hard ground, so very few supports were needed, and it was just wide enough for my shoulders to ease through. These tunnels were built by the locals to hide in when danger loomed, and also as part of the defense of the village. I did what I came to do, turned around, and headed back up the tunnel. The going up was a lot slower than going down, and I hoped that none of my charges pre-detonated before I was able to get out. From down the shaft I heard the squeaking of a little used gate opening, then the muffled sound of men talking. I hustled my pace exiting the tunnel to bright sunlight and fresh air.

When I returned, I noticed Chance had her nose to the air and smelled something. In a flash she was gone. I couldn't call her back without giving our position away in case there were other troops, so we watched as she headed down the incline at full speed.

"I recognized one of them," Reynaldo said. "He's a real mean dude, and I mean dirty mean. He was with Chance and his handler one time. Chance wouldn't do what he commanded, so he kicked her numerous times. In fact, he has a scar on his shin where Chance bit him. Then she ran and hid."

"What's Chance doing?" I asked, as he was following her with the binoculars.

"She knows the other dog and maybe feels she has found a temporary play companion," he said, handing the binoculars to me.

Chance lay down in a depression out of sight of Jaco and let out a couple of barks.

I had given the binoculars back to Reynaldo.

"What do you see?" I asked.

"When Chance barked, I was looking at Jaco, and his ears perked up. He's running to where she is."

I heard a whistle from the dog's handler, giving his position away. He was still standing beside the open gate. Jaco ignored him and kept running away looking for Chance, and as he did, Chance jumped up and started running up the hill toward us. Jaco saw Chance and took off after her with his handler whistling frantically. The dogs were of equal stamina, and as Chance neared our hiding spot, she stopped short in a slight depression; out of sight of the other troops. Jaco came running up to Chance and after the initial wariness and rump sniffing, the dogs started playing.

"They remember each other. This may be good." "You stay here, and if Jaco attacks me, you'll have to shoot. Make sure your aim is good." I smiled. "Remember, I'm your ticket out of here."

I crept out of our hiding spot and was nearly upon the dogs when they saw me and stopped playing. Chance sat down panting with her tail wagging. Jaco raised the hair on the back of his neck and started snarling when he saw me, and then Reynaldo, in the distance.

"Chance, come here, girl," I said, hoping this would calm the other dog down.

When Chance reached me, I started patting her, and Jaco came charging. Brushing by Chance's side he raced the short distance toward Reynaldo and, as he got closer, started wagging his tail and sniffing Reynaldo's outstretched hand.

"I think he remembers me," he whispered, being very wary of the dog.

"Come down here and see if he will follow you."

I held Chance so she would stay at my side. I peered down at the troops and they were in a huddle not sure what to do. Jaco followed Reynaldo through the sparse scrub but stayed behind him out of reach.

"Go back and get the sack with the snake in it, and we'll see if he follows you."

He returned with Jaco in tow. "Can I feed him?"

"You sure can, but I would like to build up a relationship with him first."

I retrieved the snake from the sack and gave Chance a little bit that she ate. Jaco didn't budge although he looked very interested. I held my hand out with another small piece for Chance. She looked at it then gingerly took it out of my hand and walked over to Jaco and dropped it in front of him. He looked at it then picked it up and it was gone. He was hungry. I called Chance back and gave her another piece which she ate. The fourth piece she wouldn't eat but kept looking at Jaco.

Very gingerly and with great trepidation, Jaco approached me and leaned as far forward as he could to get the meat. I was expecting a snapping snatch, but I was very pleased when he more or less licked it out of my hand and left me with all my fingers intact. I gave each dog another piece of meat with the same results.

"What do you think?" I said, handing him the meat.

"It looks like Chance has a companion." Reynaldo beckoned the dog over to try feeding him himself.

I checked down to where the troops were, but they were either well hidden in the jungle bush or climbing the tunnel that I had just found.

"We do have a problem with this dog," I said, patting Chance and pointing to the other dog. "If he gets near to his master, he is capable of leading them to us in which case we'd have to shoot him."

I sat there pondering our situation with the new dog.

"I think it would be wise to let Jaco become more familiar with me. You talk to him while I ease over next to you and let's see what he does," I said, bringing Chance with me.

I had kept an eye on the tunnel as I handed Jaco a piece of meat. I started to scratch his ears, then his neck, then his back with no outward reaction except sad eyes. I stood up then stood beside him patting his back and pulling him to my side, so he was touching my leg. Chance came over not wanting to miss out on the affection, and I patted them both at the same time. Nothing had changed down at the tunnel.

"Time to go," I said. "I don't know if I can trust him, but he's not showing any aggressiveness towards either of us. Keep your eye on him, you never know."

The dogs trailed behind us frolicking with each other, jumping in the air, and causing general havoc till I put a stop to it.

"Chance, come here," I said, as I knelt down patting a happy dog. "It's time to get back to work. You can play later, off you go." I pointed down the trail.

Chance ran forward to her leading position with the new dog following, but he would regularly turn back to check on us, still not too sure.

"How close are we to the river, Reynaldo?"

He stopped and looked around. Kneeling down, he patted his dog. "I think about a mile and a half that way."

There was a muffled explosion and a large cloud of dust coming from up the hill. Reynaldo looked at me, not knowing what had just happened.

"That was the tunnel exploding," I said. "When I was up the hill, I found the opening, crawled in and set charges. I thought they might try to get closer to us by coming up through the tunnel."

"How did you know there would be a tunnel? I didn't even know that."

"Through previous training we had to find and eliminate tunnels just like that one. This one was not difficult to find."

"I was worried for a moment," he said. "Good work, I wasn't sure if it was them or not."

"Well, it was them," I said, "but not anymore. I think we should forget about following the river and get to the coast as fast as we can. I've radioed for a helicopter to be on standby, and it will fly as soon as we are ready. I think we can forget about these gunmen following us, but let's be on the lookout for others. Let's go down this way where there is less foliage," I said, pointing to a small scrub of grass! "I think *they* will think we went where there is more foliage, and if anyone is following us, it will give us a little more time. What do you think? Any concerns?"

"No," he said, looking around. "I think there is enough foliage down there to hide us as long as the dogs behave."

I looked at Jaco, and he looked like he wanted to play and would take off at any moment. I looked in my backpack and retrieved a six-foot piece of rope. Making a noose at either end, I slipped the larger end over his neck without any reaction from him.

Still, with sadness in his eyes, he looked up at me. I gave him a pat, and his tail started to wag. Retrieving another piece of the snake, I gave both dogs a good meal. He looked up at me, still with sadness in his eyes not too sure and I gave him another piece of meat.

"Let's go. I'll take this one, and you handle Chance."

We started off, and from my first step Jaco marched beside me as if I was his trainer. The going was easy, both dogs behaved, and we saw neither hide nor hair of the three men from the tunnel. That night, I let Jaco off his leash, and he just lay down between Reynaldo and me. I had my arm on his back rubbing his fur.

We had plunked ourselves in a clump of trees with an outcropping of rock that gave us good cover.

"It's starting to get dark; you rest," I whispered. "Chance and I will take the first watch. It looks like Jaco wants to come but keep him here with you. Tie the rope to your wrist, then if there is trouble, hopefully, he will pull on the rope warning you."

I gave Reynaldo one of our food rations, and the dogs each a piece of meat then crawled over to my hiding spot some distance away and got settled in with Chance at my side. No sooner had we settled, than Chance started looking around.

"What is it, girl?" I whispered looking around also. I felt Chance tense long before I heard them. Down by our hiding spot, where Reynaldo was, there were two gunmen advancing on him.

I watched, and then they disappeared. I carefully crawled back to where Reynaldo and Jaco were holed up, but they were gone. I looked at Chance. "Where are they girl?" I whispered.

Chance looked at me then started crawling through the bush in the opposite direction from which we had come. Was this a trap? I thought. Had Reynaldo become homesick now that he had a local dog, and would he try to escape giving away my position?

I was about to call Chance back when I heard a faint whistle. I listened and this time Chance perked up her ears. I whistled back and then carefully but quickly changed locations, taking Chance with me. The spot I chose would give me advanced warning of anyone approaching long before they could see me.

I waited, wondering where Reynaldo was, and why he had whistled. Then, looking down the trail coming around a corner I saw Jaco leading Reynaldo back in my direction, and then I saw the two troopers following them.

The first trooper had his rifle jammed in Reynaldo's back. The second was being very cautious, looking all around rifle at the ready. They had somehow been able to lure Reynaldo and Jaco from their hiding place—or was this a trap? I felt sure Jaco would still take orders from either of these guys, food or no food. As they entered the clearing, they all stopped in surprise.

CHAPTER

What they saw was Chance, lying on her side looking like she was injured.

Jaco tore the leash out of Reynaldo's hand as he lunged for Chance, happy to see her again, but cautious as to why she was laying still.

The guard holding the gun at Reynaldo's back was startled and started whispering orders at Jaco who just ignored him as he sat beside Chance, tail wagging. Neither dog paid any attention to him, which only made him all the madder.

The guard raised his gun up over Reynaldo's shoulder and was taking aim at one of the dogs.

The first shot spun the gunman around, and he was dead before he hit the ground. My second shot hit the second trooper killing him as well.

I ran down to where Reynaldo stood shaking and put my arm around his tiny shoulder. I checked the two dead troopers, called the dogs and then led him back to our hiding spot.

Chance's ears perked up again. I looked around.

"Reynaldo," I whispered, "down there, three more. Hang on to your dog."

"Where are they all coming from?" He whispered, with a frown on his face.

"You tell me! See the one with the baseball cap on? Watch him, he is easy to spot."

The three troopers had stopped their advance after hearing the shots and were taking shelter, wondering what their next move would be, and who had fired at whom.

"They're down there," I whispered. "In that small clump of bushes."

"I don't see them," he said, straining his neck.

"You will, keep watching."

"I just saw the baseball cap. We could take them out from here, I mean you could," he whispered, with a smile on his face. "But I guess that would bring even more."

"No," I said. "I'd like to question one of them. Let's circle around behind them and see if we can capture all three." I pointed to a small hill. "I want you and Chance to circle over there, and I'll stay here till I know you're in position and safe. Give me the leash, and I'll take Jaco."

I watched as he and Chance crawled and then ran to their hiding spot. His wave was hardly noticeable but sufficient for me to know they were safe and secure. I did the same with Jaco but went the other way.

The gunmen were huddled in a small clump of bushes, the only hiding spot that gave them any cover. I signaled to Reynaldo, and our plan was put into action.

The first charge detonated in the rocks above them, where we had previously been hiding. Splinters of rock sprayed all around them kicking up numerous clouds of dust.

The second charge, which I had placed on my way down exploded a fraction of a second too late. With clouds of dust swirling around, all three thought it would be better to run to lower ground—and a better hiding spot—than face whatever was above. The third charge was larger and even more lethal and, as the gunmen ran downhill, two were hit by flying rock and killed instantly leaving the third wandering around from a hit to the head.

Chance was first to reach him, and grabbed the rifle strap with her teeth and dragged it out of danger. Jaco, who I had taken off his leash, had a farther run, and on his approach followed the stumbling guard snarling with a look of hatred in his eyes.

I approached slowly, rifle at the ready, not knowing how Jaco was going to react towards me with one of his own staggering around, but he wagged his tail as I got closer. The trooper was holding his head as blood oozed between his fingers and down the side of his neck. He was pale and his eyes were out of focus. He looked in bad shape, still alive with death knocking on his door.

As Reynaldo came running up, with Chance still snarling, Jaco looked at him and wagged his tail even harder.

"Do you know if he speaks English?"

Reynaldo looked at him then back to me.

"I don't think he can speak at all, boss. I think he is a walking dead person." At which point, the gunman fell to the ground and was still.

Constantly watching our backs, the going was easy, but the jungle thinned out, putting our nerves on edge. So close yet so far, and I had to get Reynaldo to safety. As we neared the beach and our pickup site, caution was our main concern. We found a good hiding spot in some bushes and seated ourselves looking at each other so we could look sideways and over each other's shoulders for better protection.

I sent a coded message that we were in position and ready. The return message was that the chopper was leaving within five minutes and that they were about half an hour out. Half hour on the beach with little cover, bright sunshine—me and Reynaldo and two dogs.

Something was bothering me.

"Reynaldo, I need you to answer some questions then I'll tell you what's going to happen," I said. "First of all, how did you get into the hands of those two gunmen that you said ambushed you, without me hearing any sound from you?"

Reynaldo glanced down with a worried look on his face. He kicked a rock with his shoe.

"Well, as they approached, they shot both Jaco and me with something that put both of us to sleep for a few minutes. They then picked both of us up and carried us to a different spot. I woke up, and it wasn't too long before you whistled, and they told me to answer you."

"Did they ask you any questions?"

"No, they didn't have time to, but I'm sure they were going to."

"Where did they hit you with the needle?" I asked.

"I'm not sure," he said, "but my back was to them, so maybe there."

"Show me."

He frowned then turned around lifted his shirt, and I could see a red spot where something had pierced his skin.

"Okay, all's good." I said. "The chopper will be arriving in about thirty-five minutes so keep a keen eye out for anymore gunmen."

"Okay, but what does a keen eye mean?"

"Keep a keen eye means to watch carefully."

"I can do that."

"I know you can. Now, when I give you the signal, keep your head down, and you and the dogs run as fast as you can for the chopper. I want to see smoke coming from the bottom of your sandals. Help them up, then you climb in and buckle up instantly. Hang on to them, introduce Chance to the gunner and point to the pilots, say friend. Hopefully Jaco will follow Chance's lead. If he won't, he'll have to stay, we want to get home."

"I'll be behind you, covering your back. Don't hesitate, even if shooting starts. It's important you get to the helicopter as fast as you can. They won't wait for us if the pilot sees he is in a dangerous spot. Keep running, don't look back, and remember I want to see smoke coming off your sandals."

"When we get to the ship, you will be fed, bathed, and given fresh clothes then taken into a room where you will be asked many, many questions. Do not lie or you will be flown back here and left. It's very important that you tell the truth. The dogs and I will see you before we leave the ship and are flown home. You will then be flown from the ship to the States where you will be interrogated some more. Then you will be put in a nice foster home, and you will start attending school. Everyone will tell you this, and it's very important that you always remember it. I am a nobody. You have never seen, met, or know of me. I never existed in your mind. In the States they will give you all the answers to questions you may be asked by your new friends and some who are not.

"I will arrange a meeting with you in someone's home so we can have a good talk or party in a few weeks. Down the road, when you're settled in and feel comfortable in your new surroundings, we will be able to meet more frequently."

"Now the question to you, my friend. Do you still want to come with me, or do you want to stay here?"

"I can't come live with you?" he said, choking up with sadness in his eyes.

"Sorry buddy, but the answer is no. I'm still undercover and that's why we never met."

"What about Jaco, can I take him with me?"

I hadn't thought about that. "I'll tell you what. You take Jaco, he is your dog, and I'll come and visit when Chance is in heat."

"What's *in heat* mean?"

"It means when she's ready to start babies."

He wiped a tear away. "Thank you."

We were for a while in silence with eyes on the jungle and ears straining for the sound of the advancing choppers.

We were almost home free when I saw movement in the bushes about eight hundred feet away.

I signaled to Reynaldo pointing behind his back, touched my lips, then pointed to Jaco and closed my fist. Reynaldo slowly moved, turning around and we both saw it again. I contacted the ship to warn the chopper of hostiles and to give him our exact coordinates. At this stage of the game, we didn't want to be shot by the good guys.

"Did you see the bushes move?" I whispered.

"Yes, and there was movement over there also," he said, pointing in a different direction.

"Great, just what we need!" I whispered, looking in the opposite direction.

"Keep watch while I get my drone mobile." I sent the drone up to seven hundred feet where I had a good look at the movement below. My pictures were being relayed to the ship then to the chopper. Where I had first seen movement, there were six gunmen in a huddle, pointing in all directions. I took their coordinates then swung around and looked where Reynaldo had spotted movement and sure enough there were two more gunmen looking at maps.

How did anyone know we were here? This had been happening all along. There definitely was a leak somewhere. I was being DOUBLE CROSSED. I zoomed in and could see that they were in the area we had just left. I panned out and flew the drone around but saw no more troops. I brought the drone back, and in a few moments, it was parked at my feet.

I felt my burner vibrate and checked the message.

"ETA Five minutes. Hold on to Chance and don't let her go," I said, while tying Jaco to my ankle with a quick release knot. "The helicopter will clear the area before landing, so hold tight, don't be scared. It may be rather noisy, and the bullets could come close to us. When I get the signal from the gunner and tell you to run, I want to see your sandals on fire, got it, no fooling around. Run for your life."

"I'm really scared and excited. I can do it, and I'll be halfway there before you're ready to run," he said, with a huge smile on his face. "I know I can do it."

Chance's ears perked up and I knew the chopper was near.

"Hold tight onto Chance, the chopper will be opening up very soon." The first and second rockets exploded on target, but the second group of gunmen had moved. The helicopter hovered higher looking down, then sprayed a large area with bullets, then suddenly made a drop for the ground like a mad hornet spitting fireballs and obliterating everything in its path.

The pilot, satisfied the gunner had cleared them a landing zone, landed the chopper with a thump, and a massive swirl of dust. Its engines whining and rotors spinning at near full throttle, it must have scared the crap out of the kid. "Go!" I yelled. He was off like a shot, and I was on his heels, holding Jaco by his leash, yelling at Reynaldo giving him encouragement that he really didn't need.

The gunner saw us running and, pointing in the distance with his gun thumping, signaled us to hurry. "Faster run faster," I screamed. As we neared the helicopter, I came alongside Reynaldo, picked up Jaco and hurled him onto the deck. Feet clawing on the metal plate he was able to stop before sliding out the other side. I then grabbed Chance and threw her in as Reynaldo was struggling with her weight. I jumped onboard, grabbed Reynaldo by the collar, and before his little feet hit the deck, the gunner signaled the pilot to suck air.

Guns blazing, both the gunners and choppers, we lifted, dipped, then headed for the ship in a blaze of bullets from both sides.

Reynaldo's eyes were bulging as he watched the gunner searching for hostiles while the two pilots casually flicked buttons and switches. The ground whizzing by at a welcome rate. Then we were over the water.

Buckled down with headsets on, the pilot signaled Reynaldo to come forward. He looked at me with "really?" on his face. "Go on," I yelled pointing. He settled down just behind the two pilots. It was a boy's dream come true, just being able to see and hear what was going on. As the ship grew nearer and bigger, Reynaldo was beside himself jabbering nonsense to both dogs. Whether they understood or could even hear him it didn't matter, they both wagged their tails.

As we were hovering to land on the ship, I gave Reynaldo the thumbs up and grasped the leashes of both dogs. In the rolling seas with the ship pitching, the pilot made a beautiful landing, and the chopper was immediately strapped to the deck. I unbuckled myself and stuck my head between the two pilots thanking them for the safe trip. Thumbs up from both, they continued with their shutdown.

Jumping out, I thanked the gunner, grabbed the dogs, and with Reynaldo at my side, still wide eyed, we were welcomed aboard by the commanding officer. Reynaldo was whisked away in a friendly manner—unsure what was happening even though I had explained it to him earlier on.

With both of us in separate parts of the ship, the debriefing started. Mild for Reynaldo, with cookies and milk and a few questions thrown in here and there; demanding, for me, with black coffee and water for the dogs.

Question after question. Why? Why? Why? If they had been there, they would have known the answers to why. Explaining why and leaving out one small piece of insignificant information or what seemed insignificant, resulted in more questions. I introduced the dogs to anyone who entered the room, which was better than two snapping snarling dogs being thrown overboard. Early the next morning, with Jaco in tow, I knocked on Reynaldo's door to say goodbye. He was not there, but in his best handwriting he'd written a note, saying he had been invited up to the bridge. This was good, every boy's delight.

Walking through the ship to the bridge, I passed many security guards who saluted then stepped down allowing me to pass. The last two guards were not so friendly, but when Captain Morrison opened the door to the bridge, and returned my salute, they also stepped down.

"He's over there," Captain Morrison said, pointing to a young boy dwarfed in the Captain's chair sure that he was steering the ship. "I think he will make a good captain one day."

"Thanks, Captain. The poor kid's been through a lot," I said, looking at a tiny figure sitting on a chair dwarfed by all the instruments on the bridge. "Would you mind holding the dog's leash for me for a moment, Captain?"

I walked up behind Reynaldo and put my hands on his bony shoulders giving them a slight squeeze. He was wearing a new change of clothes that looked like a navy uniform minus all the insignias. Turning around, he had a big smile on his face. "I'd like relief from my command for a short time, Captain, please?"

"Yes Reynaldo, you may step down. We have everything under control," Morrison replied.

"Well my, little friend," I said, "It's time to say goodbye."

Reynaldo's lip was quivering, and a tear rolled down his cheek. He flung himself against me wrapping his little arms around my waist. We stood there on the bridge holding each other as a father would a son with tears rolling down both of our cheeks. I was telling him it was okay. This would be better for him. I would see him as soon as I could, or I'd phone. We had both been through a lot in the last few days and would miss each other greatly.

"Remember, Reynaldo, you have never seen me, or my cover will be exposed, and many heads will roll."

He hugged me even tighter with the feeling, I'm sure, of loneliness entering his soul. "I understand, Rider, but you promised!"

"Yes, I promised, and I will keep that promise," I said, looking down at a little boy who didn't know what the future held for him.

"Remember, in a couple of months, I'll find out where you are and I'll come to see you," I whispered in his ear. "Let's go over to your dog so I can say goodbye." As we neared Jaco, he stood up and pulled against his leash. Tail wagging, he rubbed his snout against my hand. "Don't forget," I said, "Jaco may attack anyone with a gun. Your debriefers will take him away for a while to make him more of a family dog, more relaxed, not always waiting for a command. When you get him back, he'll be friendlier to everyone."

All hands on the bridge had no idea what Reynaldo and I had been through, but they showed us the utmost respect as we said our goodbyes.

"Oh, and one last thing, Reynaldo." I handed him the money and the tiny pocketknife I had kept for him.

He started crying again, and I put my arm around his shoulders. "You keep this, Boss," he said, shaking and holding his hand out palm up, with the tiny knife looking large in his tiny hand. "Then you will always remember me."

"Reynaldo, I don't need a knife to remember you, but I will keep it with me all the time."

The kid wept and even I felt a little choked up.

I thanked the captain and his crew and gave Reynaldo one last hug. I patted Jaco and left the bridge with a feeling of hollowness inside as I headed down to the flight deck, to retrieve Chance, and catch my ride. I looked up and saw Reynaldo with his face plastered against the glass waving a child's wave goodbye.

As I lifted Chance onboard and climbed in myself, I was wishing that Chance would hurry up and get into heat so that I could see Reynaldo again. The pilot was the same pilot who plucked us from the beach and understood the bond between us. He slowly raised his chopper off the deck to eye level with the bridge and hovered there while tears flowed down Reynaldo's and my cheeks. "Goodbye, my friend," I whispered, waving to Reynaldo as the pilot banked and we headed for Port-of-Spain, Trinidad and Tobago, where we would catch a flight to the States.

PART TWO

CHAPTER

Vegas was as I had left it—Chance didn't think much of it either. The buddy who stored my bike was the owner of a beat-up 99 Silverado. The truck was a real piece of shit, bald tires and cracked windows and spotted with rust, but he guaranteed me that for five hundred bucks and a case of beer it would get us home. The deal was struck. I took the truck and drank the beer.

We left the next morning with a full tank of gas, bike strapped down in the bed, and Chance riding shotgun beside me. We pulled of Highway 84 just outside Baker City, Oregon, for something to eat and more gas. The truck rode like a tank and the ride was killing us. I don't think any of the tires had ever been balanced. We both needed a rest. Chance new the drill. I threw her blanket in the bed, gave her a drink, and tied her up in the box to protect my bike. The truck was at the far corner of the parking lot, dumped under a tree, to keep Chance cool. It looked like it belonged there. Maybe I should leave it and catch a bus home. I was just finishing my greasy hash, when I glanced out the window. Through the heat waves dancing off the parking lot, it looked like some twit was agitating Chance. I paid my bill then sauntered through the heat of the day to the cool of the tree. "What's up bro?" I said, coming up behind him. He jumped, as Chances growling had deafened my approach.

"Just admiring the bike. Seen one decked out like this a while ago."

"Really? There are a few like this around."

"Where you headed?" he asked, adjusting his chaps.

"Portland."

"Sure, you're going to make it?"

"Don't know. Guy couldn't pay me, so I took his truck and dog. They both have gas, so I'm not sure which is better. I think he was glad to get rid of both." This guy looked like one of the bikers from Galt, and the way he kept looking at me, I'm pretty sure, that's where he recognized me from.

I grabbed Chances blanket, threw it in the cab, then hauled Chance out holding onto her collar. She was showing signs of dislike towards this guy. We hit 93 and headed north.

The pickup was still driving like a piece of shit. It was time for another stop. Yakima was approaching. A truck stop loomed ahead. I didn't quite make it.

CHAPTER

I saw in my mirror, a string of fully patched Harley riders coming up behind me. They rode by with pipes blazing, paint glistening, armpits to the sun, and patches showing. Some had beards that were wavering in the warm breeze and some didn't. They held onto their high-rise handlebars as they thundered by.

What a bunch of twits, I thought.

Gearing down with pipes rumbling, they had forced me off the road, and to a complete stop. I looked over at Chance. I could see the hair standing up on the back of her neck and it looked like she was ready to pounce, just waiting for my signal. Turning sideways, I patted Chance on the head. "Your turn may come later, girl," I said, looking around at a sad but mean bunch of guys.

As the grossly oversized lead biker dismounted, walked back and approached my truck, I could read the biker patch on his vest. THE HORSE'S ASS. Biker patches are upsetting to some, and being forced off the road is hell to others, and me being colored could be intimidating—but not this guy. I enjoyed harassing these guys, although they didn't know it yet. It was my job, and I expected to receive harassment in return. So, it was a toss-up as to who would win.

"Hey dude, what's up?" the lead biker asked, as he waddled toward me.

Looking around at all the bikers, I started shaking my head. "Well, I just got stopped by a bunch of longhairs on bikes. I'm on my way home from a little holiday, and here we are having a little chat on the side of the highway. Don't get too close to the dog, man, she's a little nervous of loud bikes and people she doesn't know." With that, and not looking too pleased, he withdrew back a few feet.

"You okay driving this piece of crap?" He blurted out. "I've seen better in a salvage yard come to think of it, that's more than likely where this came from. I hear you're really good at fixing bikes, might need some work done," he said, looking back at all the bikes.

"Ah, I'm not bad," I responded, looking around again. "I can usually sweeten motors up, get a few extra horses here and there. Nice bikes you guys have."

"Name's Max," he said, stepping closer again. "Saw you in town a while back. Hard to miss someone with your color of skin, riding a sweet bike like that. The boss would like you to do a few tune-ups for us tomorrow, got a couple of bikes that aren't running too well, he wants you to come by tomorrow morning at ten."

"I'll check my calendar when I get home, Max, and see if I'm free. I'm not sure what I've got lined up what with being away and all. Are you not the boss, Max?"

"You don't understand, man," he said, going a little red in the face and gesturing with his hands. "When he says tomorrow, he means tomorrow! Tomorrow, do you get it?" He said, pointing a finger at me and starting to get very agitated for no apparent reason.

"So, you're *not* the boss," I said, smiling.

Max was getting a little agitated now and moved closer to my truck.

"Keep back from the dog. Remember, she can be nasty."

"I'll shoot the damn dog," he said, pointing a wavering finger at her.

By this time the other bikers, with their engines shut off, started circling around me to give their buddy moral support, as it was starting to look like he needed it! Standing in a circle with arms crossed, they all looked the part. Big and mean with tons of ink splattered over them, tons of fat, wearing leather, rings, and chains, and most overweight. In other words, well rounded with intimidation on their minds.

"I don't think you get it," said Max.

"Actually," I said, crossing my arms, "I do get it, Max, but there seems to be a problem with you. You're the one who doesn't seem to get it. I said I would check my calendar when I get home, and see if I can fit you in. You're starting to act like you're a little hard of hearing, Max, you know that don't you?"

Max turned around to his biker buddies with a look of sheer hatred on his face not knowing what to do or say. It was obvious no one had ever talked back to him this way before.

Turning back to face me, his face was red.

"Okay asshole. We'll be at your place at ten sharp tomorrow morning to bring you to our clubhouse. Got it?"

I could see he was getting very agitated, as he thought most people would bow to his every whim, but I was not about to do that.

"Oh, I hear you loud and clear," I said, with a smile on my face. "But you're not hearing me. If I'm free, I will come with you. I need to check my calendar first. Do you and your buddies hear me?" I said, turning in a slow circle looking at them all and repeating again. "I need to check my calendar!"

Once again, he turned to his buddies addressing them in a low voice. "This guy's a real dipstick. Does he not realize what we could do to him, his bike, that dump of a truck and that mutt standing beside him?" With fists clenched he took a threatening step toward me. Chance let out a little growl that he thought was friendly.

The second step with fists still clenched was as far as he thought advisable to advance when the growl turned into a deadly snarl, with teeth bared.

"Yeah, what about the dog," he said, taking two steps back bumping into his buddies.

"She's okay if she likes you, but I don't think you're her favorite, Max. In fact, she has a very sensitive nose and smells turn her real mean, so you'd better be very careful."

"You had better keep it tied up," he growled, spitting on the ground while pointing a threatening finger at her.

"Just thinking," I said, "her name is Chance. She likes to be patted, why don't you give her a pat now, she might like that—then again, she might not. Smells, you know. I did tie her up once, but she chewed through the rope. By the time I noticed, the guy didn't look too good."

Max turned back to his hard-faced partners then back to me. "I'm going to bring some friends with me tomorrow," he spat out, "and if things look bad, you're out a dog. Got it, asshole? You better keep her out of sight, way out of sight!"

"Won't work," I said, "she can smell trouble a mile away. Better you come alone as it's easier to handle her around only one person than a group. She's so darn quick that before I have time to stop her, she is onto the second guy and I'd hate to see you and your friends disfigured by a dog."

Taking a step closer with his face red he pointed his finger at me again. "You've picked the wrong people to jack around with, asshole. You're going to pay for this big time, we don't forget!"

"Nah, Max, it's all talk with you guys. You know that as well as I do. A leather vest and a Harley, greasy hair, a ton of ink and beards. You guys may scare some people, but not me. In fact, I'm looking forward to meeting your boss to tell him what goon's you guys actually are, trying to intimidate a lone guy on the highway like this."

He was fuming, and so were his buddies. Red-faced and shaking, he and his buddies headed for their bikes. Firing up their rides, revving their motors, they left in a cloud of dust, spewing rocks, they roared down the road, beards fluttering in the wind.

I looked forward to meeting them tomorrow.

"Well girl," I said, turning around and patting Chance. "It looks like we are starting a new chapter in our lives!" She looked at me and tried to lick my hand. I pulled back not wanting this to become a habit of hers. I still wasn't sure what training Chance had, had, but it was obvious protection was one of them. I would have to start her with precise hand signals as soon as we got home, fearing she might take someone's head off with the wrong hand gesture.

CHAPTER

Next morning, I was up early in my shop, awaiting Max's arrival. Sometime after ten, I heard them coming. Max was leading three other bikers as they rumbled into the driveway, stern-faced and unshaven. It looked like they all had, had a tough night and needed coffee and more sleep.

"Morning, Max, cup of coffee?" I said, looking down at my watch. "You're late. I'm punctual. What kept you?"

"Get on your bike and let's go. I'm not in any mood for your smart-ass talk today. Let's go." He revved his motor and turned his bike around.

"Sorry, can't do that. When you weren't here at ten, I booked other appointments. Maybe tomorrow if you want to book now."

Max got off his bike rather awkwardly due to his size and approached me looking very tough—or at least he thought so. "Did you forget what I said yesterday, Rider? At ten am the boss wants to see you."

"Sure, I remember every word you said, but apparently something's been going on in your head that made you forget what I said, and besides, by my watch, its past ten already."

"Don't push me, asshole. You're coming whether you like it or not. Now get on your bike."

"I told you that I have already booked appointments because you were not here." Looking around I counted out loud. "One, two, three and four," I said, pointing at him. "Four patches and just me. Seems the odds are a little unfavorable for me, don't you think?"

Max smiled and stepping closer. "Yep, looks that way, Rider."

"Chance come," I said, and Chance who was out of site in the garage, was at my side instantly. "Now this evens the odds a little, don't you think? Remember, don't get too close… smells you know."

Max jumped back and looked at his buddies who were also looking uncomfortable. "Keep that snarling bitch of a dog away from me, or I'll bloody well shoot her." He looked at his buddies for moral support.

"Just evening the odds. I think its best if you go back and tell your boss that I was otherwise engaged today, and don't ever mention shooting my dog again, or you'll be one very sorry lad. Now tell your buddies to turn their bikes around without dropping them, and leave, and to take you with them Max. I don't want you hanging around here all day being a nuisance."

Max was spitting mad. Clenching his fists, he stepped toward me, forgetting about Chance. Chance, without any signal from me started growling and snapping. Mumbling, Max jumped back even further this time, then signaled to his buddies to get on their bikes.

"That's your warning, dickhead," Max said, revving his motor.

I knelt down and patted Chance as Max and his buddies roared up the street looking back and giving me the finger.

CHAPTER

19

My burner rang.

"Rider here," I said.

"Hey Rider, it's Julie. How are you doing?"

Julie was my next-door neighbor. Just after moving in I had been invited over to her house for coffee. It was rather awkward as Julie was a very attractive gal, great cook, good housekeeper, smart dresser and very bright. She was also divorced, with two small kids. She'd asked me for my number that first night, and I was so caught off-guard, I couldn't think of a reason not to give it to her.

"Great, actually really great. How are you doing?"

"I'm doing good thanks, how was your trip?"

"It was awesome; I had a great time. A little sun, lots of riding, hung out with my buddies, adopted a dog, and a truck such as it is, yeah, I had a good time."

"That's great. No doubt you have no food in the house, so how about coming up here for supper tonight?"

"Wow, that sounds good, thanks. Can I bring the dog?"

"By all means bring him, but leave the truck at home. Okay, let's say around seven."

"Good one, Julie. You don't like my truck? I'll be there at seven, and I'll bring a bottle of wine."

"Awesome, see you then." Julie's house was set next door on a knoll of rock high above mine. She had a well-kept yard with flowers galore. The house featured large windows and, having been recently renovated, it suited her and the kids just fine. I rang the doorbell.

"Hi, come on in," she yelled, from somewhere in the house.

"This is Chance," I said, introducing Chance to her as she came out of the kitchen. "Chance, friend!" and with that, they were instant buddies. I handed Julie the bottle of wine I had brought, wishing there were two.

"Thanks, I think we can do this bottle justice."

I had stationed Chance at the front door, not wanting her to feel she had the run of the house and to keep her away from the kids if they got up. We were sitting down, talking about my holiday in Vegas and enjoying a glass of red wine before supper, when Chance came running into the living room unannounced and put her head on my lap with a look of dismay in her eyes. She gave a little moan.

I knew that meant trouble.

"What's Chance want?"

"Not sure but this usually means trouble. I'll go check."

As I got up, I glanced down at my house and saw a shadow pass by the right rear corner of my garage. Just a flicker, but someone was there, and they shouldn't be. "Damn," I said, "I've got a problem."

"What's wrong?" Julie said, getting up.

"Stay on the couch for a moment and let me get things sorted out here."

Looking down the street I saw nothing unusual but looking up the street there was a car parked that was new to the neighborhood. I walked up the street and memorized the plate number and casually planted my tracker on his car.

As I passed by the window, I again glanced down at my house. The shadow was moving beside my house toward the road this time, then, he stopped in surprise. My motion sensor light had come on illuminating his face. It was Max, the biker who had stopped me on the highway the day before, and who I had embarrassed this morning.

Must have really ticked Max off, I thought. *The guy just doesn't get it.*

I thought he was going to have a hemorrhage this morning when he saw Chance but apparently not. He was still up and running.

What the hell was he doing sneaking around my house in the dark?

"Everything okay? You look a little worried."

"All's well." I said, sitting back down at the other end of the couch wanting to remain good friends. I didn't know what Julie's alcohol consumption was, but she was acting a little light-headed.

"Rider…" she said, standing up and falling back down. "Oh, that wasn't planned," she mumbled. "I don't know what happened there."

I heard claws scratching on the hardwood floor as Chance came charging in, with her feet going a mile a minute. She abruptly came to a sliding stopped in front of me.

Julie shot up; Chance turned around and ran back to the door.

"I have to go look, Julie, something's wrong. Chance is very agitated."

As I passed the window, I noticed a red glow coming from the interior of my house. The next moment there was a loud whoosh and a scream from Julie as two of my front windows blew out.

"Julie, dial 911, my house is on fire!" I yelled, "Get the fire department here." Julie just sat there.

"Julie, dial 911!" I yelled again as I raced out the front door and down the steps with Chance on my heels. I grabbed Julie's garden hose and started hosing down the side and roof of her house. The flames were leaping higher and higher, neighbors who heard the bang were standing in their front yards watching and waiting for the fire engines to arrive. Chance and I moved further away from the house, as the flames were reaching higher and burning my face. Steam was coming off the side of Julie's house, and it looked like Chance was wilting. I hosed her down then myself then put more spray on Julie's siding.

What with oil, grease, gas and other combustibles, it was obvious my house was going to be a complete loss. Flames were dancing high into the night sky and lighting the neighbor's faces as they looked on with concern. Julie looked up at me, and the look was hard to read. How much of it was simple concern and how much, if any, was lust.

"I have a spare bedroom downstairs you can use till you get things sorted out. I'm going to put the kids in the car."

"Thanks," I said, "I'll think about that."

We heard the wail of the fire engines coming and soon the hiss of water on the flames. The firemen backed off and soon realized it was more important to save the adjoining houses as mine would be a total loss.

CHAPTER

"Are you the owner of the house?" a deep voice said, coming up behind me.

Turning around I saw a medium built police officer with three stripes on his arm. The police officer was no rookie and his questions were direct.

"I'm Sergeant McClung."

"Pleased to meet you, Sergeant McClung" I said. "Name's Rider."

"Nasty fire, any idea how it started," he asked, shielding his face from the flames.

"I have a pretty good idea who did this," I said, turning and looking at the walls of my house as they collapsed inward.

Glancing from the fire back to me, McClung looked surprised. "You do? And how would you know that? Did you see them start it?"

"Well, yesterday while I was riding home, I was stopped by a group of patched bikers. I wasn't too friendly with one of them named Max. Anyway, this evening, I was sitting up there," I said pointing to Julie's house, "having a glass of wine when my dog gave me a warning signal. I got up to look outside and saw my yard light come on as Max walked by. I saw him leaving my property just before the fire started. At that point I didn't know that he had lit the fire. I was going to confront him about being in my yard when he came over tomorrow morning."

"Why was he coming over?"

"His boss wants me to look at a couple of his bikes, and he was going to take me over to the clubhouse."

"How long did you see him for before the fire started?"

"It was just a few seconds. Long enough for him to reach his car."

"Anything else you can tell me?" He asked. "Did anyone else see him?"

"I don't believe so. He was alone and came by car. I have his license plate number," I said, watching as the flames from my burning home leapt higher and higher into the night sky.

"Wait here, I'm going to run this number," he said, walking toward his wheels.

Returning, McClung had a worried look on his face. "So, you think he lit the fire because you gave him a rough time yesterday?"

"I would say that, that is pretty close. Is something wrong?"

"All I can tell you is that the car is not in his name."

"Do you think that he stole it?"

"No, he borrowed it."

"Well, do you think that he is, at this moment, returning it to the owner?"

"I feel pretty confident that at this moment he is either returning it or he will soon."

"If you're going to follow him now, I would like to come with you."

"Sorry Rider, we have no authority to take a civilian with us, and anyways, we will not be going out there tonight."

McClung left and I returned inside.

"Julie, I need to go out for a while. Can you put a hold on dinner till later?"

"Sure," she said. "You'll be coming back here though, right?"

"Yes," I said. "I'll be coming back."

Luckily, I had parked the beater on the street. She fired up immediately and with Chance again sitting shotgun, I started following the track to where Max had taken the getaway car. Every mile the beater covered was a bonus for the truck but very painful for Chance and me. We were out in the country, not too far from home, but far enough to call this a little piece of heaven. I was now slowly driving down a country lane, when two rock gate posts, reared up in front of me. They were once in perfect working order, but the gates now hung off their posts rusting in limbo, with little hope of restoration. I doused the beams and swung the beater across the driveway blocking any escape from anyone who decided to make a run for it. I switched the dome light off and eased out through the door, Chance following me. Through the long tunnel of trees, I could see the house way off in the distance, sitting on a slight knoll with lights out, doors shut, curtains drawn. All seemed quiet, dark, and lonely. In the haze I could see two cars parked outside, one in front of the other. I eased around the beater, looked up and saw a quick blast of light, as the front door was quickly opened, then quickly shut with a bang. The nearest car, but not to near, roared to life. Rocks spewed from its tires as copious amounts of fuel were shoveled into the cylinders. Engine screaming, it picked his way towards me through the tunnel. At the speed it was travelling I figured five seconds, then I would see it sliding sideways to a stop against my beater. I moved off the road and waited. Five seconds and it was sliding sideways toward the beater as predicted. Out the driver's door he came. Not too fast, but fast enough. I was standing there waiting for him.

"Evening Max. Good driving." He was spitting mad. And before he could say anything, I spoke up.

"Max, remember our little highway encounter?" I said, watching him start to fidget. "At that time, you mumbled something about wanting to meet me alone. Well, here we are, buddy, just you and me, and don't use the darkness as an excuse and say you can't see me Max. I'm colored but it's a light color."

As Max started to regain his composure, there was another noise, that came from the house. I glanced up to see a beautiful black car, silent except for the crunching of wheels on gravel, heading our way and fast. The car came to a silent stop. As the wing door opened, and the head lights turned off, a woman emerged. Dressed in a jogging suit and runners and with her hair tied back, this lady was dressed for action.

"Problem?" was all she said, looking first at Max then me.

Max blurted out. "Yea, this is the asshole that I was telling you about."

"I see," she said, looking me up and down. I stood there, and so did Chance, waiting for them to make their first move. She clicked the wing shut then put her fob on the hood. To me this meant that she wanted to know where her fob was when needed and didn't want it falling out of her pocket. I was standing at the back corner of her Tesla; she was in the middle, and Max was at the front. It was a smart move, perhaps the same thing that I would have done, if I was in her shoes, but not smart enough. She was tall and lanky and lacking in looks, but maybe she was good at... cooking, defiantly not fighting. She should have been able to execute her move perfectly, but her timing was totally off. The kick missed, and I just stood there. She looked embarrassed and dumbfounded; Max looked totally let down. Now that she was a partial step closer, she tried the same move again. This, I figured. When her foot moved, I stepped back then instantly forward missing the kick and grabbing her temporarily in a choke hold then putting her out for some time.

Max was on the move. He charged around the lady and tried to bowl me down. I sidestepped and buried my fist in his gut, way in his gut, leaving him helpless, writhing and laying with the lady on the ground. I opened the Tesla door, took the papers out, then did the same with Max's vehicle.

CHAPTER

I fired up the beater leaving Max and his friend to fend for themselves and headed back to my house, which was still smoldering, and would require a fire truck to stand by all night. It was late. I was tired and upset though I had lost was very little. Most of the house contents were government property. I was thinking whether to go to the nearest motel when I felt a warm arm slip through mine. It was Julie standing there in the moonlight and, from the ambers still glowing, I could see a tear in her eye. "Are you alright?" I asked, thinking something was seriously was wrong.

"Yes, just upset for you," she said, giving my arm a squeeze.

"It's all covered by insurance," I said, thinking of the hours it was going to take me to list everything.

"Want to come in and have a cup of coffee?" she said, giving me a little smile.

"Actually, I would like that, and maybe a bit of the supper. We haven't eaten yet, and I'm famished."

Looking at my house one last time, and waving at the firemen, we went to her SUV and retrieved the sleeping kids.

"A little wash wouldn't hurt either," I said, looking at my sad state of affairs. Drinking the coffee, eating a great leftover supper, thinking about the fire, and relishing in Julie's beauty, I became very lightheaded and when she asked again about the spare bedroom downstairs, I said "yes."

Leading me into the bedroom Julie suddenly turned, and I found myself wrapped in her arms. Her kiss was gentle at first but grew more demanding as our arms entwined. Suddenly Julie jumped up startled, almost sending me crashing against the dresser, as a banging on the door pierced the night.

Chance raced to the door.

"Who do you think is at the door at this time of the night?" she asked.

"I don't know, but you answer it, Julie. It's your home."

"Okay, but what if they ask for you? What should I say?"

"Give me a call, and I'll come up."

Julie slowly opened the door with the help of Chance, who was trying to get out. "Rider," she called from upstairs. "It's for you."

"Sergeant, it's good to see you again. Do come in."

"Actually, let's talk outside."

He turned to me as we neared the sidewalk. "There is something I need to tell you off the record, and if I don't it will bother me. I normally wouldn't speak like this, but I think you should know. These people you are dealing with can be very dangerous, forceful, and destructive. This fire could be just the beginning, and I don't want to see you or anyone else get hurt. We have had dealings with these people before, and it wasn't good."

"Yeah thanks. I understand that totally. I had an encounter with Max and a lady tonight. I don't think you will be hearing about this from Max."

"Better tell me about it."

"Well, I went out to where Max was, and I left unscathed."

"How did you know where they were? You didn't follow them and what do you mean you were unscathed?"

"Okay, here is the thing. I have my own contacts within law enforcement."

"It sounds like there's a story there," he said—and it didn't look like he was in the mood to leave without hearing it.

I looked around. "Okay, between you and me, I am working undercover for the DEA. My job is to infiltrate this motorcycle gang."

"Wow, I knew there was something different about you."

"My color? Just joking. There is something different, I'm not one of them."

"What happened with Max?"

I told him and his eyebrows shot up.

"There are a couple of people in this town who have a lot of influence about the goings on here, and that is where one of the people live. Is there anything else you want too tell me about tonight?"

"Not really, I left both of them resting on the ground."

"What did the lady look like?"

"She was tall and slim, dressed in what looked like expensive clothes. Not the best looking of ladies. Short dark hair, and I saw dark rimmed glasses on the passenger's seat when I left. She had the look of a lady who wanted to be in control, and she was driving a Tesla. The most expensive model. Black and beautiful. The car that is. The car was ten out of ten. I don't think she even rated."

"Oh great. She is the daughter of one of the influential people I was telling you about."

"I think I hurt her pride more than I hurt her."

"Now you really need to watch your back."

CHAPTER

It was late afternoon, the day after the fire, and I was sitting in Julie's living room thinking about my contact Tony, when my phone vibrated. A lengthy coded message came through requesting a meeting. Thinking of how I was going to get away from Julie for a few hours, I decided to tell her I had to go down to the insurance company to sign papers—and would she mind looking after Chance as I would not be back till after supper?

"Not at all," she replied. "Will you be sleeping here tonight?"

"Yes, thank you," I replied, "and I shouldn't be too late."

I patted Chance goodbye and headed out the door. The cab I caught let me out in a downtown parking garage where I made a quick exit through the back door, and caught another cab to another parking garage, where I did the same. My destination was a dirty, sleazy restaurant, and upon entering I wasn't disappointed. Worn countertops, threadbare curtains, dirty windows and floor and seats that had not weathered the test of time too well.

In the far corner sat Tony, wiping his cutlery on a not too clean napkin. Before approaching, I looked at all the scruffy looking patrons and figured if they didn't have diarrhea before they arrived home, they would be very lucky. The food not only looked like it had been scraped off the floor but smelled like it too.

I sat down without acknowledging Tony, as the waiter shuffled over in his oversized garb, with a filthy apron being held tight by his oversized midriff. I ordered a Coke in a can, unopened, and Tony did the same. Neither of us felt like eating. Neither of us felt like looking around at the decrepit state of the restaurant. Neither of us wished we were here.

"Okay, Rider, here's the deal," Tony said. "We have purchased a new home for you about three blocks away from your old home. I think it will fit our and your needs better than the last house and we have possession in two days. See, the government can work fast if it wants to. Shortly, we will have a team in there placing cameras and painting. I placed enough money in your account to buy yourself two more motorcycles, replenish all your tools, and furnish the house. Go easy on the bikes and you should be okay. In a few days, a member of the biker gang should approach you as before. Get yourself set up and ready to roll. Here is a key to the house, and you'd better let neighbors see you looking at it before your move-in date."

I left by the back door with key in hand and caught the first cab I saw. I went to the local Kawasaki dealer where I bought a low mileage 2006 Kawasaki 900 touring bike. Red with gold pinstriping, spoked wheels, new tires and a full tank of gas. A beautiful looking bike. Night and day compared to my beater.

It didn't make as much noise as my burnt Harley, but enough noise to make a guy feel good. The power was ample, the back seat was large enough for Chance to sit on, if she was careful, and the chrome spokes added a deluxe eye-catching flavor. I drove over to my new house and was not disappointed.

Although the new house was only three blocks away from my old house, it was in a better neighborhood, with a well-kept garden, and an attached triple-bay garage. I parked my bike in the driveway and sauntered around the back.

The back yard was more than sufficient for a dog to run around in. There were large ground-level wood decks, newly constructed and still releasing the smell of cedar. It had a completely fenced yard, and a large stand of trees cutting off the view to the house at the back. It was sprinkled with a few shrubs and four fruit trees, plus plenty of green grass.

I returned through the gate to the driveway, climbed the three rock steps to the front porch, and fished the key out of my pocket.

"Hello there."

I turned around to see coming up the sidewalk a very large, muscle ridden guy. I'm six three and tipped the scales at 230 give or take—this guy was a little taller and easily outweighed me by thirty pounds. Sprouting a close cut, full beard, this guy looked like he could be a bouncer, and could definitely take care of himself.

"Name's Grant," he said, walking closer and holding out his hand. "I just live up the road, saw you turn in here. That's an eye-catching bike you got there."

"Thanks, she's a beauty all right. Rider," I said, shaking his hand. "Yeah, it's a nice bike I just bought it."

"Buying the house?" he asked, raising his eyebrows.

"Well maybe, waiting to see what the owners say about my offer. I should know in a few hours."

"Terrible thing happened here," Grant said, shaking his head. "Really bad, it shook the whole neighborhood."

"You mean in the house?"

"Yeah, double murder. Real messy. The police never found out who did it."

"How long ago?" I asked, having my curiosity tweaked.

"Some time ago," Grant said, looking around. "Never found out if it happened in the house or if they were planted here after they were killed. Weird couple though, both in their mid-thirties. I think they got mixed up in drugs, but that's only my two-cent's worth."

"Do you know what they did for a living?" I asked, not sure I wanted to go in the house.

"Well that's the funny thing. He had a motorbike similar to yours, and he would leave the house every morning between eight and nine, returning in the midafternoon, then go out again in the evening. His wife very seldom left the house, but she did a lot of entertaining. I was talking to him one day and casually asked him what he did for a living? He looked at me and you know what he said?"

"No, no I don't, should I guess?"

"He said, 'Why don't you mind your own bloody business,' and then turned and walked away leaving me standing there with my mouth open. I didn't like the looks of him at all. I never talked or looked at him again. He was one creepy dude."

"Wow, maybe I should back away from this deal," I said, feigning innocence, with a look of surprise on my face.

"No, I think you'll be okay. I watch the neighbors' houses around here. I'm not nosy, just curious. I'm sure it will be fine."

"When was the last time you were in the house?" I asked, not sure he was really as genuine as he appeared, or even lived up the road, and not really caring.

"Oh, about two years ago, I think."

I wasn't sure whether I should befriend Grant or give him the slip. He might be beneficial to me if he watched the neighborhood, but I had a funny feeling about him.

"Want to come in and take a look around?"

"No, I'm... well, okay. Sure, why not? I have nothing pressing at the moment."

I opened the door.

CHAPTER

I woke up to a throbbing head. Looking around, I could see that I was tied up in one of the bedrooms. Where was Chance when I needed her? The bedroom door slowly opened, and there stood Grant in all his muscular glory.

"Ah, I see your still with us. Just checking to make sure you're okay. You're one heavy prick to lug around, you know that?"

"Yeah, and you're one hell of a neighbor! They needed a big airhead like you to take me down," I said, wishing I hadn't opened my mouth. Just moving my jaw hurt my head like hell.

"You don't look too bright laying on the floor yourself, and by the way," he said, reaching into his pocket, "does this actually belong to you?" Holding in his massive paw was a small object that looked the size of a toothpick. It was Reynaldo's pen knife. Trying to sit up with my head pounding, it felt like my skull was split in two. My hands were tied to an O-ring screwed firmly into the floor, limiting my movements.

"Make yourself comfortable. You're going to be here for quite some time," he said, with a big smile on his face.

"What gives?" I said, wishing again that I hadn't spoken as my head felt like it was going to explode.

"You'll find out soon enough." He turned and left the room, locking the door behind him. I rolled over carefully, taking in my surroundings. The room was completely bare, without even a chair. The window was curtainless letting in a stream of light, killing my eyes. Looking around, the only removable thing I saw in the room was the metal hot air register in the floor, and it looked like it was out of my reach.

I stretched out as far as I could, and after many tries, and ignoring my pounding head, I was able to get my foot on the edge of the register and eject it from its saddle. Thinking I was a contortionist—twisting, grunting, and squirming—I was able to work the register behind my back where my hands could reach it. Working the rope tying my hands together, while listening for Grant's return, I started rubbing them against the outside edge of the register, which was not very sharp, but I hoped sharp enough. Eventually I was able to cut through the ropes and release myself. I then reinserted the heat register.

I heard him coming down the hall, and resumed my prone position on the floor. Hands behind my back, as if still tied to the O-ring. I lay still as if still in pain, which I was. After inserting the key, he slowly and carefully opened the door.

"I see you've made yourself comfortable. Shouldn't be too much longer."

Lying on the floor I just looked up at him saying nothing.

Retreating, he locked the door again, and I was able to stand up nursing my pounding head. I looked out the bedroom window into the back yard, and absentmindedly touched the back of my head, and instantly knew that was a big mistake. I heard him coming again, the click of the key in the door.

I reacted quickly and, luckily for me, Grant was careless this time.

One quick blow to his nose, a punch to his mid-section, and as he buckled over, a knee to his already damaged nose, left Grant lying unconscious on the floor and me trying to hold my head together, as the throbbing was almost unbearable.

Searching Grant, I found my knife and my phone. I called Julie. "Hello?"

"Julie, it's me."

"Are you okay? You sound strained and terrible."

"I'm okay, but I need you to do something for me now."

"Anything, what is it?"

"I need you to bring Chance to my new house. I'm three blocks away at 4605 Amblewood Drive. You can walk, but don't waste any time. Drop her off outside, don't stop or come in, and don't come back here without first letting me know."

"Okay. Got it, I'm leaving now, and I'll be just a minute, but you don't sound very good."

"I'm not, but we'll talk about that later."

"Okay, I'm on my way."

I hurried around the house as best I could, getting the layout and familiarizing myself with every room, the location of light switches and the stairwell. I checked the lower area, and the house looked better than I thought. I looked in on Grant again, checked his bindings then went to the front door. I saw Julie, Chance, and her two toddlers, walking down the sidewalk looking for my address. I whistled, Chance stopped, looked around then raced for the front door where I was standing. I waved goodbye to Julie and the kids and shut the door.

"C'mon, Chance, we have work to do." Tail wagging, she followed me down the hall where Grant was still lying unconscious. "Guard, Chance!" I said, pointing at Grant. She looked at me then I saw the hair rise on the back of her neck. I left them there with the door open, hoping Grant wouldn't try anything stupid before I returned.

My bike was as I left it, so I fired it up and raced the three blocks to Julie's house arriving there the same time as her. Racing in, I said, "sorry," then ran downstairs and retrieved what I was looking for, raced upstairs, and as I was heading out the door Julie yelled!

"Your head! You're hurt. Here, take these," she yelled, throwing a bottle at me.

"Thanks, I'll be back as soon as I can, then you can clean me up." I jumped back on my bike and headed back to the house. Grant was just waking up, and Chance was just starting to growl. Grant looked up at me with bleary eyes then over at Chance.

"If you keep still, and don't move a muscle, the dog will not harm you. But if you decide to play hero, someone will be transporting you to the hospital, in a heck of a mess, as walking or driving will not be an option."

The wait wasn't too long before I heard the distinct rumble of two Harley's bouncing down the road. Gliding to a stop in the driveway, twisting the throttle one last time, giving that annoying useless rumble, both ignitions were shut off, and the largest, meanest muscle-ridden looking humans I had ever seen, swung their legs over the seats of their bikes, and proceeded up the walkway to the front door.

As they shuffled up the sidewalk, I had my phone out ready to dial 911. When they reached the last step before the porch, I flung the door open stepped out, and in total surprise to them gave each a horrendous punch that left their noses imbedded in their nasal cavities. One of the neighbors must have dialed 911 because I heard sirens coming from quite some distance. Both guys grabbed their noses in unison trying to stop the flow of blood cascading off their chins. Another chop to the neck had them laid out on the ground.

A quick search found their weapons.

I raced into the bedroom where Grant was and found him still laying on the floor.

"Get up, big boy, your free time is up," I said, releasing him from the O-ring but still keeping his hands tied behind his back.

Returning to the front door, I had Grant lay down on the grass, with his two buddies "Guard, Chance." It was my favorite sergeant, walking up the sidewalk hand on his holster.

"What happened?" McClung asked. I walked out of hearing range and told McClung what had happened.

"We know these fellows very well. They belong to one of the drug gangs in town. I think they figured that you were going to set up base here and continue where the previous couple left off."

"Well they're yours. Just get them off my property."

The house was perfect—triple garage, painted concrete floors, well-lit with built in workbenches. The kitchen had all the amenities a house could hold, and the whole ambience of the place gave a warm welcome feeling. I felt at home.

With Chance planted firmly on the back seat of my bike, I returned to Julie's house. That's when my phone buzzed.

"Rider here."

"Hi, it's McClung. Bad news. One of our prisoners has escaped from the hospital, were not sure how yet, but we'll get him."

"Which one?" I asked, thoroughly exasperated.

"The bearded one, his name is Jake. Apparently, you hit him hard enough to rattle his brain."

"Not hard enough, McClung. I should not have held back. How could he have escaped?" I asked. "He could hardly breathe."

At the hospital, I was given the goon's room number. Walking down the corridor towards his room, I was met by two big police officers, chatting and drinking coffee.

"Can't go in there," the slimmer one said.

"Oh, and why would that be?"

"The fellow in there is under police custody."

"Really, how do you know he's still in there?" I said, looking at the closed door.

They both looked at each other, and then headed for the door. The lights were out, and the window was open with a slight breeze moving the curtains. The bed was ruffled but empty and there was a low beep coming from some piece of equipment, that was meant to help keep him alive. He was not in the bed nor hooked up to it.

The two officers looked at each other with grave concern, then let out a sigh. The goon was sitting on a chair in the corner of the room, waiting to go up to surgery. I walked over to him, said a few words, then left.

I found Grant in the emergency room, sitting on the edge of the bed, looking downcast. Two police officers were stationed outside the opened curtain, keeping a close watch on him. "Grant, how's your head?" I asked, knowing that mine was in worse shape than his.

"We're going to get you for this," he whispered. "Those other guys have no trouble getting even, and I'll be there to help them."

"Grant, this was all your doing. You hit me first."

I returned to Julie's to pick up a chair and some blankets. I had her run them over to my house in her SUV while I sat with the kids. Returning, I was prepared for a lonely evening, but I was wrong. As dusk approached, I heard what sounded like eight bikes coming down the street. I was wrong again; it was only three. Grant and two of his other buddies.

CHAPTER

"McClung?"

"No this is Dave; can I help you?"

"It's Rider. I have been having trouble with a local motorcycle gang, and it looks like more is brewing."

"Yes, I read last night's report. I'll have someone over there on the double."

I went downstairs and opened the garage door as they pulled into the driveway, with a look of incredulity on their faces, especially Grant's.

"Off my property, boys," I warned. The second biker got off his bike and walked in my direction. "I won't tell you again, get off my property." With that, the younger one, who was very quick for his size, faked a punch with his left hand and swung with his right.

I blocked the punch and twisted his arm popping it out of its socket. This left him incapable of doing anything except cursing and jumping around from the extreme pain. The larger one came at me, and I wasn't quite so lucky. He just barreled right into me, knocking me over and reinstating the previous pain I had suffered from my earlier head injury from Grant.

The first and only kick was aimed at my head.

But it never landed.

By the time I had hauled Chance off him, he was in bad shape. What they didn't realize was that Dave and his officers had arrived blocking anyone's escape and saw the whole thing. While we were waiting for the ambulance, the three were cuffed, two behind their backs and the little guy, his feet, as his arm was still out of its socket.

I pushed three Harleys into the garage and chained them up. I had some very nice-looking bikes in my garage. I locked up and returned to Julie's house.

—

After a hearty breakfast with Julie and the kids, Chance and I headed back to our new home. Rooms were being painted, and perimeter security cameras were being installed with cameras hidden on the inside. I left the tradesmen to do their thing and went shopping. By the end of the day, I had everything ordered to set up a new house. With Julie and the kids' help, I had all my furnishings, paintings, linen, cutlery, electronics, BBQ, scatter rugs and many other odds and ends, but the most important were my tools. Everything was slated for delivery the next day. Julie had wanted to spend the first night with me in my new home, but I really didn't want to get that involved. I had too many other work-related jobs to keep me busy.

Chance and I were down in the garage sorting my tools out when we heard them coming. The poor neighbors must have wondered what had moved in. Three of them all fully patched, cigarettes dangling from their mouths, shades on, no smiles and covered in ink from head to toe. Tons of it. All three giving their bikes a little too much throttle before shutting them down. They dismounted and lined up like a firing squad.

"Morning, boys," I said, with a smile on my face. "How can I help you today?"

"Hear you had a bit of a run-in the other night," the leader said.

"Not too bad," I said smiling. "Just had to let the boys know who was boss around here, that's all."

"I hear reconstructive surgery is needed in a few cases."

"Yeah possibly, I guess, but it can only improve their looks."

"We would like you to take a look at one of our bikes."

"What's up with your bike?"

"It's not mine. It's Bud's. The damn thing won't start. He thinks someone cut a couple of wires on it."

"Well, bring it in. I'll take a look."

"Can't do that."

"Can't do what?"

"Bring it in."

"Is there something wrong with you guys?"

"Not licensed."

"Not licensed, when did that stop you guys from riding. Come to think of it, when did it stop you from doing anything?"

"Get on your bike and follow us," he said. "We haven't got time to waste, listening to your bullshit!"

I turned around and pointed into the garage. "Too busy at the moment, boys. I just can't afford the time right now."

The three looked at each other.

"What! I don't think you heard what I said. Get on your dam bike and follow us!"

"I don't think so. You don't even have an appointment, and you're just lucky that I'm giving you my time right now, so, if you'd like to make an appointment, I'll get my book."

"Get on your bike," he demanded, clenching his teeth with spittle being thrown from his mouth in humongous proportions as he spoke.

"Look, you can't just ride up here and kidnap me, besides, I'm very busy today, and if you did kidnap me, I'd stand out like a sore thumb. After all I do have colored skin."

I looked in the garage, and Chance was not to be seen— as I planned.

"Kidnapped!" he yelled at me with more spittle being thrown from his mouth. "We'll kidnap you if we bloody well want to!" he yelled again, pointing a stubby finger at me. I wondered if the rest of him was stubby like his finger.

"You get on your bike now, dickhead!" he yelled, shaking and pointing that stubby finger of his at me again.

"Can't, none of these bikes are running yet."

He slowly started advancing toward me using his sleeve to wipe his chin somewhat dry. He came up to me and leaned close. "I'm not going to hurt you just yet," he said, in a quiet voice, "but you just wait."

"I know you're not," I said, smiling and showing him a mouthful of perfect white teeth.

"How do you know that?" he said, leaning close again.

"Because, first of all, I don't think you would be able too, and second you just said you wouldn't, and I know you wouldn't lie. You look like the honest type to me," I said, smiling again.

"Shit," he said, with drool leaking out of his mouth again. "What kind of an asshole are you?"

"Well, as you said earlier, I'm really good at fixing bikes, and I'm equally good at getting under people's skin, so stick that in your pipe and smoke it," I said, under my breath so the others wouldn't hear.

"I'm losing face here, asshole," he whispered, "and to lose face in front of other patches is bad for both you and me. Do you get it?" He said, leaning close and spraying me again.

I made a show of considering that for a moment. "Okay, well how about this," I said. "Why don't you try asking me instead of telling me and see if that works."

He clenched his jaw so tight I imagined I could hear his teeth creak.

"Will you get on your dam bike and follow us, Rider?" He said.

"Well, you didn't use the magic word, but that's okay. Rome wasn't built in a day," I said. "You lead, and I'll follow. I'd hate to see your buddies disrespect you." I pulled the 900 out and called Chance. I locked the doors, and when I fired up the bike, Chance jumped up behind me. I followed Drool, with the other two following us.

—

The clubhouse was not too far away and not what I expected. The outside was a total disgrace for the neighborhood. It was a standalone house with wood siding that needed scraping and painting and a concrete driveway heavily stained with oil and full of cracks with weeds growing in abundance. Ratty off-color blinds were drawn across windows. Double front doors bore signs of having been repaired more than once after police break-ins. An unkept lawn in the front was full of weeds and discarded crap. I couldn't see the backyard because of the fence leaning against the house, but I expected it was worse. There was paint missing on the window frames and garage doors.

Gutters were detached and full of leaves. Downspouts hung loosely by one bracket and runners of ivy were climbing up the sides of the house. It could only generously be called a fixer upper—most would call it a shit hole.

I got off my bike. "Let's go, Chance."

"No way," Drool said, pointing at Chance. "No dogs allowed. She stays here!"

"Give me a break, man. I'll bet you've had a lot of dogs in there." I said, smiling and looking at the clubhouse.

"She stays."

"Okay. But tell the boys not to go near her. She hasn't been fed yet today." After a special code was entered in a box housed beside the front door, the door was opened, but not before we were seen through the peep hole from the inside. While walking down the filthy carpet in the hallway, I could not see into any rooms. All the doors were closed, but lights were blinking on all the security cameras as they tracked our progress. We entered the garage through a solid wood door clad in tin for extra protection against fire and break ins, with a commercial security lock fastened to it.

And there it was! Candy-apple red and green, raised handlebars, everything that could be chromed was, and everything that shouldn't have been chromed, was chromed anyways. Spoked wheels, fancy pin-stripping, and a leather seat. The only thing missing were streamers off the end of the grips. This bike had been built from the ground up using Harley parts, and with the long front rake, it was a showpiece, a real beauty and made from stolen parts.

"Wow, that's a beauty. What's the problem here?" I asked. Not being able to take my eyes off it.

"Won't start."

"Where's the key?"

"Don't know."

"You don't know where the key is," I said (boy, these clowns were bright). "Is that because it's stolen?"

"Well," Drool said, smiling and looking at his buddies, "it just appeared here one night."

"I see," I said. "So, it just mysteriously came through that door all on its own, and without a key? If I leave my garage door open do you think one will appear in my garage?"

"Don't get smart. So, what's the difference?" Drool said. "It's here, and you're going to fix it."

"I need you to put plates on it. I'll hotwire it and drive it home."

"No bloody way. You're going to work on it here."

"Actually, I bet you could hotwire it faster than I could, and I bet with your eyes shut, Drool."

"No way," Drool said. "The bike stays here, and so do you. It's not leaving this garage"

"I don't have any tools," I said, looking around and taking in the whole garage.

"Get our tools, Jake," Drool demanded.

Jake reappeared with what looked like bargain basement tools. One twist and they would be stripped, toast.

I disconnected the battery, and as I looked around noticed that this bike was built to conceal drugs. I removed unnecessary parts to get a better look inside.

"Ouch," I yelled jumping back, "this is unreal!"

"What's wrong?" Drool yelled, rushing over to me.

"Look at this," I said, feigning innocence. "Did you know about this?"

Under the cowling and in triple sealed bags fitting snug to the gas tank were small tightly packed bags of what looked like heroin.

"That's why you can't take the bike home," Drool said, and if word gets around about this, you are dead meat. Got it?"

"Oh yeah, I understand," I said. "I get it, just like a doctor. Privacy of information." I removed the required part and said they could come and get me in two days. I could have made a key in an hour, but I needed time to get my letterhead and business cards made up. After all I was a legally qualified mechanic.

I fitted a key to the bike ignition as soon as I got home, then worked on my Kawasaki, had lunch with Julie, then pretty well stayed around the house enjoying myself and Chance. Two days later, the three of them came down the road. Pulling up, all three got off their choppers looking mad as hell and headed for the garage where I was working.

"We need to talk, and you need to listen. There are rumors that you have been banging up some guys really bad around here," Drool said, pointing his stubby finger at me.

I didn't want to get him to riled up and start spitting, so I stood and listened.

"If you so much as touch another of our chapter guys, you'll regret it for the rest of your life and if *anything,* you see or hear in our clubhouse is ever exposed to the outside, you're a goner, you're going down. No questions asked, do you understand?"

I gave him a smile. "Are you finished?"

"I don't think we will ever be finished with you, dickhead!"

"What you said about your members is not a rumor. It's true, and the same will happen to you, and these guys here, if you provoke me. Now," I said, holding up the mechanism and key, "do you want this part installed in the chopper or not?" He glared at me, turned around, and started walking to his bike.

"Hold on there, gringo," I yelled. Drool stopped and slowly turned around. "Well, now I have something to say to you. If you or any of your patch members or followers ever lays a hand on me or my dog, I'm going to respond to a degree that may not be acceptable to you. The fellows you were mentioning earlier, they were very lucky. I was in a good mood that day. Now, do you guys understand what I just said?" I looked at all three in turn so Drool wouldn't lose face.

He pointed that stubby finger at me again. "You're walking on thin ice, dickhead, and I'm sure you're able to count. There is only one of you."

"Pal, there has always only been one of me, and I'm still standing. You come here with a whole army and you're the one complaining?"

He stopped in his tracks, thought for a minute, swore under his breath, then continued to his bike. Arriving at the clubhouse, they used the same procedure to get me into the garage. I reinstalled all the removed parts, making sure not to disturb the drugs. I hooked up the battery and asked if they wanted me to fire it up.

"Yeah sure, let's see how it runs," Drool said, moving back.

"Open the doors boys," I said.

"No way," was Drool's reply.

"Can't fire it up without the doors open, could pop an ear drum or, worse still, asphyxiate us all."

"Jake, open the doors."

I rolled the bike partway out, called Chance, and put her away from the bike. I turned the key and had to think where the start button was hidden. After almost deafening everyone in the garage, I shut her down. There definitely was a miss in the engine.

"Needs work. There's definitely a miss in the engine," I said.

"Yeah, I could hear it. Let me see if he wants you to tune it."

I walked around the bike, admiring it—but actually taking in every corner of the garage. Pretty bare except a few tools and a three-foot by four-foot piece of plywood laid into the concrete floor and flush like a door. I pushed the bike back inside close to the plywood. Walking around the bike again I purposely walked on the plywood and just as I thought, it was hollow. Glancing around again, I noticed three cameras, and they were all well-hidden. Extra heavy-duty locks on the garage doors, as well as the entrance door to the house. The garage windows were sprayed white with heavy bars screwed into the frames. The inside of the double garage doors was reinforced, and there were dirty footprints on the concrete floor coming from the plywood door.

Drool returned. "Yeah, he wants you to tune it up, but it must be done here."

"Sounds good, how about tomorrow at ten? I'll bring my tools."

"No way, no one is here until noon to let you in."

"Sure, noon is great," I said, as I slipped the bike key into my pocket. I was led out to the parking lot where Chance was waiting. I spent the rest of the day organizing my garage and went to Julie's for supper. Her excuse was that the kids wanted to play with Chance, so I might just as well stay for supper. Chance was so good with them. They pulled her ears, pulled her feet, pulled her tail, pulled her fur, lifted her gums laughing, checked her teeth, poked her eyes and climbed all over her. All the time she was wagging her tail and asking for more. When that was done, they chased her around the house giggling and squealing. Chance was in her glory, always coming back for more.

I was standing at Julie's window looking down at where my old house once stood. An excavator and dump trucks had spent the day loading and hauling the debris away, leaving a bare foundation waiting for another house to be built. Julie came up behind me and put her arms around my waist.

"Kids in bed?" I asked.

"Yes," she replied in a husky voice, "I told them that if they were good, Chance would go to sleep with them so all three are in the same bed."

"Let's go look." We crept down the hall. There was Chance in the middle of the bed with a child on each side, each having one hand over her back, and each claiming sole possession. We crept back out, leaving the door open in case Chance wanted out.

"Sit down. I'll get us coffee," Julie said, heading for the kitchen.

Returning, she sat next to me and lifted her feet up on the couch. "Well," she said, "tell me about your day, anything exciting happen?"

"No," I said, "nothing special. I worked on a couple of bikes, went for a short ride, picked up some parts, and sorted out my tools."

"Sounds like quite the day," she said, starting to fidget. "I was going shopping, and as I passed the end of your street, I saw three fully patched riders heading your way. On the way back, I saw the same three leading you somewhere. Know those guys, Rider?"

"Nope, don't know them, but they may want some work done on their bikes."

"You really like working on bikes, don't you?"

"Yes, I do, and I also like being around beautiful ladies."

"Ladies," she repeated.

"Well, yes, there is Angela, Victoria, Wendy, and you—"

The jab to my knee stopped me short. That wasn't a playful jab but from someone who at one time or another had been trained in survival. I didn't let on that she had dropped a card.

"So where did you go with the bikers?" she asked.

I thought I might as well tell her where I went and tease her at the same time.

"Oh, just for a little ride around the town, showing our bikes off, then to their clubhouse."

"Clubhouse," she exclaimed, sitting up suddenly. "You're kidding me. Did you feel safe? This is unreal."

"I felt very safe. With all those guys around, who's going to harm me? They're great protection; I didn't have to worry about anything!"

"What's it like inside, or can't you tell me?"

"Sorry, but I'm sworn to secrecy, what with girls and all. They asked me not to talk to anyone about it. You know what it's like?"

"Come on, you can tell me."

"Nope, not even a little."

"Oh, I guess it's top secret in there."

"Sure is. Guards everywhere. A metal detector on entering then a strip search by a scantily clad real blonde. I'll be making many trips back there."

"A strip search?"

"Yeah, it was very entertaining. She stripped. I searched. That's how I new that she was a real blond."

"You're kidding me? And you're going back tomorrow?"

"Yeah, need to work on a few bikes."

"Fancy bright-colored bikes with lots of chrome and pin striping?" she asked.

"No, they're all painted black. I think these guys do a lot of night work," I said, smiling at her.

Chance rushed in all agitated. "What is it, girl?" I said, getting up. She ran to the door. I walked to the window and looked out. Nothing there. I opened the door and Chance ran outside and jumped on my bike. "Hot damn," I said. "I'll be back shortly."

I fired up the bike, turned it around and headed towards home three blocks away. I stopped at the top of the street and parked the bike. I crossed to the other side of the road and as my house came into view, I could see my garage door was open and two guys standing looking at the bikes. I watched for some time to make sure there were only two, then by the cover of parked cars, I started to cross the street keeping Chance close. I quickly retreated when I heard a vehicle turning the corner at the top of the street.

It was a cube van, and it was going to back into my driveway. I dialed 911, deciding to leave this problem to the police. There was only one person in the van, and Chance and I could handle the three, but at the end we would need the police. Looking under the van, I could see one of the guys trying to phone out and getting very agitated. I hadn't noticed their mode of transportation, but guessed it was bikes parked somewhere up the street.

Chance and I walked up the side of the van standing in plain view. No one had noticed us as they were too involved in cutting the bike chains.

"Break and entry, possession of stolen property, aggravated assault… The list goes on," I said, in a loud voice.

"Get lost, meathead," was the reply.

"Now that's not a kind thing to say when you're in someone's home and stealing his bikes."

In the distance I could hear sirens nearing. I wondered if the neighbor had also called 911 as I had asked.

Confusion reigned. Sirens were arriving; dog and a man were blocking any escape, break and enter charges pending.

"Let's get out of here," the smaller one yelled looking for an escape route.

"Not so fast!" I yelled. "We need to have a little talk."

The driver was standing looking a little confused, so I wasn't too concerned about him. The other two started for the door. "Chance," I said, "guard!" She ran forward and started snarling and snapping at the legs of the two bikers. Not knowing what to do, one of them pulled out a knife.

That was it. "Chance, attack!" By the time the police arrived our hero was in bad shape. His partner stood ramrod still, shaking in his boots and not moving an inch. McClung was on duty, which was fortunate for me. I put Chance in a corner.

"Another break in, Rider?" he asked, as he was handcuffing one of the bikers, and looking down at the other who was hollering something about my mother.

"I'm bleeding to death, man. Get an ambulance. Hurry up!" He yelled, getting more agitated.

"No, you're not going to bleed to death, my friend," I said, "you're going to die from rabies!"

His eyes flew open and a look of horror flashed across his face. "What do you mean *rabies*?" he stammered in a very agitated voice.

"Actually," I said, "she had her rabies shot yesterday, and so you might be lucky. The hospital will know though, they will watch you closely to see if you start drooling and snapping, or you may just start spitting, when you talk. Not sure, but it's not pleasant."

"Is there nothing I can do?" He said, forgetting he was going to bled to death.

"Sorry man, no, there is nothing you can do. I feel bad about this, but what I'll do for you is tomorrow, I'll take her to the vet, then I'll let the surgeon on duty at the hospital know what the results are. Do you know anything about rabies, man?"

"No, I've never heard of it."

"The worst thing is that you may never be able to have an erection again."

"Really?"

"I'll check with the surgeon. It may be Viagra for the rest of your life."

"No man, how could I live like that? But you will check with the surgeon, will you?"

"Sure," I said, "I hate seeing guys your age snapping and drooling." I think I saw a quick smile flash over Dave's face. I picked up the phone Dave had taken from our prone biker and turned it on. I pushed the phone picture then the time. The last call he was trying to answer was from a number I recognized. The jammer that had been installed to cut out incoming and outgoing calls had worked perfectly! Good thing I had remembered to turn it on.

CHAPTER

"Do you know these guys, McClung?" I asked, shaking my head in disbelief.

"Yeah, and it's good to catch them again. They both have huge rap sheets, and these two you don't want to mingle with."

I asked McClung if I could talk to the driver alone. I took him into the house and sat him down at the kitchen table.

"I've got to run back to the garage, don't move and Chance won't hurt you, I'll be right back."

"I won't move," he said, with a look of concern on his face.

I returned with both the bikers bike keys in my hand and sat down across the table from him. "Anything you say in this kitchen, even the fact that we were talking alone, will not leave this house. Do you understand what I'm saying?"

A look of grave concern came over his face. "Yeah. Yeah. I'm cool man."

"Okay, which gang are you with?"

"The one you were with this morning, fixing the green chopper."

"Oh great!" I said.

Looks like I can expect a visit from my three friends.

"How long have you been a member?"

"I'm not a member. The other two are, but I'm not."

"Criminal record?"

"No, just speeding."

"What are you riding?"

"An older Honda Valkyrie."

"Okay, I suggest you return the truck, head back to the clubhouse. Be prepared, though; they're going to grill you so tell them everything except coming up here. Why don't you bring your Honda around tomorrow, and I'll take a look at it for you?"

"The cops aren't going to charge me for driving the truck here?"

"I don't know for sure. McClung and I will discuss it, but I feel sure that if you cooperate, we can work something out." Returning to the garage, a crew had been called in to clean up the blood, while McClung was patiently leaning against his cruiser, waiting for me.

"Think they will be back?"

"They'll be back sometime tonight to cause havoc."

"Keep me informed about any goings on, and what do you think about the driver?"

"I'm thinking he may give me some inside information." McClung jumped in his car and sped off, while I went over to talk to the driver again.

"What's your name?"

"The cops have it, but it's James."

"Okay James, I've spoken to the cops and at this moment they have decided not to press charges, hopefully, I'll see you tomorrow. Now jump in that truck and get out of here."

As I walked down the road, I saw two awesome bikes. First, I drove one bike home and then the other and chained them up. I was tired and ready to head back to Julie's. Jumping on my bike, I drove slowly giving Chance some exercise, by letting her run behind me.

I had my hand up to knock on the door when it flew open. "What took you so long to get back here?"

"Well, first of all there were a couple of guys who broke into my house and were trying to steal my bikes, so I had to wait for the cops to come, and then I had to clean up the mess."

"You didn't fight with anyone did you?"

"No, I just listened and talked."

"I'm glad you were not hurt, but how did they know you would be out?"

"Beats me," I said. I didn't know whether or not Julie knew she was just digging herself deeper with all the questions she was asking, so I let her carry on.

"Well, I hope they didn't get the bikes."

"No, they didn't, but the police got them."

For a split second a look of grave concern flashed over her face. She was flustered. "Well, as long as you're okay."

"Yeah, I'm fine except I left my phone here."

"I found it on the couch. I'll go get it," she said. When Julie returned, she looked gray and beaten. She sat beside me.

"Rider, I have something to tell you, but you must keep it between us."

"That's fine, I think I can do that."

"I was once married to Frank, the leader of the Horse's Ass, and my two kids are his. We were divorced because of his occupation, but I still do work for Frank because I'm scared of him."

"You don't need to tell me this, Julie."

"Yes, I do, please listen. I was paid to make friends with you. I was paid to invite you over tonight and keep you here while those guys were over at your house. I was not told why. I tried phoning them at your house, to tell them that you were on your way over, but my calls would not go through. I have been told that, in future, when I go into your house, I am to have a good look around, in other words, spy on you. They are looking for information about you, any information. They have a tight hold on me, and there is nothing I can do. If they find out that I have told you anything, anything at all, the kids and I will suffer."

She burst into tears and covered her face with her hands.

"I'm so sorry, I didn't want this to happen, not this way. You're such a nice man. I'm telling you this, because I want to remain friends, and maybe you could help me get away from Frank. I don't know what to say. I did something unthinkable, just like Frank and his gang members do. Pressure from Frank has turned me into a person I don't know, and don't want to know or be. I'm stuck." She flung her hands to her face and started crying again, even harder than before.

I saddled closer to her and held her sobbing body. When she stopped, I wiped the remaining tears from her face.

"Julie, I knew some of what you were doing, but didn't think you were that involved with the gang. I will help you as much as I can, but we need to work on this together. We'll start now by figuring out what you're going to tell Frank."

By the time we had hashed out what she was going to say her tears had stopped.

"Yes, I can remember all that," she said. "He will be calling me as soon as he gets word of what happened."

"Are you having an affair with Frank or anyone else?" I asked, hoping the answer was no.

"No," she said, with a tone of surprise in her voice.

"Okay, I believe you, but if I find out that you have lied to me, you're on your own. Let's go over this one more time. Tonight, or tomorrow, whenever Frank calls, you show him or them your phone with the phone calls you made. Don't suggest why the phone calls didn't go through. Let them make the suggestions and figure it out themselves. Don't mention Chance, just say I jumped up and said I had something to show you and would be back in a few moments. If he asks what took me so long to get back, tell them that after going home, I went looking for a bottle of wine, which I brought back. I'm not going to tell you anything that goes on at my house or anywhere else concerning the gang, then you will not have to make up excuses when he asks you questions, and that way if he tells you anything you don't know, it will be a complete surprise. Got it?" I said, looking into her eyes.

"Got it," she said.

"I have to go. Come by tomorrow with the kids, and you can have a good look at my house," I said, winking at her.

I rode home, with Chance racing once again behind me. I'd have to let her win next time. I heard the engine but didn't see any lights as the car pulled out behind me. Narrowly missing Chance, the car followed me into my driveway. Getting off my bike, I opened the clip holding my knife. Doors left open, the three thugs raced from the car and surrounded me. Chance who was running down the road behind the car stayed in the shadows.

"What's up guys?" I asked, turning in a slow circle taking them all in. Two fit, one heavy. No weapons showing. Deadpan faces, these must be three of Frank's best. "Why is it that Frank always sends three against one?" I asked. "You guys need some training or what?"

"You know what's up," the fat one, Drool said, "I warned you."

"Hold on a moment, gringo," I said, keeping two in my vision at all times. "Your buddies broke into *my* house and were caught in the act."

"Don't think so," Drool said, starting to move closer.

"Well, you had better think again," I said, starting to turn slowly.

Taking a step closer and not knowing what to do with the moisture building up in his mouth he turned around and spat—thank goodness away from me. "Don't get smart with me, asshole."

"Well perhaps if you and your fine-looking friends here were to get the facts straight, you wouldn't have had to make the trip over here tonight and get all riled up."

"Shut your bloody mouth, asshole," he said, stepping closer and removing the ugliest knife I have ever seen. He was quick, and as his two buddies started to circle me, he slashed out with his knife lacerating my left upper arm. It was deep, it was long, it was nasty, and it hurt—and it bled like hell.

I grabbed my knife and cut Drool before he realized we were even. The cut was long, deep, and nasty just like mine. In the split second that it took me to cut Drool, Chance had knocked the guy down behind me and was having a go at him, which left me with the third one. The fellow on the ground was having a real tough time with Chance, which drew both their attention for a few seconds. I placed a good kick to Drool's knee that knocked him down directly in the path of Chance. I turned in time to see the last remaining guy coming at me with a knife aimed at my stomach. I grabbed his arm then realized I was getting weak from loss of blood and did not have the strength I required to hold him off.

"Chance!" I called.

The biker turned, wrenching his wrist from my grip and, with knife extended, waited for the advancing dog. I didn't know if Chance had any training with thugs with knives, but I could see this could be a fatal wound. Staggering back, I threw my knife with my left hand burying it deep into the back of his left arm. The pain must have been extreme as he dropped his knife reaching where my knife had buried itself, but his hand never reached it. Chance hit him with such a blow that when his head hit the concrete, I knew he was out for the count.

Chance stopped and looked at the prone figure lying on the ground then turned back and stood guard over the others. I ripped my shirt off and wrapped a large piece around my arm. I retrieved my knife from the still prone gang member, stood up wobbling and looked at the blood covering my driveway.

The police arrived without sirens, and in my woozy state, I thought I recognized one of them. I sat down, calling Chance over.

"Good work, girl," I croaked, patting her. She let out a woof then I rubbed her head against my leg. The officers were looking at the three men lying on the ground wishing the ambulance attendants would arrive soon. Two ambulances and three bikers. The first two to receive attention were the biker Chance had first dealt with, then the biker she knocked down. As they approached me my head started swimming.

The cop I recognized walked over and looked around at the mess.

"I don't think they like you very much, Rider. If you keep going like this there will be no more members left. Can you tell me what happened?"

As I climbed onto the stretcher, I told him the story.

"Well," he said, "we will lock them all up this time."

"Which neighbor phoned you?" I asked, fighting nausea.

He looked at his notes. "The same as last time."

"Good, I'll have to thank them."

"I'll let the ambulance get you to the hospital, and when you're stabilized, we'll get a statement."

"Sounds good, I'm pretty weak at the moment."

"Yeah it looks like a pretty nasty cut, we'd better get them all to the hospital."

I beckoned the police officer back over. Fishing in my pockets and retrieving my keys I handed them to him. Chance looked not too pleased. The officer looked down at her with a wary look on his face. "Come here, Chance," I whispered. "Friend," I said, pointing at the officer. "You can pat her now if you want," I said, in a weak voice. "She would like that." Tentatively he reached down and patted her head. She moved closer asking for more. "Okay, Chance, into the garage," I whispered. "Open the door for her please, and lock her in."

It would mean an overnight stay in the hospital as I needed to get my blood back up to normal. It would be a little longer for the other three then off to jail awaiting bail if they could get it.

I arrived home late the next morning with a headache, arm throbbing, antibiotics, and forty-eight stitches. My bike was still in the driveway, all the blood cleaned up, and the car gone. Either stolen or taken by the police, I'd have to look at my surveillance cameras to see who took it. I phoned Julie and asked her to bring the kids over to play with Chance and to bring me some lunch. I went into my office and turned on my surveillance monitor. The time flashed up one AM. Looking at the surveillance monitor, a car slowly drove up and a figure emerged in a hooded jacket. A figure I recognized.

CHAPTER

I heard the kids laughing as they ran up the sidewalk. I went to the door with Chance who was showing more excitement than me, opened it and welcomed the mob. Chance was in her glory, and soon she had the kids chasing her all over the house.

"Rider," Julie exclaimed, "what happened? You look pale and your arm is swollen. You had better sit down."

"Yeah, it's a little swollen, and I do feel weak, but I think that I'll be okay."

"What happened?" she asked again.

"Well, when I came home last night, I was jumped by three patches in a black car. They had followed me home from your house. That's about it."

"Did they get away?" she asked.

"Yeah, they knifed me in the arm then left leaving me weak and bleeding. I was then taken to the hospital, and here I am. And what did you do last night?"

"I went to bed shortly after you left and got a good night's rest."

"Good, you're looking awesome," I said, giving her arm a squeeze and knowing that she was lying.

The kids were being a little too noisy downstairs, and I was a little worried. I told Julie to look around while I went down and checked. Returning, I found Julie in my office looking at the TV screen. "What's this?" She asked, in a somewhat strained voice.

"Apparently it's you. You retrieved the car last night, and you have been lying to me."

Julie lowered her head, turned around, went downstairs, found the kids and left. After she was gone, Chance and I went to the kitchen and ate the lunch Julie had brought. Well, actually Chance ate it. I wasn't feeling that good. It was after supper that I first heard, then saw them coming again, four this time and ones I had never seen before. Chance started growling, so I had her stay behind me hidden as I opened the front door.

The leader was in his early forties. He was tall and muscular with longish hair. He was also well dressed and walked with easy authority.

"My name's Frank," he said. "I wanted to introduce myself and apologize for the trouble my guys have been causing you. May I come in?"

"Thanks," I said. "That's civilized of you. Come in, the others can wait on the step."

My arm was starting to throb and so was my head. Frank walked in and saw the dog. He looked at the door, and in his mind was figuring if he could get to the door before the dog.

"Don't worry, she's okay."

"What're you basing that on," he said dubiously. "She's disabled a number of my members."

"Yes, I guess you're right."

"I'm okay in here?" he asked.

"You're okay, I think."

He looked at me then turned towards the door. "Not that way, Frank. Over here, sit down."

Frank and I both sat on chairs facing each other, then he turned his so he could see Chance.

"I came to tell you that I've ordered my guys not to bother you anymore. We had a meeting this morning, and it was unanimous that they had started everything."

"Good," I said, tongue in cheek. "Sounds like you've got an okay bunch of guys there." He smiled the first smile since meeting Chance.

"They're okay."

"What about Julie?" I said.

He didn't miss a beat. "She's off the leash. I told her I wouldn't bother her anymore."

"And when did you tell her this?"

"Just before I left, I phoned her and told her that she was free. She said something interesting though. She said that she wished she had met you under different circumstances."

"Well, shit happens," I said.

"Okay, I'll leave you now and see you at the clubhouse, when your arm's better." He then looked at Chance uneasily.

"You're okay," I said. "She's good." As they walked down the sidewalk, I waved to my neighbor. I sent Julie a text, telling her what had transpired and that I would see her when my arm was better. Blood was still trickling from my wound, so I thought I should lie down for awhile. It was getting dark when I heard a faint knock at the door. I looked at my watch then at Chance.

"Who is it, girl?" I got up off the couch still feeling weak and went to the door. Julie was standing there with a big smile on her face.

"May I come in?" she asked.

"By all means," I said, feeling my blood gushing through my body. "Where are the children?"

"Asleep in the car. I'll go get them."

I couldn't help her with the kids so sat back down on the couch.

With the children snuggled down in bed asleep, and Chance between them, it was time for a serious talk. Julie returned with appetizers and two glasses of wine. Sitting on the couch with her feet tucked up facing me, she looked forlorn.

"I don't know where to start," she said.

"Well, start with a sip or two of wine," I said, taking a big gulp of mine.

"That's better, and the second is helping even more."

"Okay, here we go! Frank called yesterday and said I needed to do something for him. He wanted me to keep you at my house till it got dark."

"And how did you plan to do that?"

"Unfortunately, you'll never find out."

"Then I was to get you to go home. He never tells me why, just do it."

"And if you were to say no, what would he do?"

"I haven't said no yet, but I suspect he'd send a couple of his goons over the next night to pay me an unpleasant visit. He's threatened that when I've hesitated."

"He told me that you're free now. Do you trust him?"

"No, after saying I was free, he told me to take a good look around here before leaving."

"Yeah, I suspected that much."

"One good thing though, he said, he would keep his payments up."

"He has to do that regardless. Don't let that bother you. Though I suppose he could think the payments were for a future favor, not money to bring up the kids."

"I know that's what he's thinking. How's your arm?" she asked, leaning over and touching it.

"Ouch, that hurts," I yelled, pulling my arm away a little too quickly.

"Let me see. Oh, it's been bleeding. I'll change the dressing for you."

Pulling the bandage off and looking at my arm, I thought she was going to faint. "I'll be back in a moment," she said, running to the bathroom holding her mouth. Bandage reapplied, she looked better and I felt better.

CHAPTER

Next morning, I was up early and left to keep an appointment with Tony, at our usual dump of a restaurant. I arrived by taxi the usual way, and found Tony sitting in a corner eating a big dish of slop.

"You should try some of this, it's actually pretty good," he said. "I think you would like it, and oh, what happened to your arm, it looks bad?"

"It's sore, bad, swollen, looks ugly and it's not functioning at the moment, thank you very much!"

"Is this something that happened last night?"

"It'll all be in my report."

His lunch looked like something nameless, something that shouldn't have been let out of the pot or the kitchen.

"Suit yourself," he said, "look at all the people in here eating, it can't be that bad of a place."

"Yea, I'm looking really hard, Tony. The good, the bad, and the ugly are in here."

As I glanced around, I noticed the poor quality of shoes, lack of teeth, unkempt hair, and a very muscular guy coming through the door, who looked totally out of place—like we did. I glanced at Tony then back at him. I was sure I had seen him at the clubhouse the other day.

"See that fellow who just walked in?" I said, looking back at Tony.

"Yeah."

"Watch him," I said. "Watch him closely. Tell me his every move."

The fellow was huge and obviously on a mission. Tony kept me informed on his movements then said, "It looks like he's double-crossing the chapter, he just has that look on his face."

"There's a Chinese fellow who just slipped out of one of the booths near that big fellow, and he's walking into the kitchen with a parcel under his arm. I think the big guy gave it to him."

"Keep watching," I said, "and tell me everything that's going on."

I sat there with my back to the big guy watching Tony's eyes darting from patron to patron.

"Another guy just walked in, and he's scrutinizing the room. Now he's walking over toward the first guy that walked in."

Tony and I both hit the floor as shots rang out. Tony, with a look of concern on his face, had his pistol out. I was clutching my arm trying to keep it immobilized, and in its sling. It was hurting like a hot damn.

The Chinese fellow who had walked into the kitchen apparently wasn't happy with the contents of the package and was pumping bullet after bullet into both of the large men.

"Rider," Tony yelled, over the sound of bullets being pumped into the two big guys. "When he finishes, we need to get out of here and fast."

"You're kidding me, Tony," I yelled, still holding my throbbing arm. "You haven't finished your meal, and I was just about to order some slop."

There was pandemonium in the restaurant. The cook suddenly materialized with a knife in each hand. The gunman, seeing the cook coming at him with two knives, turned, but had already spent his last shot. Out of desperation, he flung his pistol at the cook. He was too far away to do any damage, and it just made the cook all the madder. The cook came fast, jumping over people and knocking over tables, yelling as he advanced on the gunman. Without his gun, it was no contest—he was soon lying on the floor hacked to shreds. Hmm! I wonder what Tony thinks of his soup now. Who knows what goes into it?

"Let's go," Tony yelled, "follow me."

Tony, brandishing his gun, led the way. I was on his tail, holding my arm to stabilize it while jumping over fallen furniture and pushing screaming people out of the way.

We walked down the street separately and entered another equally disgusting restaurant where we ordered lunch. Sirens wailed by outside.

Tony and I discussed thoroughly what had been going on and how I should proceed.

"One last thing, Rider," Tony said, looking around the restaurant again. "We have tapped Julie's mobile and home phones, and if anything, life-threatening comes, I will send you a coded message."

After then telling me to look after my arm, we parted ways.

CHAPTER

I had my stitches out a week later, a quiet week without any visits from Frank or his patch members. Even though the doctor had said my arm was healing nicely it was still swollen and felt like a hot poker was stuck in it.

Two days later, I fired up my bike and went for a short ride. The turning of the throttle and squeezing of the front brake on the right handlebar did not pose a problem but squeezing the clutch on the left handlebar, sent jolts of pain up my arm and into my shoulder.

At noon the next day, I went over to the clubhouse to see Frank.

I wasn't sure which door to go to, so I choose the front door. I felt sure they were watching me on their hidden cameras. I had an eerie feeling something strange was going on and that was confirmed when the goon who answered the door looked at me as if I had just committed a murder.

"What do you want?" he growled. "We're in mourning."

Morning? I thought.

"Sorry, but it's afternoon now," I said, "It must have been a tough night for you? Frank instructed me to come over and see him today."

"Frank is in no condition to see anyone. We just buried his number one man."

"Oh, man, I'm sorry," I said, with a look of great concern on my face, but I really didn't give a damn. "When he's feeling better, have him give me a call, and I'll come over and work on the bikes."

Without a further comment he slammed the door in my face.

Considering what I had seen happen at the Chinese restaurant, I was wondering if I should tell Frank or just let it rest. I drove over to Julie's and was greeted with a big hug.

"Where are the little ones?" I asked, looking around.

"Nap time, thank goodness," she said.

I walked over to the couch with Julie following me and sat down.

"How are you?" I asked, wondering whether Frank was still pestering her.

"More to the point, how is your arm doing? It still looks swollen."

"It's really painful after my little ride, but I think the ride is doing it good. No pain, no gain, you know."

"Where were you riding before coming over here?" she asked.

"I drove over to Frank's to see about working on his bikes but was denied access."

"Not one of those days?"

"What days," I asked with a frown on my face.

"Some days they are packing drugs, and the place is locked down like a fortress. They have members positioned around a two-block radius and others cruising around the main intersections, keeping a watch for cops. How they get the stuff in and out I have no idea. When I was married to Frank, I was allowed over any time I wanted, but had to phone first, and if Frank or one of his men answered and said that Frank wasn't in, that meant don't come over we're busy."

That made me think of the plywood I'd seen on the garage floor. I'd have to check it out the next time I was over there.

"No, I don't think it was drugs or they wouldn't have opened the front door. He said something about a funeral."

"Oh yes, that would have been Hook who was shot in some Chinese restaurant on the other side of town. I read about it online. Hook was his number one man. I heard the gang's going to get even."

"Did you know this Hook character?" I asked. "Did you see him around when you were there?"

"Oh yeah, I knew him. He was a cruel one. He tried to take advantage of me a few times and there was almost a war when Frank found out. Then things calmed down and they were the best of friends after that. Hook was huge and had a real mean streak. Beat the crap out of the girls that came around on party night if they didn't perform for the guys. Another time he cut a finger off one of the new recruits because he said he was stealing drugs. The kid hightailed it out of town, and we later found out that he had nothing to do with it. Hook had set him up to look like he had."

"Sounds like a nice guy, someone you'd like to hang around with. Do you think Frank knew he was going to that Chinese restaurant?"

"Frank knows everything everyone does and when they do it. I wouldn't doubt that he has my house bugged, I wouldn't put it past him."

"How long were you married to Frank?"

"Do you want to know to the second or the day? It was four and a half miserable years, and I hated it. He would sit in his office all day unless he had a meeting. There were always other women around, and I expect with him sometimes. The police kept a close eye on me. I only had other biker ladies for friends, and it was lonely. You wouldn't believe how happy I am over here and away from him. Sure, we had the best of everything. Nice cars, beautiful home, ate at nice restaurants, and jewelry, but it bothered me where the money came from."

"You seem to be doing okay now. Nice house, monthly payments, kids are happy, and at one time you had a nice guy for a next-door neighbor. Why do you think Frank sat in his office all day?"

"Well, I heard—but I could never confirm—that he had ties to someone in the government here. In other words, he was paying off a government official for information, and the government official had direct ties to someone in South America and knew when drug shipments were being sent. Frank's not dumb. If I asked too many questions, or the wrong question, one that might have him reveal too much information, he would get very mad at me. You know that he owns the house two doors down from the clubhouse."

"No, I didn't know that, I just go there to fix his bikes."

"Well, be careful, he will try to get you to deliver for him. He's done it many times before, with no connection coming back to him. He has everything backed up so far that when the police catch someone, they think will lead them back to Frank, it always ends in a dead-end trail."

I had come over a day earlier with my detector, and it showed that there were bugs planted in Julie's house. But the other thing Julie didn't know was that when I was in her house, I had planted my own device that neutralized all existing bugs when I entered the house until after I exited the front door.

"Hmm, interesting," I said, glancing around the room as if bored with the conversation. I was tiring and needed rest. Leaving before the kids woke up would be a good thing.

The drive home, although only three blocks away, again hurt my arm like hell.

I sent Tony a coded message that we needed to talk:

come to my house at eleven am tomorrow

Our understanding was that Tony would bring his Honda Shadow over, and I would do some work on it. I would mark his name as Mike in the appointment book just in case anyone had the gall to look. It was also understood that, under no circumstances, would Tony take off his full-face helmet while at my house, for security reasons.

At eleven sharp next morning, I heard him coming and opened the garage door so he could drive in. There was no valid reason to close the garage door as it was such a nice day. Tony kept his engine running, opened his saddlebag and pulled out his frequency jammer just in case the place had somehow been bugged.

I walked over, twisting the throttle a few times listening to nothing. I stepped close to Tony.

"Julie said that the big guy killed at the Chinese restaurant was Frank's number one man. She also said that they had had their differences but had since patched them up. However, she did say that the big guy, Hook, had made a few passes at her and when Frank found out he was furious.

"I think that yesterday was a setup," I said. "I also think that Hook was the delivery guy and the drugs were substandard, or poor quality or shortchanged or not there at all. I also think that the Chinese shooter who was being paid in drugs, was not part of the restaurant but had an agreement that he could go into the back to check the contents. Or maybe all the drugs were there but he was being paid by Frank to eliminate Hook for some reason. The little Chinese cook got a little mixed up and ruined things for the Chinese drug dealer."

Tony's phone buzzed. When he finished, he said, "That was the office. Julie had a call from Frank, and she said you didn't know how the drugs were getting out."

The Shadow needed a new front tire, so I put Mike's name in my appointment book to have it installed in three days' time.

The next day I heard a lone bike coming down the street. I greeted the biker in my driveway. "What's up, buddy?" I asked, curious as to why he was here.

"Frank sent me. He wants to see you tomorrow morning at nine to work on his bikes."

"Okay, I'll be there," I said listening to his bike. "You got a problem in there I said pointing to his motor, sounds bad. It doesn't sound like it will last long without a little repair."

He looked at me, frowned, and then left.

CHAPTER

At nine the next morning, I approached the clubhouse and noticed a beehive of activity. Bikers were placed a few blocks out, hidden to the inexperienced eye. There were more bikes scattered around outside, and two guys were standing near the front door looking at everyone and everything.

I knocked on the front door and when it opened none other than Drool was standing there.

"Hey man," I said, "you never did tell me your name."

"Kool, that's what you call me asshole, Kool! What the shit do you want?" He said in a nasal voice.

"Now, Drool," I said, smiling at him.

"Not *Drool*, you asshole, *Kool*, and if you call me that again we're coming after you!"

"You mean you and these two other guys standing guard here? Kool, I can see that English is not one of your better subjects, and if you'd like some lessons, I'd be happy to help you out." I said, trying to aggravate him.

"Go shit yourself, you stupid bastard."

"Now Kool, that's not a nice way to help someone who wants to help you."

I looked at his face, and from the look of it, it had more stitches crisscrossing it than a softball had. Come to think of it, he had more than likely been batted around more than a softball.

"I thought we had settled our differences and could now be friends," I said frowning.

"Shit, you're a stupid ass, you know that, don't you?"

"Come on, Kool, just because you look better than you did last week, doesn't mean you have to be upset with me. Just think what people would say if you always looked ugly? Now we can call you pretty boy."

I saw the swing coming and leaned back like Cassius Clay. This made him really mad and he was about to swing again, when a loud voice stopped him short. He halted in midair and hissed at me. "I'm not finished with you yet, asshole."

"Well Kool, you'd better be careful there, I don't know if they can reconstruct faces like yours a second time. I've seen them come out looking like a plate of spaghetti with cheese sprinkled on top. Pretty ugly actually, much worse than before."

Frank appeared at the door and greeted me with a warm smile, signaling Kool to leave.

"Come to work on the bikes?" he asked, watching Kool retreat.

"Yeah, I can order what parts I'll need, and then come back when they're in and work on the bikes. It would still be better if I could work on them at my place," I said, hoping he'd refuse.

"Order the parts and come back here," he said.

"Perfect."

My arm was still very painful and there were still some jobs I could not do without help so the few extra days would be beneficial in the healing process.

Frank left me in the hands of someone I hadn't met before. Down the same hall, through the metal clad door, and into the garage.

"Frank wants the green one, that silver thing, and the baby blue one running like a top," he said, pointing at the three bikes.

I fired all three up, listening and determining that there was no real problem that a change of spark plugs, a little tweaking up, and an oil change wouldn't fix. It was going to be interesting seeing if he offered drugs for payment instead of cash.

Arriving home, my arm was as painful as it had ever been. Chance met me at the door with no outward warning signs.

"C'mon, Chance, let's go for a run," I said, getting back on my bike.

Around the block we went, Chance following the bike till the throbbing in my arm was so bad, medication would be needed to subdue the pain. Getting off the bike, we both ran upstairs heading in different directions, for different reasons. Chance to her food bowl for a snack then a drink, and me to the medicine cabinet for a pill, then the kitchen for a glass of water.

CHAPTER

When I found the drugs hidden in Frank's green bike, I decided to have a look at the other bikes in the garage. The first was a beautiful baby blue, with contrasting pinstriping in darker shades of blue. I measured the gas tank inside and out with no luck. All the measurements matched. There weren't too many places on this bike where drugs could be hidden except the tires. I removed the valve releasing all the air. Inserting through the valve stem a special wire I had, it measured as it should. I filled the front tire while releasing the air from the rear. Inserting the wire, *bingo*! The tires were filled with drugs. The other bikes, not having the paint job of the baby blue one, outshone her with all their chrome. One of the other bikes had the same rear tire. I'd have to order two new tires and remember to bill Tony for them. They now became McClung's property. One of the bikes had a single-shot pistol installed in the left handlebar. This would hit anyone standing beside the bike. I looked a little closer to the rear fender of a candy apple red bike. It looked nice, but if you were to slide your hand up inside the fender and place your other hand on top, you'd notice that your hands were quite some distance apart.

I'd need to order a new fender and bill Tony again.

I heard the bike at eleven AM and knew it was Tony coming for his new tire. I opened the door and Tony drove his bike into the shop.

"Good morning."

"Yeah," he said, "it's turning out that way."

"You're going to have to change the tire, Tony. I'll show you how. I still can't do too much with my hand."

"You've got to be kidding," Tony said, looking at his hands with a look of disgust on his face.

"No, I'm not kidding. A person in my condition should be lying on the couch drinking beer, with his feet up not getting his hands dirty or even standing here telling you what to do. Now let's get on with it."

While Tony changed his tire, we discussed Julie.

"You know, by the sounds of her voice, she is still in love with Frank and tells him everything you guys do and say. She's going to invite you over for dinner so she can pump you about the Chinese fiasco. I want you to go but be very vague and don't ask her any questions. Frank has something big going down, and we're not sure what it is. Just keep your ears and eyes open. Not long after Tony left, UPS arrived with Frank's parts. Chance slept, I ached, and Julie called me for supper. All five things that I figured would happen, happened. What I didn't know was how I was going to get the information about the clubhouse that Tony required.

Another one of Julie's attributes was that she could cook. The meal was delicious, and Chance got her fill from the kids who were flipping food on the floor.

Relaxing after dinner, I was waiting for the interrogation to start. The kids were in bed, and Julie was sitting on the couch with a glass of wine in hand. She turned to me with a worrisome look on her face.

"I had a call from Frank today. He wanted me to find out all I could from you, about the Chinese restaurant shooting, and that's why I invited you over for supper tonight. Frank's orders. Like I said, he'll never leave me alone."

Sighing, she took a good sip of wine. "He didn't say, but there was urgency in his voice. He wanted answers. He knew you were there. How he knows that, I don't know."

"How would he know that I was there? I stopped by for a light snack and left in a hurry after the shooting. I didn't know he was involved till just now when you told me. Tell him I was at the bike dealer down the street and dropped in for a drink. That's all I said, except it was pretty gruesome."

"Sounds good," Julie said, "I'll see if that will satisfy him."

I had Julie change my dressing, and although it was still swollen and looking ugly, she didn't run from the room this time. I headed home for a good night's rest. Chance chased me home for her exercise, which was a good thing, because she could be busy tomorrow.

CHAPTER

I loaded the beater up and arrived at the clubhouse at nine the following morning with spark plugs, oil, and other related parts, all neatly packed in boxes. I had left all the boxes piled outside the garage door, feeling pretty confident that any normal person wouldn't steal anything from this clubhouse. If they did, they wouldn't be normal or around for long. If a club member stole them, where else would he put them except in the garage.

I knocked, waited, then knocked again. Finally, the door was opened by a large bleary-eyed, pockmarked guy who looked like he could inflict serious pain, as well as receive it.

"Yeah?" he said in a real snarl. What do you want?"

Oh, I could tell instantly that I was going to have fun with this guy, and he was going to make my day.

"Morning, brother. I'm collecting for the Salvation Army," I said, looking down at my feet as if very nervous and a little embarrassed.

"The who?" he growled again. "And I'm no brother of yours, so drop it."

"The Salvation Army, brother, you know, when you were a kid you would see them marching in parades, blue and red uniforms, Christmas time, ringing bells," I said, still looking down.

"Not today," he said with a big bad-breathed yawn while starting to shut the door in my face. I put my foot out, stopping any further movement. He didn't know what to say or do.

"Just a few dollars, brother," I said, looking up. "It's the Salvation Army who gives 93% of the money you're going to give to me to help those in need. The neighbors, said you were loaded and would make a large donation. Every bit helps, brother."

"Get out of here before I stomp on your bloody foot, and don't call me brother again."

"Easy my man, it's for a very good cause, you can't give to a better one. Somewhere around here, I was told there was a house that sells drugs, well the Salvation Army helps people get off those drugs, maybe you need their help, brother?"

Now he was seething mad being called brother and having to deal with a persistent goon who wouldn't give up.

"Get off this property and get off it now," he bellowed, clenching his fists and stepping toward me.

"Did I say something wrong? This isn't the house that sells those drugs, is it?"

"Your times up, buddy" he said, lining me up for, I'm sure, one of his powerful punches.

"Whoa, I didn't mean to upset you that much. Why are people like you so cheap?" I asked, shaking my head.

"See that sidewalk, if you're not on it in three seconds, you won't be collecting money but stars. Now get the shit off this property."

I needed to get into the garage to check on the plywood inserted into the floor.

"Okay, okay," I said, "but see those boxes over there."

"So, now what are you selling!"

"I'm here to fix the bikes; Frank made an appointment for me to come here today."

"You're what?"

"I'm here to fix Frank's bikes. Now I need to get in."

"You're not coming in here to fix anyone's bikes. Your nothing but a door-to-door, colored, charity collector."

"I'm here to fix Frank's bikes under his orders."

"You wait here and don't move."

I walked back to my truck and sat on the tail gate, patting Chance and watching the front door.

Just as expected, Slab reappeared, yelling. "Come here! I told you not to move."

"I know you did, but I got tired of standing."

"No fixing of bikes today."

"And why would that be?"

"No one here except me."

"You're not worried about the two of us being alone in the house, are you brother? Man, that's a tempting offer, but not today. I have a headache, so don't you worry. I won't take advantage of you, and besides, you can help me fix the bikes."

"You've come on the wrong day, and your talking to the wrong guy, now get that piece of shit," he said, pointing to my truck, "out of here, and take your boxes with you."

"Well at least open the garage door, and I'll stack the boxes in there."

"Can't do that."

"What do you mean, you can't do that. You're saying you don't know how to open a garage door? Give me a break. Here I'll show you," I said, stepping towards him.

"Look, just get lost; go peddle for money from someone else."

"Hey, that's a good one coming from you 'Cheapo' and no, I won't go somewhere else. I'm coming in, and I'm going to work on those bikes, whether you like it or not. Frank's orders."

He gave me a shove back, luckily on my good shoulder, which neither Chance nor I liked. As he was slamming the door, I was able to get my boot wedged in which, with a little help, flung the door back open hitting him on the head, and stunning him more than he already was.

"What the hell are you doing, little man?" he yelled, clutching his head with both hands.

"I told you that I have come to work on the boss's bikes. You're making me feel unwanted, like I'll be sorry to leave but eager to return. What's your name?"

"Spanner." (A spanner comes in an open end or a closed end, it was obvious that this Spanner was an open end).

"Spanner?"

"You deaf or something?"

"Sometimes Spanner, sometimes. It just depends what garbage is being shoveled at me. It's Spanner, as in wrench?"

"That's right," he said, with a smile on his face, "and strong too."

"Yeah, I can see that, but it's not always strength that counts, sometimes technique, if you know what I mean? Sometimes spanners come open-ended and can also come in a very short version, any relation?"

"Get out of here asshole before I—"

"Look, I don't want to have a problem with you, Spanner, but if you don't cooperate, nasty things could happen here."

"Get out of here, asshole."

"Chance," I called.

"What the dick is she doing here?"

"Don't talk like that or she'll attack. She has a thing about swearing. Very smart dog and more than likely understands more English than you do. In fact, she can bark the alphabet."

"You're kidding," he said with a look of concern on his face.

"Yeah, and with her eyes shut. I'm surprised she hasn't attacked you yet. I guess she's a little deaf also, she couldn't hear too well sitting over there in the beater."

"You're in big trouble, you know that?" Spanner said, looking like he would like to attack me.

"Not nearly as much as you'll be in if I don't get those parts inside. Frank will be royally pissed off with you."

I started walking quickly past him. He grabbed my good arm and swung me around almost lifting my feet off the ground. Chance had him by the pant leg. As he started to draw his free foot back for a good kick, he loosened the grip on my arm. It was enough for me to pull free and bury my fist in his gut then an elbow to the head. I heard a crack and hoped it was his head and not my elbow. I stepped back.

"I'm going to call the dog off, but next time she will head higher so be careful."

"Go shit yourself, asshole!"

"Told you not to swear, didn't I? Now we're both in trouble. I'm in trouble because you don't like me, and you're in trouble because the dog doesn't like you."

"Get him off me," he yelled, holding the doorframe for support and trying to kick Chance off.

"It's a *her*, Spanner, and you better treat her with respect, or she gets really riled up! You know what women are like?"

I pointed and Chance came and sat next to me.

"Hands on the wall, Spanner," I said, giving him a shove backwards.

"You're in big shit, dickhead," Spanner said, turning slowly. Not too sure of himself anymore.

"Be careful, Spanner, that was getting close to a swear word."

"Let's see here, two knives, some drugs, and what's *this*? Oh, and what's *this*?"

"Don't point that thing at me," he yelled.

"It looks like a tire gauge that holds one bullet, one shot, correct?" I said, turning the tire gauge over in my hand. "Keys, cash, and an emergency light of some kind with a red-light flashing. Very interesting. What's with the blinking red light, Spanner?" I asked.

He looked at me with scorn on his face and was about to speak, then he looked at Chance.

"You wouldn't," he blurted out.

"No, I wouldn't stoop as low as to chew your pants, Spanner, but Chance would, just answer the question. What's the blinking red light for?"

"Go shit yourself."

"Chance!"

"Okay, okay, I push it and help comes," he blurted out.

"What help, Molly Maid? We all know she would be very welcome here."

"No, anyone who is free and can get here quickly," he uttered, looking down at Chance.

"Okay, Spanner, where is everyone?" I asked looking around.

"I don't know."

"Is this like you don't know how to open the garage doors." I clicked my finger and Chance was pulling his pant leg again.

"Okay, okay, get the dog off," he yelled kicking at Chance with a look of terror on his face. "You're a stupid bastard, and you're going to pay big time for this."

"You're actually lucky she hasn't bitten you yet. She's quite persnickety about what she eats, too much fat there I expect. Could be her diet, you know what these ladies are like."

"They have gone to a different chapter for a meeting, and I don't know what the meeting is about, or when they will be back."

"Okay," I said, pocketing the paraphernalia. "Let's get the garage door open."

When we entered the garage, I counted seven bikes. Six from before, and one, presumably, that was Spanner's or stolen.

"Now, here is what is going to happen, Spanner. I'm going to sit you in a comfortable chair in one of the other rooms. Chance will be guarding you. Don't move or reach for anything. Keep your hands at all times where she can see them. Don't talk to her or anyone else. For goodness sakes, remember to breathe, shallow, but breathe. Don't swear, and you may come out of this looking better than Kool."

His eyes flew open. "Chance and Kool?" He stammered.

"Yep, she had a good feed on him" I said, shaking my head in sorrow. "Poor Kool, he just wouldn't listen, now let's go."

We walked into a sparsely decorated room with a bed, a chair, and a phone. The carpet was dirty which matched the brown painted walls. With a look of despair on his face he watched me unhook the phone, tie his hands, and then push him into the chair.

"You're in big trouble man," he growled, shaking his head, "big trouble!"

"Those are the last words you will speak for a while, Spanner. If she attacks it will take me some time to get over here, and if I don't hear her, well, you know what your buddies look like."

I went back to the garage and, with my device, turned off the security cameras. Then I phoned Tony.

I got six oil pans out and, without warming the engines, took off the filters and started draining the oil. I then removed the parts that needed replacing and placed them on the floor next to the respective bikes. All this was done in a hurry with my arm throbbing. My phone rang. I didn't answer but went outside to meet Tony. I gave him Spanner's keys, alarm, a little dope and the tire gauge gun.

"Don't shoot yourself," I said, as he looked at the tire gauge gun.

"Hot damn," Tony said, turning it over in his hand. "Where did you find this little gem?"

Tony had his team's work cut out for them.

I told Tony that, if I wasn't around when he returned, he was to leave everything in the far corner of the garage and then hightail it out of here. I said goodbye to Tony then cautiously returned to the garage and went down the hall to check on Spanner.

"Need a drink of water or anything?" I asked Spanner while rubbing my greasy hands on my pants.

"Just get out of here," Spanner growled.

"Be careful," I said as Chance perked up her ears.

He was obviously worried what would happen to him when Frank and his buddies got back. I returned to the garage and lifted up the garage door so I could hear the rumble of any Harleys approaching better than if the door were down. Next, I looked at the concealed hatch in the floor. I checked for any signs of security but saw none. Carefully lifting the hatch, I saw locks all around the perimeter on the inside that could be activated with a remote device locking anybody in or out. I could see no way to jimmy them without damaging the hinges.

I lifted the hatch. There was a wide wooden staircase leading down eight feet or so and it was dark. I hurriedly looked around and found a light switch—not hidden but requiring thought to find. It was placed up in the floor joists. I wasn't sure about turning the lights on, so I chose to keep using my flashlight instead.

Heading down the stairs, I stopped, debated, then decided to close the hatch behind me. I reached up and silently returned the hatch to its floor position on hidden hinges, then continued down into the darkness. I turned my flashlight on, and when I reached the bottom step, I froze. It looked like my last step onto the concrete floor, would also be onto a pressure sensitive switch, to sound off an alarm somewhere, and to someone other than me.

I only spotted this because my flashlight showed undulations in the concrete floor and a slightly raised portion around the pressure plate in front of the bottom step. With overhead lights on this would not be visible. Shining my light along the wall, I saw hundreds of white plastic bags all neatly stacked and numbered. More shelves down the middle and back held more drugs. The far shelf supported a large arsenal of weapons. I was tempted to run.

The room the same size as the double garage above. I looked around, shining my flashlight. Through the shadows, I thought I saw what looked like a door at the far end of the room. Looking for more sensor plates, I eased my way closer. I checked the door; something was wrong.

I had to get out of here, but where did the door lead? I tentatively reached for the handle then stopped just before touching it. Hard to notice, but the handle was on the same side as the hinges. Why?

Shining my flashlight around and looking closer I could see that the handle was an alarm, pull, push or touch it and an alarm would sound. This meant that the door with no active handle was a pressure sensitive door.

I touched the door on the opposite side of the hinges, and it released itself allowing me to pull it open. In front of me was a dirt tunnel about five feet high and leading in a straight line as far as my flashlight would shine. I retrieved a transponder and buried it in the dirt. That's when I heard voices coming from down the tunnel. I turned my flashlight off and listened.

The sounds were coming closer. Someone was coming through the tunnel. I slowly shut the door, turned around and crept backed into the drug room. I had to get back upstairs into the garage. As I once again shone my flashlight around, looking for the stairs, I noticed a small device that looked out of place on the middle shelf. I took my camera out and hurriedly took pictures of the door, shelves, and firearms. Avoiding the sensor plate, I cautiously climbed the stairs and pushed on the plywood hatch. The hatch was locked, it wouldn't budge. It was solid. My heart stopped beating. I carefully shone my light around the perimeter. All looked good. I put my back against the hatch and pushed again this time harder. There was no movement. It still wouldn't budge. It must have locked itself when I shut it. Either that or someone came into the garage and locked the door from above.

Shit, nowhere to go, now what? I was running out of options.

Sweating, using my back, I pushed again. No luck. I listened. Nothing! All was quiet and dark. I could hear mumbling getting closer. I was about to retreat and hide amongst the shelves which was about all I could do, when I decided to give it one last push. As the door flew open, a pair of black boots, then jeans, then a Glock, greeted me.

"C'mon up!" the voice said.

As I climbed out the Glock followed me up.

"Find anything interesting?" The voice said.

I slowly looked up, then let out a sigh. It was Tony. He had been standing on the hatch but had not realized it. Heart pounding, I instructed Tony to drop the items he had picked up earlier in the corner and to get out and get out now, people were coming.

"They're on their way back Tony! Go! Go!" I whispered. I turned around and headed back to the room where Chance was guarding Spanner.

"Spanner," I said, "listen, and listen closely. They're on their way back. If I untie you and you come to the garage and watch me, they will never know anything happened here and you were doing your duty by watching me all the time."

"The cameras," he said. "What about the cameras?"

"I've turned them off but will turn them on in a second. No cameras have been on, but they will be when we walk back into the garage."

"If you say no, Spanner, you know you will be in deep shit, but if you come to the garage, Frank will never know. Quick, what's your answer?"

"Yes," he said, "let's go."

I just hope I could trust him. "Remember, Chance will be watching your every move." I untied him. "Okay, back to the garage, pick up your keys, which are in the corner, and I'll turn the cameras back on while you take me to the can. This way we will not be in the garage when they return."

"Okay."

"Let's go. The cameras are on."

With the cameras now on and Chance in tow, Spanner took me through the house to the bathroom. He waited in the hall while I went in. I explained to him that I would stay in the WC till they returned and that way they wouldn't see us in the garage. I checked the bathroom window and it looked like it was barred but would open. I turned on the cold water and let Chance drink while I went back to the window. The door started to open. I quickly dropped the device outside. I took the towel I had thrown over my shoulder and started wiping my hands.

"You in there, Rider?" Kool yelled.

"Yeah, just freshening up for you, Drool, sorry, I mean Kool. Don't know why I always say drool, sorry man. I'll try harder next time."

"Frank wants to see you."

"Okay, tell him I'll be in the garage."

"His office, asshole."

"I have too much work to do, and besides I'm dirty. He can come to the garage." Chance was sitting at my side eyeing Kool.

Kool looked down at Chance with hatred in his eyes.

"I'll tell him."

I returned to the garage with Spanner following me.

"Hey man," Frank said, as he strode into the garage, "I see you have a good start, but I need you to call it quits for the day."

"Do I have time to dump oil in these engines? Hate to see someone start one of the bikes without oil. That would be the end of the engine."

Frank thought for a moment. "No, come back in a few days."

"Okay, I'll just clean up a little, put some of this stuff out of the way."

"No, I want you to leave *now*. On second thought, up against the wall, I want to search you before you leave." Frank said, gesturing towards the wall with his hand.

"Pardon me!" I said, with a look of shock on my face. "You want to search me, Frank?"

"I want to search you before you go. This way you'll never know when I'm going to do it again."

"Okay, fill your boots," I said, walking over to the wall.

It was quick, it was fruitless, it was needless—and it was thorough.

"I'm outta here Frank," I said, looking downcast. "I'll see you in a couple of days."

Returning home, I stopped by Julie's to see if she wanted to come over with the kids for a barbecue that night. Julie was on the phone and seemed very upset. She looked up with a look of puzzlement on her face.

"What's wrong?" I asked.

"That was Frank."

"Shhh…" I whispered. "Let's sit on the back steps and talk."

Beer in hand, we headed outside.

"Frank is very agitated about something," she said, after her first sip. "He thinks you were snooping around today. Can't put my finger on it, but I don't think he trusts you."

"I don't know why, Julie. A guy by the name of Spanner let me in and watched me the whole time I was working on the bikes. I was doing well till I was told to leave."

"Hmm," Julie thought, "did you go anywhere else in the house?"

"To the bathroom, and I glanced in a couple of doors on the way down the hall."

"No, it's not that. He said, something was missing."

"I don't know. He searched me before I left."

"He what?" She said, with a surprised look on her face.

"Yeah, and I was surprised too. Here I am, working for the guy, and he does something like that. I feel like collecting my money and not going back. Let's forget about this. Are you coming over with the kids for a barbecue?"

"I don't think I should. I'm sure Frank will be calling me at all hours of the night to talk."

"That's fine," I said. "I'll catch you another night then."

I was relieved. Whatever I had dropped out the bathroom window was something important, and I had to go and get it as soon as it got dark. I said goodbye to Julie and headed out the door. I had to pry Chance away from the kids. I had a quick shower, a quick supper, and a quick phone call, to make sure Julie was okay. With Chance on the back, I headed toward the clubhouse taking back roads and approaching from the most populated area. I parked four blocks away and started my approach. Chance knew something was up and was behaving as if we were on a mission.

In the dark, we proceeded through backyards, through gates, over fences, and past whatever got in our way. Two blocks along I spotted the first sentry. He was sitting in a house across the street, casually smoking a cigarette. I put Chance in the lead and moved very cautiously, not wanting to start any dogs barking or run across Ma and Pa sitting in the back yard enjoying the barbecue like the one that I had just missed.

Chance stopped. I could see lights on in the clubhouse and never thought till then that the tunnel I had been in ended up in one of these houses. The house Julie had told me about. Chance wouldn't move, and that was a bad sign. I lay down next to her and watched. She was right! In the yard of the next house, which was two houses from the clubhouse, were three men huddled together and talking in hushed voices. From my position I couldn't hear what they were saying, but I recognized two of them. The first was Kool's friend with the pushed-in face. He was still bandaged up and glowed in the dark. The second was the truck driver—who I still needed to have a serious talk with—and the third, the strongest looking of all three, looked like trouble.

If there were three outside, how many were inside? The only thing I could think of was a decoy. I coded Tony, and within five minutes a police cruiser went by, lights flashing, but without sirens. It worked. All three left their posts and went to the front of the house after the cruiser had passed to see where he was going. Chance and I made a dash for the next yard where we were able to conceal ourselves.

From my pocket, I took the cloth that I had used to wipe the mystery device, and I let Chance sniff it. I pointed toward the bathroom window, and away she crawled. I could only see her because the moon was partially out, and she had a blonde coat. She was nearing the window when I heard a muffled shot then a yelp. I could see the shooter who was looking away from Chance, and was walking toward whatever it was he shot, thankfully not her.

Chance was now under the window and had turned around heading back toward me. Two men after hearing the shot came running out of a side door that I hadn't seen before, and they noticed Chance.

"There's that dog!" I heard one of them yell. He raised his gun. I whistled. Chance jumped up and ran, bullets were chasing her. She came running towards me, dropped the device in midstride and kept going.

What the hell?

A decoy! She was smarter than I was. My best bet was to head toward the clubhouse as everyone else was running away from it. Four more guys came running out of the same door. I waited till they came thundering past, and then I headed at full gallop toward the clubhouse parking lot. Without wasting time, I found what I was looking for and left in a hurry.

The racket was deafening without earplugs, but I had no choice. Around the block I went, waking up all the early to bed goers, and then headed toward my bike as quietly as I could. I ditched Spanner's bike in a culvert, wiped the handlebars clean, retrieved my bike and felt a thump on the back. I had no time to turn around but knew it was Chance when I felt her warm head pushed against my cheek.

My only safeguard was to go to Julie's and when Frank called, and he would, she could say I was there for supper. As I headed down Julie's street, I saw two choppers in her driveway. I made a hastily turned around and headed home.

Into my garage I went. I changed into work clothes, hid the device, and then opened the plug to drain the oil in my bike. I spun the filter off then turned to a Goldwing a customer had left for a tune up. Sitting on a stool, working on the bike, I heard them coming. It sounded like the whole fleet but turned out to be four. I put Chance in a corner then sat down beside the bike again. They came into the garage through the opened door, shoulder to shoulder. I hoped my friend was watching and had dialed 911. This wasn't looking good for me.

"Gentlemen," I said with a big smile on my face, "what can I do for you?"

"You know bloody well what you can do for us," the meanest of the four said, spitting on the ground and adjusting his belt.

"Well I can only work on one bike at a time, not four, even I know that."

"Smart-ass, where is it?"

"Where is what?"

"We're going to shut the garage door, and teach you a lesson," the leader said.

I heard the sirens, then it was quiet.

They were still mouthing me, and oblivious to what was going on behind them, when McClung walked in.

"What's going on here boys?" McClung asked.

The leader blurted out that they were just leaving. "We were asking him about tuning up one of our bikes. Right, Rider?"

"Yeah, next week anytime, boys."

One by one the boys fired up their bikes, and one by one they turned them around, then one by one they left, screaming down the road.

"Where is Chance?"

"She's on guard sitting over there out of sight. Chance, come here girl."

Chance came running up to McClung to be patted. Chance did something I had never seen her do before. She sat in front of McClung and lifted a paw to be shaken.

"First time I have seen her do that, McClung. You must be very special. She'll be riding shotgun for you next."

"Could be a good thing," McClung said. "Could use a female who doesn't speak back all the time. Oh, did I say that Rider?"

213

CHAPTER

I sent a coded message to Tony telling him about the trapdoor, the drugs, the arsenal, and the tunnel I had found. His reply came almost immediately.

we need to meet ASAP

My phone rang. It was Julie.

"I need to come over and have a talk," she said. "it's important."

"No, I'll come to your home."

"Okay, but not for half an hour," she said, sounding stressed.

"Got it."

I said goodbye to McClung, locked up, jumped in my beater, and stashed it a block away. As I neared Julie's house on foot, the two bikers who were previously there were walking down the sidewalk towards their bikes. I didn't recognize either of them. I watched as they left then walked back to my truck. Fifteen minutes later Chance and I were at her door.

"Hi," I said, "you look like you have been put through the wringer."

"And the dryer," she said. "It was terrible."

Chance squeezed by us and headed for the bedroom where she climbed on the bed between the two kids.

"I had visitors tonight," she said, looking worried. "They were not very nice and threatened me."

"Let's start at the beginning. Do you know them?"

"I do now."

"Are they from Frank's gang?"

"No, they're from another gang, from out of town, and they're mean."

"Do they know that I am here now?"

"No, but if they drive by, they will."

"No, they won't, my truck is parked up the street."

"I'm scared, Rider. They threatened to do things to me no man should ever talk about. These men are wicked," she said, as tears started flowing down her face.

"What did they want?"

"They said you stole something from them, and they want it back."

"What did I steal?" I said, not wanting to let her know what I had—and why these guys had come and not Frank's.

"Frank has been storing stuff for them, and they want it back."

"What did they threaten to do to you?"

"I can't talk about it; it's not human."

"So, they think you can get info from me if I had any?"

"They know I can."

"Did they leave you a number?"

"Yes."

"Okay, here is what you're going to do."

"I can't do that!"

"Yes, you can, go to my house with the kids, park your car in my garage, put the kids to bed in the spare bedroom, and you can sleep in mine."

Julie left with the kids, and I seated myself comfortably on her couch, waiting for the doorbell to ring.

The knock came to the door a half hour later. By Julie's description, I was facing the two mean looking thugs, who had threatened her.

"Where is Julie?" the closest said, with a smirk on his face.

"This has nothing to do with, Julie. It's between you and me."

"Get picked, meathead."

"As I said, Julie is not involved in this."

"Where is it?" the second goon said.

"Where is what? This is the confusing common denominator," I said. "You're confusing me. I have no idea, who you are or what you want."

"Frank, said you took something from his place today, while you were over there, and we want it back."

"Now we're getting somewhere, gentlemen," I said. "Frank thinks I took something of his?"

"No, not his. *Ours.*"

"This is getting very confusing for me. I'm a mechanic and that's what I was doing at Frank's today. How or why would I take something of yours from Frank's when I had one of his boys sitting by my side babysitting me all day, and Frank searched me when I left? Did he tell you that?"

They looked at each other trying to fit the puzzle together.

"You saying that you didn't take anything?"

"There was nothing to take except parts, and they're still all there, lying on the floor beside the bikes."

"Okay, we're going to have a talk with Frank, and if there is the slightest chance, we think you're lying, we will be back, and it won't be pleasant."

"Fill your boots, boys. I'll be waiting."

I turned my phone on to check on Julie and saw from sheer exhaustion she was sound asleep in my bed. I then phoned McClung and told him the story.

"Okay, Rider, I'll be waiting for your call. This gang has its clubhouse forty miles out of town. We think that they are partners in the drug trade with Frank."

I heard them coming a half hour later. I phoned McClung, but his line was busy. Dang, isn't that always the way. Their bikes parked, they lumbered up the sidewalk to the front door. I was sitting on a chair facing them, when they both burst in with knives in hand. My partner, Chance, was crouched out of sight waiting for a command. I jumped up and threw two knives. One grazing the right ear of one goon and the left of the other. Unfortunately, the second throw was with my damaged arm and due to the pain, my aim wasn't so accurate. One goon suffered a nick the second lost half his ear. They both stopped in their tracks noticing two more knives in my hands. As the blood started to flow, they both had a concerned look on their faces.

"What the shit was that all about?" The leader yelled, looking at his partner's ear lying on the floor.

"That's your warning," I said, balancing two more knives in my hands.

"Drop your knives, boys, and turn around slowly. Don't be air heads." Good thing they were standing on hardwood floors or they would be scrubbing carpet from the blood flow. As they both turned around slowly, something didn't feel right, and I was correct. I hadn't seen the Billy club up the sleeve of the nearest goon. As he turned, he dropped the

217

club out of his sleeve and into his hand. Turning quickly and stepping forward, he reached out and hit my damaged arm a horrendous blow that lit my eyes up with every color in the rainbow. My arm and head exploded with pain.

I dropped my knives as I fell to my knees with white flashing through my eyes. I clicked for Chance, who had the first goon knocked over in surprise and was gnawing on the second. I was too dazed from the pain to even gain mobility, but I noticed Chance had returned to the first and was having a go at him again. Blood was everywhere, and I was leaving my contribution behind also. The first goon I attacked had bleeding lacerations everywhere—as for the second, I couldn't tell as Chance was jumping all over him as he wrestled trying to get away from her.

"Rider, call the dog off!"

Looking up through glazed eyes, I saw McClung and his troops standing back by the door—they didn't want to get too close to Chance.

"Chance," I mumbled.

Chance looked at me then went over and sat next to McClung. I slowly got to my feet, wobbling and holding my damaged arm. I looked down at the two guys laying on the floor moaning. I could hear ambulances coming and felt comfort in that.

"What happened?" McClung asked, looking around at the carnage, then at the blood flowing off my damaged arm.

"Both entered Julie's house without knocking, and this is the result. They want something that I don't have, but they won't tell me what it is. They're both from out of town and working on Frank's info."

"Seize their bikes, then get them to the hospital under tight security, then back to the station for questioning," McClung ordered, shaking his head.

My arm was a mess. My cut had been opened even more with the blow exposing muscle and bone, it hurt like a son of a gun.

The goons were not happy campers as the attendants worked on them both trying to stem the blood flow from many punctures. They all kept a wary eye on the dog.

"She's okay," I said weakly to the attendants, hanging onto the couch for support as dizziness came and went.

I pointed to one of the attendants, and Chance started walking towards him. He became very nervous and the goon looking through a blood-covered face started moaning again.

"Just stay there," I told the attendant, "and she will sit by your side. She's very friendly to most humans. It's guys like this that upset her." Chance walked over and nuzzled her head against his arm.

"You're okay, she likes you." I said, to the attendant.

"What about me?" one of the other attendants said, without looking up from what he was doing. "I think she likes me too."

"She's not sure about you," McClung answered. "You're wielding a needle."

"Be careful, I hear she goes bananas if she sees one."

The attendant put a tight bandage around my arm to help hold things together till I got to the hospital.

"McClung, do you mind taking Chance home with you? I don't know how protective she will be here with the cleaners coming and going."

"I'll put her through her paces, and don't you worry. She will be a new dog when you next see her."

I arrived back at my place in the morning to find Julie and the kids playing in my back yard. I told Julie what happened, and then scooted her out with the kids. I needed a quiet rest.

CHAPTER

Shortly after Julie left, McClung arrived at my house with Chance.

I felt sick. Coming up the sidewalk was McClung, with his face all bandaged up. What had Chance done to him? I went to the door stumbling due to the pain, medication and lack of sleep. Opening the door McClung looked even worse close up. Holding onto the door jamb for support I croaked. "What happened?"

"It was my fault. I thought I could give her a command, and she turned on me. My wife then jumped on her pounding like heck, and then she stopped."

"I'm sorry, I was sure you were the best of friends."

"Well, friends or not friends, you can have her back," he said, shaking his head. Then he started laughing. "Got you—it wasn't Chance."

"It was just a little mismanagement on my part, I should've known better, but you should see the other guy."

"I don't understand."

"Well," he said, grimacing with every word, "I had a call to a domestic dispute, which is the worst. I was standing back listening to both sides of the story, when the guy halls off and hits me smack in the face. I go down trying to get my gun out. The lady has turned on me also, and I'm on the floor with both wailing on me. Kicks to the body and face. Chance was in the car with the window only partially down so she couldn't get out. How she did it, I don't know. But suddenly she was there, and let's just say the situation turned around pretty quickly at that point. Both of them were taken to the hospital with numerous puncture wounds, and here I am thanks to Chance."

"That's my girl," I said.

"And how are you feeling?"

"Terrible. Worse than last time. Feels like my arm has been cut off and not sewn up. Doc says he was able to mend everything up inside good as new, but I'm not sure."

"Well if it helps any, you look the way I feel."

"Thanks! And so, do you."

"Do you feel like talking?"

"Yeah, okay. What's up?"

"Tony has been telling me personally all about the motorcycle gangs you've infiltrated. When you and I are a little better, we will be conducting a raid. The goons you met last night wouldn't talk, but thanks to you, we found important info on their bikes."

"McClung, before you tell me anymore, will you go to the kitchen and make us a cup of coffee, I really need one."

"Sure, I could do that."

I sent Tony a text asking about McClung. "He is clean! Tell him everything," was Tony's reply.

I got off the phone as my coffee arrived. I told him about the device, drugs, armament tunnel, and which house it was.

"I didn't know any of that. Maybe we had better get this raid underway as soon as possible."

"You know," I said, "there are always rovers driving around keeping watch, lookouts in the surrounding houses, and hidden cameras. I think the best approach would be to take the rovers out first, then the lookouts, then the house where the tunnel ends and then the clubhouse. This way, if our plan works, they will head down the tunnel to the house where we will be waiting."

"Sounds like it might work. I'll sleep on it, but I will station patrolmen in our safe houses to keep watch on them."

"You know that I have pictures of the drugs and weapons, which the judge may want to see."

"Okay, let's meet tomorrow morning with Tony," McClung said.

CHAPTER

38

I met McClung and Tony in the mayor's office. The chief of police was also there in all his splendor. As the meeting progressed, a date, an approach, the number of officers both local and outside, the temporary jails, interrogators, paddy wagons, communication system, cell jammers, tow trucks, ambulances and other important items were all discussed.

The date for the raid was set for two days from now.

Julie called regularly, but I wouldn't let her come over, telling her that the kids were too noisy for me at this point. Finally, in desperation—or under direct orders from Frank—she hired a babysitter and came over, the night before the raid.

"Come on in," I said.

"You look terrible," she said. "Are you still not feeling too well?"

"I feel like a truck ran over my arm. Would you change the dressing for me?"

"Oh, this does look sore and maybe infected. Did they give you any antibiotics to take?"

"Yes, they did, and I've been taking them regularly."

"First, let's talk about your arm."

"Okay, it hurts bad."

"How did it happen?" she asked, getting exasperated.

I told her.

"Where are they now?"

"In jail, I expect."

"You had a visit from that cop sergeant?"

Now how does she know that? I wondered.

"McClung," I said.

"And where is Chance? She didn't run off, did she?"

"Yeah, with all the violence that's been going on, I guess she had, had enough, wanted a quieter home, so she took off. They found her in a happy house. I think she smokes pot now."

"You're kidding me. Where did they find her?"

"Down at the Salvation Army, good people you know! They fed her, bathed her, brushed her and gave her a place to sleep. I don't think she even picked up any bugs, and they didn't charge her."

"Really," Julie said, eyes wide open.

"Yeah, and you know the best part? When they found out I owned her, and they couldn't contact me, they put her in a cab, and sent her to the police station."

"No, you're kidding me."

"Yes, I'm kidding. I had nowhere to leave her, so McClung took her home with him. Look, I'm sorry, Julie, but all of a sudden, I'm feeling really rotten, I need to lie down. I really feel terrible."

"Okay," she said, getting up.

I think she was glad she could now go home and phone Frank. I closed the door and went to bed.

—

Next morning, after a restless night, I was sitting enjoying my coffee when there was a knock at the front door. When I opened it the kid who had driven the truck was standing there.

"Are you okay?" he asked, looking at my arm.

"No, not really. Why, what's up?"

"Frank wants to see you."

"Man, I don't know. If he wants to come here, maybe. But ask if he can wait a few days. I can't even drive my bike."

"Yeah, it looks really bad, but you have the truck."

"That thing, it would open all my stitches it bounces around so much. Here, take a good look." I showed him my arm where I had just taken the bandage off to give it some air. He turned around and started gagging.

"It's okay; it's just a little gangrene setting in. The doc is going to see if it will heal before cutting it off."

Up it came! All over my flowerbed!

"I'm sure it will be okay, though, don't you worry."

Wiping his mouth on his shirtsleeve, he said he would forward my message.

CHAPTER

The raid was on. It was arranged that at four AM, I was to meet McClung to be picked up two blocks from my house. Everything was in place. None of the officers knew what was happening but would get a call at home and be given instructions where to meet. I had one working arm, so I wasn't of much use, but I still wanted to be there.

That night I set my alarm and went to bed early, waking up at two AM with the buzzer sounding. After fumbling in the dark, I realized that it wasn't the radio alarm, but the front door. I looked out the bedroom window, but no bikes were to be seen. I armed myself with a knife and Chance. Staggering to the door, I flung the door open, knife in hand ready for the unwanted and standing there was the kid, the truck driver, the one who said he wasn't a club member.

"What the heck are you waking me up for at this time of the morning?" I demanded.

"Sorry Rider, but I needed to talk to you this afternoon but felt sick. Can I come in?"

"Come in and sit over there." I said, upset of being deprived of sleep, which I badly needed.

"What's so important that you couldn't have spoken to me later on today?"

The kid looked at his boots, then stood up.

"I shouldn't be here."

"Sit down and start talking." I demanded.

He looked at me for over a minute thinking and thinking.

"Well?" I said.

"Frank is after you, and he's coming with five guys at three this morning." He blurted out.

"How do you know this?"

"I'm one of the five."

"What's his plan?"

"He said, you and the dog wouldn't leave this house alive. He is really ticked off."

"Should I see if I can have the house armed with police?" I asked.

"No, he said he would kill anyone in his way."

"Why are you telling me this?"

"I was forced into the gang and want out. The only way out is in a coffin."

"And if you don't show up for the kill?"

"He will be after me, I'm dead meat either way."

"What about Julie?"

"He has no use for her and would just as soon see her gone also."

"Tell me about the clubhouse."

"I know he has video cameras all around the exterior as well as interior. His office he keeps locked up; the rest is just rooms."

"Have you been anywhere else?"

He looked down, dejected, and I felt sorry for him. His days were limited coming here.

"Yes, under the garage is a room full of drugs and an arsenal. There's a tunnel leading to a house outside that five guys live in. He keeps guys posted outside twenty-four hours a day."

"Do you know where these guys are?"

"Yes, precisely. I was on duty when you went over the other day."

"If I help you, will you forget about your appointment with Frank tonight and talk to Sergeant McClung?"

"You know I'm dead meat just coming here, but yes, I will talk to him."

I phoned Sergeant McClung and had him meet us at the pickup spot in fifteen minutes. Time was running out.

"Where is your bike?"

"It's parked up and around the corner."

"Get it quick! No lights or engine, and we will hide it in my garage."

I got dressed, armed myself, and ate something. With a blanket thrown over James's bike, we headed outside. Sergeant McClung was a little disturbed to see James come on board.

"James was forced into working for the club. He wants out, but there is no way. Frank and his guys are coming to my house at three in the morning, no one gets out alive."

"And let me guess, James here is supposed to be one of the guys."

James looked at his shoes.

"McClung," I said, "what if we lay in ambush and wait for Frank, take them down, then your fellows will be free to raid the clubhouse."

"Okay Rider, we don't have much time. I'll get you eight men; you wake and warn the neighbors then figure out what you're going to do?"

"James, are you armed?"

"No man, but I've hunted. I can shoot."

"This is the plan I worked out…"

I explained it to him in complete detail.

"Will Frank be calling you, if you're not there with him?"

"Yeah, many times I would expect."

"Okay, give me your phone."

"Why?"

"If he starts calling you, you'll become distracted, and I don't want that."

"No, I'm okay."

"I want your phone, and I want it now," I said, "or the deal's off."

He handed it over to me slapping it in my good hand. I turned it off then pocketed it. I saw movement up the street. It was two thirty, and Frank and his gang were getting close, hiding in the shadows.

"Back here, James." I ordered. I made sure James was always in front of me so I could keep an eye on him. Glock in one hand and knife in my sling, I backed up slowly, keeping an eye on the movement up the street. My phone vibrated.

"Troops are leaving the attachment now."

"Hurry, five patches have arrived. Text me when two blocks away and hold. No sirens, no lights, but hurry."

The five were making their way down the street very slowly. I could see what appeared to be Frank, giving orders and pointing. Without warning, all five ran down the sidewalk hiding behind the parked cars and then hiding behind the car we had been positioned behind, five minutes before. I touched James on the shoulder. Holding my fingers to my lips in a 'be quiet' gesture.

Chance knew what was happening and began shaking. I petted her to calm her down. The thugs were positioned behind a car, casing out my house. A dog started barking down the block, easing the tension, and then a baby could be heard two houses down. Frank ran towards my house followed by his four heavily armed shooters. What I was hoping was that they would break down my door and enter the house. That way they would all be contained.

Flat against the house in the flowerbed, and inching their way to the front door, Frank suddenly stopped. He signaled one of his men to check the garage door. The dog kept barking, the baby kept crying, my phone was vibrating, and my alarm was sounding because the garage door had been opened. They stormed in and closed the door behind them.

CHAPTER

"We're two blocks away."

"Send one man down behind the north houses. Leave the others where they are, and you come down and see me, I whispered into my phone."

I told the deputy what was happening, and instructed him where to place his troops, and not to fire until I did. Back he went, and in three minutes I could see everyone in place.

I turned on my phone and watched Frank running from room to room. It looked like he was beyond mad. I phoned using the number I had retrieved from Julie's phone.

"Yeah!"

"Give yourself up, Frank. You're surrounded."

"What the hell? Tell James he's dead meat."

"Frank, look—"–*Click*– He hung up.

I kept the police informed of what was going on. Frank was in my office looking through all the drawers but found nothing of interest, so he headed for the garage. I could see his crew standing at the windows behind the curtains. It looked like four, but it was too crowded to tell. I called again, this time on the house phone using James's phone.

"You are dead meat, man," Frank, yelled into his phone.

"Sorry, Frank it's me. Just come out with your hands up and it will be over."

"You think I'm an idiot? I've got better plans than that dickhead." –*Click*–

I turned my back to James. I did not see nor hear the blow coming. "Frank, this is James, I did as you—"

And those were the last words he spoke.

I could hear mumbling, but my senses had not yet returned. I lay still trying to figure out what had happened. Then I realized it was not mumbling I heard but Chance tearing something apart. I stood up, wobbling from the nausea, and saw Chance throwing something around. In a weak voice I called her over. Looking around I saw fragments of James's clothing. I heard the phone ringing in the distance and with Chance's help, I found it.

"Yeah?"

"James?"

"What, uh, no," I said, in a somewhat incoherent voice. "It's Rider."–*Click*–

I phoned McClung and told him what was happening. He suggested we turn on the cell jammer and let them sit. I turned on the house cameras and saw that Frank and his boys were in the garage looking at the bikes. In the garage were six operable bikes and the Goldwing. I informed the police that they were going to make a run for it and to shoot when the target was in sight. I had two police in the backyard move to either end of the street. I looked at the garage again and all five bikes had been turned around facing the door. I could see that two had gas cans in their hands and were going to set the place on fire. I dialed 911 and asked for a fire truck and three ambulances with no lights and no sirens to move in within one block.

Two of them burst from the garage, screaming, brandishing firearms, engines roaring. My first shot got one of them in the chest. He dropped his can of gas in order to have both hands on the handlebars. Making the sharp turn out of my driveway is as far as he got. The second shot from one of the police sent him flying off my beautiful blue bike, and both went careening down the street, in a heap of metal intertwined with flesh and fire.

The second rider made it onto the street where he was hit by a direct shot that sent him plowing into my already downed bike and rider. Gas spilled, engine still running, the ensuing fire was not pretty, but there was nothing we could do. There were still three riders to go. Seeing the havoc and the fire down the street unfolding a singular rider shot out of the garage.

I was helpless to do anything as my head was throbbing and my arm was bleeding again. The third rider, with the most powerful bike, gunned the motor creating a roar that could have woken up people three blocks away. Underestimating the power of the engine, he did a back flip, sending bike and rider flying into the night sky. Man, and machine landed in a tangle of flesh and metal, gas and oil—no medical attention would be required. Another bike ruined.

Where were the last two riders?

CHAPTER

I turned on my camera and saw the two remaining in the house running up the stairs to my office. In the turmoil, the police thought they had found all the gang members. I told them to take cover and asked for their best marksman. He arrived and, surveying the carnage left behind by Chance, looked at me with awe in his eyes. I turned on my phone and showed him where they were located in the house.

Holding his rifle steady, pointing at the most prominent of the two, he slowly pulled the trigger. His target spun around and fell to the floor.

The shot member got up with help from his partner and headed for the bathroom where they were fumbling through my medicine cabinet. They returned to my office again where another bullet hit the same goon, spinning him around again and dropping him to the floor. He lay still.

I radioed McClung. "One's down. Chance and I are going in. Check the bikers on the road to make sure they are all dead."

Even though it looked like one was dead, I couldn't take that chance. Chance and I struggled up the road, hiding behind parked cars, crossing the street out of sight of my house, down the street, hugging my neighbor's houses to my garage door. It was still open, smelling of exhaust fumes and devoid of most bikes. I turned my cell jammer off, but my phone would not pick up my security cameras. Two gas cans were slowly dribbling their contents on the driveway where they had been dropped in a rush to get out.

I gave Chance a pat and tightened her leash. I walked over to the electrical panel and tripped the main breaker. Back to the basement stairs, remembering where every squeak was, we slowly crept up. The door at the top was slightly ajar, letting a small shaft of light filter through from the full moon. Chance was shaking, and so was I.

Keeping my eye on the hallway, I texted my shooter to come around to the front door, and to open it quietly then push it hard enough to hit the wall with bang—but to stay outside.

Two minutes later, Chance's posture told me he was at the front door. I heard the handle turning, the door swinging open then a loud bang. The front door opening and banging camouflaged the sound of the basement door opening. I was in the hall.

My computer room was the first door on the left, spare bedroom second door, and my bedroom, first door on the right. They had been in my computer room, but they had moved. My computer room door was open, but all others closed.

I texted for stun grenades to be tossed into the front rooms, one at a time and spaced apart.

The first was in my office and after smashing glass and a stun boom, Chance and I ran in. There was blood on the floor, on the wall, on the chair, but no one in the room. I shut the door and helped my earplugs by covering my ears.

Crouching down waiting for the second boom I looked at Chance with her own specially made cap on. She seemed unfrazzled.

—Boom—

Peering out into the hall, a door was hanging on one hinge at a precarious angle. Into that room Chance followed me with no result.

Chance was moaning and trying to tell me something. I was trying to read her body language when, across the hall, the bathroom door burst open and there stood Julie, with Frank holding a knife to her neck.

"Julie," I said stammering. "What are you doing here?"

She just looked at me with a smile on her face.

"Let's talk, Frank?" I said, stalling for time.

"Nothing to talk about," he said, clutching his midsection. "Julie and I are leaving here alive, and you and the dog will be wondering what happened."

I slowly moved away from the bedroom door and towards the basement, pulling Chance with me.

"Not so fast," Frank said, pushing Julie out of the bathroom and into the hall still with the knife pushed against her neck.

"Why are you treating the mother of your children like this, Frank? If anything happens to Julie, you are going to leave your kids orphaned."

"Nothing is going to happen to Julie, unless you make it happen. Like I said, we're leaving together."

I could see Frank was getting weak from loss of blood. I made to rub my sore arm and in the same move retrieved my knife. When the third boom came, I threw my knife, Julie screamed as Frank moaned, then released his grip on her, Chance attacked, and Frank twitched then laid still. Julie looked down at Frank then attacked me pounding on my chest sobbing and screaming. "You ruined everything; you ruined everything, why did you do it?"

Love is blind, I thought. Little did she know that Frank was going to kill me and have it staged like Julie killed me in a blind love-ridden rage, then Chance would attack Julie and Frank would be free again.

Sobbing and using me as a pillar to hold her up, I realized that it was all a show with Julie. She thought she and Frank were going to run away, and I ruined everything.

My phone vibrated again.

"Rider."

"They're all dead outside."

"Frank's dead inside, but Julie's here. He brought her as a hostage."

"I'll call the ambulances and fire truck in."

"Good," I said. "Arrest Julie, but make sure her two kids are taken care of, she has two. Bring two cars up here, turn on the reds then knock on doors and tell people all is okay. I'll take four officers and help the others at the clubhouse. James, the driver, is across the street. I wouldn't go look. Your assumption of him was correct. He double crossed me."

Chance and I jumped in one of the cruisers and headed down to the clubhouse.

"Never seen anything like that, Rider," Dave said, shaking his head. "Bikes ruined, men burnt, it looked like a horrendous traffic accident."

CHAPTER

Dave was of middle age, medium height, and medium plus weight. He was one of the ones called in at the last minute. Even Chance noticed that he had garlic on his breath that would have disabled any of those bikers if he breathed on them. It was overpowering. My eyes were watering, I had to open the window—Chance was luckier, her window was open with her head fully extended outside.

We tore down the street towards the clubhouse with neither lights nor sirens.

My arm was as bad as ever and hurt even more with every move. The operation was starting within five minutes, so we parked four blocks away in a double driveway to help conceal the ghost car. We listened to our phones as the car radios were transmitting false transmissions to misinform the gang members listening in on their police scanners. If it was an emergency, either a cell was used, or the transmission was followed by two beeps.

I called McClung, and he said he thought they had captured all the roaming and staked-out gang members, as well as the club members from out of town. They had raided all the club member's homes and hangouts and were now heading for the clubhouse.

"Okay Dave," I said, "sounds like we can head on down to the clubhouse."

I made sure Dave walked behind me and Chance—otherwise it would be like breathing unwanted diesel fumes from a throbbing engine parked next to you at a stop sign.

McClung was certain he had everything under control. The stakeouts had been arrested. All their houses had been searched using search warrants with guards posted. Local hangouts were raided then watched, and all people involved were in holding cells. The out of town gang members had been arrested. I had done my part so far, now it was the clubhouse and adjoining residence to be raided.

McClung was in the FBI control trailer, that had been moved to within two blocks of the clubhouse. He was manning the phones and watching live video from those who were wearing police issued action cams. All landlines and mobile phones had been jammed at both locations, power was to be shut off as soon as I gained entry to the clubhouse, and vehicles were ready to block the escape of any motorbikes. Walking into the command trailer, I spotted McClung busy on the phone.

"How's it going, McClung," I asked, listening to the entire hubbub going on.

McClung had a look of concern on his face as he spoke. "Rider, you said there was a room full of drugs, and arsenal under the garage. Well I'm worried they will blow it up before we get there."

"I'm not sure they will. With their leader out of contact, I don't think they would risk a move like that without explicit instructions. Besides, I have his phone and there have been no calls sent yet. The other option is that we gain access to the house and then go through the tunnel and up into the clubhouse. I have a set of keys that I took from Frank, which will be keys to both houses."

McClung turned around to address his squad leaders standing behind him. "Well, *you* heard what the man said. Which do you think is best?"

"Personally," one of the leaders said, "I think we should go through the garage door of the clubhouse, because of Chance's abilities. We're going to need the exterior cameras blanked out, and as soon as Rider enters, he can pull the main switch, shutting off all the power to the clubhouse. They may have a generator backup, but we'll know that when the breaker is flipped. The backup could come from the other house, but on my surveillance, I didn't see any exterior generators."

"I also think going to the clubhouse with Chance is the best option," McClung said.

"Have you notified the neighbors?" I asked.

"Yes, they have all been contacted. They were all told to not look out any windows or answer any doors. We have jammed their phones and cut their landlines just in case. We informed them that when this is over, we will turn on the police sirens and knock on doors. We have five minutes! Let's get in position, men."

CHAPTER

Chance and I took up positions with six SWAT team members behind the neighboring house, waiting for the signal to proceed to the clubhouse. The other gang house had its share of law enforcement officers waiting to storm it also. Chance was looking at the SWAT team that was with me with concern on her face. I called the leader over and pointed to Chance, then to his team. The leader put his thumb in the air as acknowledgment. I knelt next to Chance and pointed to the leader who was standing next to me and whispered, "friend."

Chance sniffed the leader's hand then sat down. I pointed to the others and Chance did the same, requiring a pat from each. Frank's phone was vibrating; I pulled it out, checked the number, then sent a message to McClung. In one of the houses someone was looking for Frank. Five seconds later my phone was vibrating. "Go. Go. Go," was all it said.

With Chance on a leash leading, we carefully rounded the corner of the house to the garage door where I started trying keys—at the same time, one of the demolition experts was placing explosives around the perimeter of the door as a backup. The others were scanning for hostiles. I had four keys to try. The first didn't work. The second didn't work. My time of surprise was running out. The third didn't work. The explosives were in place. Inserting the fourth and last key it didn't work either. "Shit!" I said under my breath. *Our plan is not a surprise anymore.*

I had not really scrutinized the keys closely, and as I stepped back from the door; I ran my fingers over the key undulations. One had undulations on *both* sides. I turned around suddenly almost knocking the explosives expert over, and turning the key over, it slid into its sheath. The door swung open, and Chance and I stood back while the SWAT team cleared the garage. I took the leash off Chance, and she ran for the inside garage door, while I raced for the breaker.

In the dark we could hear someone yelling and heading down the hall. If they were yelling, that meant there were others in the house. I clicked for Chance, and she was by my side. The SWAT team had positioned themselves to take out the first patch, as he came fumbling into the garage. The door flew open, and a female came in feeling her way to the breaker. Two SWAT members had grabbed her from behind; covering her mouth, cuffed her and had her on the floor under guard before she knew what had hit her.

Chance and I stood guard. The SWAT team members called clear, as they ran down the hall, checking the rooms. Gunshots sounded and an injured SWAT member was hurriedly brought back to the garage, along with three gang members and two girls. I called the SWAT leader over to the trapdoor. "This is the way to the drug room below. I didn't see any devices around the door, but the bottom step onto the concrete has a sensor plate. In the far corner you will see a door which leads to the tunnel. Do not touch the door handle, it's an alarm, but push on the other side of the door and it will open automatically. There is a light switch, but it may light up the tunnel as well, warning others. There's lots of artillery and drugs down there! Be careful."

"Mark is injured," the leader yelled at me, "but he's strong enough to watch over this bunch. I'll take three with me and leave Paul to help you clear the remaining rooms."

I flipped the breaker back on and looked down at the members sitting on the floor.

"Well, well," I said, "what do we have here? Is that you Kool?"

"You're friggin' dead meat, man."

"Kool, how many times have you repeated yourself, you said that last time we met, and I'm still here."

"Get lost, asshole!"

"You're looking good, pretty boy. What with that new face and all? You'll look even better to your friends in the pen."

We thought it best to check all the rooms again. Chance and I stood ready at the first door. "Empty," Paul yelled.

Chance showed no fear at the second and third doors. These three had already been cleared, but we were checking anyways.

Standing outside Frank's office, Chance started to shake and moan. I put my hand on the handle as if to open it, and Chance backed away. I signaled to Paul, that there could be someone in there. As he drew nearer, he signaled for me and Chance to move away from the door.

With my arm still bleeding, head throbbing, stomach churning, and mind wandering, I backed away.

The door was flung open, and a stun grenade was thrown inside. Paul followed closely behind. With the sound of the grenade going off, the leader in the basement—feeling concerned—sent one of his members upstairs to help. I turned around and almost crapped my pants, not expecting to see a ninja running down the hall towards me, gun drawn.

They brought out two more members, cursing and swearing.

Paul and Nick, the two SWAT team members, left to deposit the two gang members in the garage with the others, while Chance and I went down to the other end of the house. This area was quite clean and well decorated. Julie must have had a say in that. Chance entered the living room but stopped at a side door that was shut.

I put my hand on the handle, and Chance backed away. Two SWAT team members returned and threw in another stun grenade. Out came two more members and two girls. This must have been party night.

We were given the go ahead to enter while the four were handcuffed and taken to the garage. Chance was shaking. So was I. I knelt down and patted her.

As Paul and Nick returned again, I held up one finger and pointed to another door in the room. They each threw in a grenade then entered. I heard scuffling and entered the room with Chance. It was a large room, tastefully decorated, but the way a man would decorate it. All the pictures, or at least all those still remaining on the wall, were hanging crooked. There was paper scattered everywhere, and a gun collection had been knocked off the wall. The two patches were lying in wait and took the two SWAT members by surprise as they entered. The two patches had the upper hand, knives were out, and blood was flowing from several wounds. The men were getting weaker. I couldn't help but hoped Chance could remember bad from good.

I pointed and Chance got into the ruckus by attacking a gang member. This left Paul—as weak as he was—the option to help his buddy if he could. I texted for backup, called Chance off, then put her into the other fight.

Four men were lying on the floor either from exhaustion, severe knife wounds, or from Chance. Help arrived none too soon, as Paul needed immediate attention for a severe knife wound to his stomach.

I called over the SWAT member who had just arrived.

"You can take care of this mess, call in the ambulances, and back up to protect them. Cuff these patches, attend to Paul over there but don't move him till the attendants arrive. Let the attendants do that, Chance and I are going to check the rest of the house."

The kitchen was clear, the bathroom was clear, which left one remaining room. Chance and I hugged the wall as we crept nearer to the door. I looked down at Chance and she was shaking as well as me. The door was open. I was weak, Chance was charged, and the air was electrified.

Behind me was a couch with a pillow on it. I turned around and in excruciating pain grabbed the pillow, then, as a decoy, threw it high in the air through the open door. As Chance ran in, I followed gun drawn.

Sitting on the couch was a girl wrapped in a blanket. Chance had not attacked her, but was standing close to her growling, and baring her teeth.

"Are you alone?" I asked, looking around the room and pointing my gun at her.

"Yes, I'm alone," she replied, shaking.

"You're not lying, I hope. It could be bad for both of us," I whispered, in a weak voice. I looked around the nicely decorated room and saw no other doors or hiding spots.

"Stand up slowly and keep your hands where I can see them, with no sudden moves or the dog may attack."

She looked at Chance with terror in her eyes then stood up slowly, clutching the blanket as if she was cold.

"Drop the blanket!" I said.

"No," she replied in a firm voice.

"Drop the blanket and drop it now," I stammered in a weak voice.

Chance must have noticed a change in the girl's voice, as she started growling and snapping at the girl. She dropped the blanket.

'Holly shit!" I said, looking away. "Pick it up and cover yourself! Where are your clothes?"

As she bent over to retrieve the blanket, I had to admit she was a beauty.

"Why are you alone in here?" I stammered.

"I was in the other room. I ran here when I heard all the other noises," she whispered, clutching her blanket tight to her again.

"Let's go get your clothes," I said. still pointing my gun at her.

I took her arm and she led me into the room where the four had been fighting. It was a mess, blood was puddled everywhere, pictures askew, furniture broken, holes in the walls and the smell of blood tinged our nostrils.

"I can't go in there," she said, holding her mouth.

"Yes, you can."

"No, I'll be sick."

"Be sick then, let's go."

"Where are your clothes?" I said again, glancing around the room.

She pointed. "In that room."

It was a door none of us had noticed before.

"What's in there?"

"Money, papers, and my clothes," she said, looking worried.

"Let's go."

"I can't." She was frightened.

I tightened my grip on her arm and propelled her over and between the carnage and into the adjoining room.

As she had said, there was money, papers and clothes.

"Grab your clothes, and let's go back to the other room."

Clutching her clothes—what there was of them—we left the room and proceeded back through the rubble again.

"I'm going to step outside while you put your clothes on, but I'm going to leave Chance in charge. If you make any sudden moves, pick anything up but your clothes, or try to touch her, you will wish you hadn't."

"Don't go!" she pleaded, looking at Chance. "I'm scared of dogs."

"You'll be okay."

"Don't go," she said, her voice rising. "I'm scared of dogs, and I'll scream. I will. They will think you touched me. You have to stay."

"You'll be okay," I said getting weaker.

"Can't do it," she yelled. "I'll scream!"

"Chance won't hurt you, as long as you behave."

"You go, and I'll scream!"

"Okay, hurry up then."

She dropped her blanket and picked up the flimsiest of paraphernalia I had ever seen. I couldn't take my eyes off it, or her. Where was this going? (Got to be on the lookout for concealed weapons you know; Safety first). It was smaller than a thong and a little bigger than a postage stamp. After wiggling into it I could tell it was made for her. Shorts then a T-shirt. I could tell all three pieces were not cheap. She looked good.

"What's your name?"

"Tiffany, but you can call me Tiff."

"Who do you know here, Tiff?"

"I'm Kool's girl."

"Oh man," I said under my breath. "You must be kidding me."

"Why would I be kidding you? I'm Kool's girl. We're working together."

"What are you working together on?" I asked, wishing I hadn't.

"Just stuff," she said, with a smirk on her face.

"Hands behind your back."

"What for? I just let you watch me get dressed, and now you're going to cuff me. I'm not hiding anything. No, I won't turn around."

"Pardon me, you'll do as I say. Now turn around."

"No!"

I clicked my fingers and Chance did one growl.

"Okay, okay!" She swung around so fast that I didn't see the swing coming. It landed with a mighty blow right on my damaged arm. Pain shot through me like a bolt of lightning. My eyes flashed white, my knees buckled, and I landed on the floor, weak from loss of blood. I was embarrassed that a little thing like this had dropped me to my knees and doing little for my ego.

"That's for—"

That's all she got out before Chance had one of her pretty legs in her mouth. She screamed, I gained my senses and called Chance off.

"I told you not to move suddenly," I said weakly.

"I'll move suddenly if I want to," she screamed, looking down at Chance realizing she had spoken without thinking about the dog first.

I was starting to think she was dumber than a gatepost.

One SWAT guy came running when he heard the scream. Blood was dribbling from four small puncture wounds on her leg, but it was nothing serious. Chance must have thought she had nice legs, to bite her so gently. And she did. I gave out a groan as the ninja helped me up, then he caught me as I started falling again. I sat on the couch, and as I did, I put my hand out for support. I felt something hard, picked it up and saw that it was a memory stick, that must have fallen out of someone's pocket.

"That's mine and Kool's," Tiff said, reaching for it. "Give it to me now or I'll scream again."

"You can scream all you want, Tiff, because where you're going nobody will hear you scream except your cell mates," I said, in a weak voice.

"Where do you think I'm going, big boy?"

"Jail!"

"What for?" Tiff yelled, with a smug look on her face. "You guys can't do anything to me." She started to scream, and the SWAT guy grabbed her by the arm and hauled her to the garage dancing on one foot as he propelled her along to sit with her friends and wait.

I put a leash on Chance and asked one of the SWAT team guys to take her over to the command post and deposit her with McClung. A stretcher came and they hauled me past a still kicking-at-nothing Tiff. Poor girl she didn't have a clue.

—

"Well Rider," the attending surgeon said, "I see you've been getting into trouble again. Let's take a look. Oh! That's nasty! Did I hear that you were struck down by a petite slip of a woman? Amazing the damage, they can inflict, isn't it?"

249

"Those dang SWAT guys," I said. "They just can't keep their mouths shut."

"You need blood, my man, then intravenous, then up to the operating room. We need to put you out this time to clean your arm up good. Any questions?"

"No questions. I'm so tired that the anesthetic will do me good."

I woke up two hours later but didn't remember anything. Then I fell asleep for another four hours. After that I sat up, kicked my legs over the edges of the bed—then quickly put them back in a horizontal plane as severe pain and nausea set in. I was in the hospital for two days and had no idea how the raid had gone. The nurses said two men came to see me, but she wouldn't wake me.

CHAPTER

It was two AM and my second night in the hospital. I was lying awake, facing the door, waiting for the nurse to come in with my painkillers. The door opened a crack, spilling light over my one closed eye. The lower eye was partially opened, allowing me to watch the door. The door slowly opened a little further, and I could see what looked like a nurse wearing a mask and cap silently slipping through the opening. My nurses didn't wear a mask and cap. I was lying on my good arm, which was holding one of my knives. It was useless unless the intruder came within a foot of me. The door quietly shut, and in the glow of the green lights shining off my monitors, I could see the intruder hesitantly approaching my bed slowly and focused. Through the folds of the sheets I was straining to see if she was holding a weapon. As she drew nearer it appeared both hands were empty.

"Rider," she whispered, "can you hear me? I'm not here to hurt you, but to warn you. Listen closely and keep quiet. I can't tell you my name, and you will never see my face, I want to tell you there are two gang members that you don't know about, and they were not found in the raid. If you will do me a favor, I will give you the info you require about one of these guys. The other, whose name is Gus, will show himself in an unfavorable way to you and you can deal with him then."

"What's the favor?" I croaked, still clutching my knife.

"This man needs to be, shall we say, silenced. Do we have a deal?"

"No, we don't. I don't go around doing people favors like that."

"Okay. I see that I have started off on the wrong foot here. There is another gang member who you have never seen and who you will never hear about. This fellow is Frank's boss. He is taking matters into his own hands. In two hours, he will be coming through that door to kill you, be prepared. It's you or him." She made an abrupt turn and was out the door in a flash.

I grabbed my phone from beside the bed and quickly made a call. It was picked up right away.

"Police department."

"Who's the sergeant on duty at the moment?" I asked

"It's Sergeant Smith." "Put him on please." The police and I were in position across the hall at three AM; It was Sergeant Smith, and I and one of his trusted members.

Four AM was my medication time, and through the small glass window, we could see the doctor on duty slowly working his way down the hall going from room to room.

"Here comes your medication, Rider," Sergeant Smith said. "Do you want me to call the doctor in here?"

"No, I think it's better if I deal with this pain. Let's see what his reaction is when he sees the mannequin we placed in my bed."

We all crowded around the small window like a bunch of school kids, waiting to see what the doctor's reaction would be.

The doctor pushed my door open, and without entering, he fired two shots into my bed. Sergeant Smith flung our door open whacking me in the head. Spiraling backwards, I landed on my good arm amongst a host of hospital bedpans which scattered across the floor making one hell of a racket.

From my prone position on the floor, I heard two more shots fired and, looking up, saw Sergeant Smith and his trooper running from our room. I struggled to get up, making a terrible racket, pushing the metal bedpans out of the way.

Blood was flowing freely down my face from the gash the door had inflicted on my head. I found an extra gown and pushed it against my forehead somewhat stemming the flow of blood.

In the hall Sergeant Smith was standing over the dead body of the slain assailant, trying to figure out who he was.

"What happened to you, Rider?" Smith asked, looking at my head.

"Just another war wound. Nothing they can't patch up here," I said, still clutching the gown to my face.

The corridor was sealed off, and all those who were able to get out of bed to see what the commotion was were sent back to bed.

"Did you recognize him?" I asked, staggering back to my bed, waiting for someone to come and stitch me up.

"Yeah, he was one of our more prominent figures in town. We'll have to try to figure this one out. Something's not right here. His involvement is something no one knows about. He always seemed so clean and straight. A real pillar of the town."

CHAPTER

On my second day after entering the hospital, which was McClung's day off, he and Chance came to pick me up. Chance was beside herself. I've never seen her so excited.

"Did you forget to feed her, McClung?" I asked.

"Are you kidding, she ate us out of house and home. I kept telling my wife Ann not to feed her so much, but she did, so I had to work overtime just to pay for the extra food bill. Tomorrow, if you're feeling up to it, Tony wants to meet us at ten AM for a debriefing and to fill you in."

"Sounds good, I won't bother asking you any questions now. Just getting home to a quiet place will be nice."

—

My house had been cleaned from top to bottom, the bikes been taken to a shop, and all appraised for damage. It was the baby blue one I was worried about. I listened to my messages, which only included three important ones. The blue bike was a write-off, but the appraiser contacted the builder, and for $65,000 he would build me a new one.

Julie called, and said through tears—although I could not see them—that she had a court date and wanted me to attend with her. Just so happens that's the day I would be conveniently out of town. Dang, I was so looking forward to helping her through all her misery especially that which she caused me, and the last call was disturbing.

> *"You may have thought that you got us all, Rider. But there is one remaining and I'm going to get you."*

I checked all my monitors and alarms then lay down for a much-needed sleep.

I awoke to hear something ringing. Stumbling half-daze, I managed to get to the door, where Chance was waiting. It was Julie.

"Aren't you going to invite me in?" she asked, showing me that big beautiful smile.

"Ah, yeah, come in. I was sleeping. Want some coffee?"

"No," she said, letting out a big sigh.

"What's up?"

"What do you mean 'what's up'?" she said. "Aren't you glad to see me?"

"After the other day, no, not really, Julie."

"Well, you're going to be when I tell you what I've done."

"Why would what you've done interest me?" I said, wishing she wasn't here.

Julie looked at me with a look of genuine shock on her face.

"What do you mean?"

"Julie, in case you don't remember, three nights ago, standing right *over there*," I said, pointing to the bathroom door, "you screamed at me that I was just a pawn and said

255

that you and Frank were going to run off together, and live happily ever after. That was, of course, until you realized that Frank was setting you up to get rid of me. Now that you've lost him, you're coming after me. It's not going to work."

Julie stood up, hands on her hips, looking down at me with fire in her eyes. I didn't dare stand, in case she hit me.

"I'm not the least bit interested in you, Rider," she said, storming out of the room and slamming the door behind her.

I had to admit she was beautiful coming or going, mad or sweet, she looked darn good. I looked at Chance. She looked at me. I shrugged. Chance licked her lips.

"Well girl," I said, patting her head, "it's just you and me now. Think you can live without playing with the little kids?"

I locked the door, took a painkiller and went back to bed. I don't know how long I slept but not very long before the doorbell awakened me again.

"C'mon Chance, this time she's not coming in." I opened the door, and there stood Tiffany.

"And what can I do for *you*?" I asked, keeping my bad arm behind the door, and out of her striking distance. Tiff was a very nice-looking lady; it's just that I was pretty sure drugs had altered her mind. She was standing there looking down at the little pink flip flops on her feet not knowing— or unable to remember—what to say. Her hair was done to a T, her makeup, although minimal, looked like it had been professionally applied. She was wearing a short skirt that hid very little, maybe she only had a little to hide, and a halter-top that showed quite a bit of cleavage with still lots hiding.

I stood there looking down at her cleavage (Tiff was very short).

She slowly brought her eyes up to mine.

"You think I'm dumb like most of the other girls, don't you, Rider? You think I go with a guy just because I want excitement, don't you? And you think that all the guys in the club have had me, don't you? You don't know," she said, as tears started to flow down her face. "Well, you're wrong. I'm not that kind of a girl!"

Great, I thought. *I just get rid of one and another appears.*

"Why don't you come in and tell me why you're here," I said, keeping my arm as far from her as possibly, possible. I was nervous about this lady. She could do serious damage.

"Sit on that chair," I said, taking the couch opposite her. "And as long as you don't move, Chance won't bite you."

She crept over to the chair with a watchful eye on Chance.

"Would you like a coffee?" I asked. *Dang, I didn't mean to say that.*

"Yes please," she answered.

"Well, you'll have to make it then, I'm not feeling that good."

Returning with coffee, I kept my good arm between us. Sitting across from her, she was a very pretty looking lady. Knees on the chair to keep her legs away from Chance, she smiled at me.

"Why did you come here, Tiff?"

"I wanted to tell you about myself, and give you some info," she said, fidgeting with her dress or what little there was of it.

I was enjoying the coffee, and every time I looked at Tiff, I forgot about my arm. She was a beautiful specimen.

"I have never been in jail before, but I heard things that night."

I sat up and started paying attention to her.

257

"First about me," she said. "I'm single, twenty-six, never been married, have gone to college, have a degree in fashion design and that was my first time at the club. I met Kool in the emergency waiting room, at the hospital. I think he had a broken nose or something, or maybe no nose at all. I was there because I had put a sewing needle into my finger and needed a tetanus shot. We started talking, and Kool told me that, if I wanted to meet some nice people, who could supply me with drugs, he could do it."

"I told him I wasn't interested in buying drugs, free drugs, selling drugs, delivering drugs, doing drugs or anything to do with drugs, so he could stop, and not talk to me about drugs again. He looked down at me then and tried to smile. I could tell it hurt because he couldn't smile.

"Then he says, 'That was a test because I won't have anything to do with people who do drugs either.' And after he said that, I thought he was okay."

"When I found you the other night, Tiff, you said that was your first time at the club, is that right?"

"Yes, the first time, I'd been there about an hour."

"Why did you not have any clothes on?"

"Oh that," she said, putting her head down and blushing.

"Kool told me to bring jeans and a warm top. I was in the adjoining washroom changing when I heard all the ruckus. I grabbed a sheet and ran to the other room. I didn't want to have anything to do with him. I don't think he's as nice as he puts out to be."

"Yeah, but if I remember correctly—and I have a very good memory for things like this—you were not even wearing that 'thing' such as it was."

"I had a warmer *thing*, as you call it, to put on."

"A warmer thing," I said. "That wouldn't be hard—there was a lot you could add to that 'thing' to make you warmer."

Tiff looked down at the hem of her skirt and started fidgeting with it.

"Have you seen or heard from Kool since that night?" I asked.

"No, not a word, and I hope not to."

"Okay, what about that night? What did you hear?"

"Okay, I'll tell you, but you need to promise me—I think I can trust you—that you will not divulge where you got this information from."

"Yes, I can do that for you, but first I need to eat. I'm feeling weak from lack of food. Let's cook dinner then we can talk while eating."

"That sounds really good," Tiff said. "I haven't eaten all day, thinking about coming to see you."

"Can you cook?"

"Can I cook? Probably better than anyone else has ever cooked for you. I've taken so many cooking classes I feel like I should be the instructor sometimes, and other times I *know* I should be."

"Well, look in the fridge. There are a lot of goodies in there. Make something up, and I'll cook the steaks if I feel up to it. But first you have to promise *me* something."

"I can do that, what is it?" she said, with concern on her face.

"Promise me you won't touch my arm, or even breathe on it, ever again."

"Oh, I'm really sorry about that, and I promise it won't happen again. I felt slighted by you, and all the others, so I struck out."

"You certainly did, Tiff."

I was looking forward to Tiff's cooking. So many friends over the years have told me what good cooks they were, and they didn't even know how to beat an egg let alone turn on the stove or know what a spatula is.

"Would you like a beer or something?" I called from the couch.

"No thanks, I drink very little, but you go ahead, I don't mind."

"I'll get a beer," I said. "Call me when you want the steaks put on."

"I'll get the beer for you, and I've lit the BBQ to warm up for you."

There was a lot of idle chatter, and chopping going on in the kitchen.

"Thanks," I said, now starting to feel badly about all the things I had thought about her. A very pretty lady in a short, short skirt, delivered my beer in a very tall glass with very little head on it.

"Okay, let's eat!" she said, heading back to the kitchen.

I struggled up, tired, my arm starting to throb again, and went into the kitchen. There was a tossed salad with pieces of mandarin oranges, strawberries, and slivers of almonds sprinkled on top, with a homemade dressing on the side. The steak was sizzling and cut into small pieces. An opened baked potato on the plate, with a slab of melting butter, covered with sour cream, cheese, bacon bits, and chives sprinkled on the top. Salt and pepper were present. Water was on the table, and from the stove, she brought asparagus tips, diced carrots, and cream corn. All my favorites.

What happened? I thought.

"When did you first learn to cook?" I asked, tasting everything with sheer delight.

"In high school, I wanted to be a chef, so started taking courses, but come graduation I wanted to be a clothes designer, thus college."

"Did you put your designing to work?"

"Oh yes, I started designing clothes, then started making them. Now I have a small business."

"Still going?"

"Still going; it supports me."

"Was that tiny *thing* you picked up the other night and put on, one of your designs? It was so small I was wondering what you were going to do with it."

She looked down in apparent embarrassment. "That's one of my bestsellers."

"Really, and what does it sell for?"

"Money," she said smiling.

She also had a sense of humor.

"Around twenty-five dollars," she said. "This skirt and top are also mine."

"And how do you sell them?"

"Oh, well, I model them for good looking guys like you," she said, blushing again, "or I go to trucker's trade shows, and strut around. They hoot and holler, it's really great, even gives me a little exposure, so to speak."

"Quite some exposure," I said. "You're kidding me, aren't you, Tiff?"

"Nope, the truckers love to see me modeling that thing. Sometimes I can't keep up with the orders. Other times I go to nightclubs that hold what they call, model night. I walk across the stage, and the orders pour in. It can be a little embarrassing at times, but money is money and other times I do personal modeling. This can get a little dicey, so I have to watch myself."

"Get real!"

"Yeah, I'm joking on both counts. I can't believe I just said that. You're bringing out the worst in me. Well," she said, with a smile, "three months ago I signed a contract with a well-known chain, and things are moving very well. I have a house not far from here with six staff in my basement—I've turned into a nice little factory. Very quiet, unobtrusive, with one delivery a day." She smiled. "I don't want to upset the neighbors you know."

"Let's talk about what you heard in jail the other night."

"Well, we girls were put in one of the temporary holding cells, with some guys in the cell next to us."

"The girls really didn't say too much, and I wouldn't have known what to ask them, but they were talking about prostitution and nightclubs. I was glad to get away from them." She turned and met my gaze then. "But the guys were talking about a guy named Gus—he was out of town that night, and they kept saying Gus would get him. He is the only one out, and he will get him, he owes us." She shivered looking down, then looking across the table into my eyes again. "Kool was in that cell, and he said Gus would put an end to that double-crossing Rider. That's when I knew you were good and that I could trust you. Are you in any danger, Rider?"

I chewed on a perfectly cooked piece of steak—not that it needed much chewing—and thought about what I could tell her, then started at the beginning with the broken noses, the knife fight, and how Chance has saved my life many times.

"You're an undercover policeman?"

Oh, what thoughts ran through my mind, when she said that!

"No, not really but I can't discuss that right now. This supper is absolutely awesome," I said, picking up a piece of asparagus she had cut up for me, and putting it in my mouth.

"What puzzles me, Tiff, is how all these groceries got into my house?"

"Well," she said, with a gleam in her eye. "When Tony was interrogating me, he figured I was not associated with the motorcycle gang, so I asked about you. I told him I owed you and would like to cook you a nice dinner. I went shopping, he met me here, and I put everything in the fridge. I bought enough for three meals."

"That was really nice of you, Tiff. Now I want you to listen closely to what I have to say, but first I would like to introduce you to Chance."

"No," she said with fear in her voice, "he bit me once and he will do it again."

"It's okay," I said, getting up and walking over to her and putting my good hand on her shoulder. "She won't bite you again."

She stood up, and in a weak voice asked me to hold her hand.

I called Chance from where she was standing in the living room.

"Tiffany, Chance is a girl not a boy."

A small flicker of a smile crossed her face.

As Chance entered the room, Tiff swung around and hugged me. Being careful of my arm she put her head on my chest. "I can't look. I'm terrified of dogs."

Chance looked at me then got up and sat behind Tiff, waiting for a pat.

"She is behind you, Tiff, waiting for a pat."

"I can't," she struggled to say. "I just can't. I'm too scared."

"Give me your hand."

"No, I can't."

"Chance, go lie down, girl."

"Okay Tiff, Chance has left. Let's go sit on the couch."

I took her trembling hand and led her to the couch. She sat next to me, flipping her feet up so they were off the floor.

"Chance, come here girl." Chance walked over again, and sat by Tiff, putting her head on her lap, waiting for a pat. Tiff arched her back trying to get as far away from Chance as possible. I reached over and ruffled her ears, Chances ears that is, then took Tiff's hand and did the same.

"She's good, Tiff. She likes you, and now that your friends, she'll protect you."

"I'm still scared, but she does seem to have a nice side."

Chance jumped up, startling Tiff, and ran to the door.

"Tiff, go down the hall and sit in my office, do not come out or make a sound." She didn't move right away. "Tiff, when I ask you to do something like that, I need you to do it before the words are out of my mouth, now go." Tiff got up, picked up her pink flipflops, and watching Chance, she ran down the hall to one of the bedrooms. I kept Chance out of sight and opened the door while keeping my damaged arm hidden, behind the door frame.

Kool and two of his buddies I had not seen before stood in a semicircle at the door. His buddies looked like they could take care of themselves.

"What's up, Drool, thought you were in jail?"

"It's Kool, asshole."

"Okay Kool. Want to introduce me to your buddies?"

"You're never going to hear their names, asshole. I want Tiffany," he said, drooling as usual, but not spitting yet.

"I'll be right back." I hurried to the kitchen returning with a paper towel in my hand. "Here Kool, you need this."

He swung out with a barroom punch narrowly missing my chin, which made him even madder. His two buddies moved closer; fists clenched. "Don't lose your cool, man. Tell me what you want?"

"I want that little thing, Tiffany," he stuttered.

"Yes Kool, but does Tiffany want you? That's the question."

"Damn rights she does, and you have her."

"What do you mean, I *have* her?"

"She is here, and she shouldn't be. She should be with me."

"I don't think she even wants to be seen with you, Kool. You look like you just emerged from a pile of discarded clothes left on the floor. Look at you, man, you're a disgrace! Well, I guess she figured you were in jail and wouldn't be getting out. Not every girl wants to hang around with a thug."

"I'm out on bail, and I want her."

"Well Kool, neither you nor your henchmen are going to get her, so turn around and leave."

The three of them tried to get to me all at the same time, but the door would only allow one through at a time. They were pushing each other with no great advancement. I turned around and there stood Tiff and Chance. Tiff stepped in front of me.

"Kool, what are you doing here? I've been listening to your conversation, and not only do I find your language absolutely repulsive, but your attitude toward me is disrespectful."

"I want you, Tiff."

I didn't see it coming—nor did Kool—but I heard it hit. It was a slap starting from the hip coming up with all the force that little lady could muster.

Kool stepped back from the slap, his newly patched face reddening, and his ego shattered, in front of his buddies.

"You little, bitch," he yelled, his hand at his cheek. "I'm going to get you for that."

"Look at me, Kool," Tiff said, "I weigh a hundred and ten pounds soaking wet. You and your buddies with all your fat must weigh well over seven hundred pounds. All three of you are standing there looking like a bunch of idiots, which you are. Now get off this property before I kick you off."

"Not going anywhere without you, little lady, not without you."

"Whack," the second blow was harder than the first, knocking him back again. Now he was spitting mad and insulted, and started spitting when he talked.

"You little, bitch, when we get through with you, you will never be the same again."

His buddies were not in the habit of watching a domestic fight, where one of their buddies was losing. They both stepped forward to help Kool when Chance, snapping and snarling, attacked the first muscle-ridden guy.

My good neighbor must have heard the commotion, as I heard sirens nearing. Dave, McClung's number one man, was first on the scene. Running up with his gun drawn to the tangled mess lying on the ground, he took complete control. Chance had been called off, and none too soon.

The paramedics soon arrived, and they temporarily stopped the flow of blood that was staining my sidewalk. Both boys looked in bad shape, and Kool was holding his face cursing and spitting, while trying to explain in a foreign language, what was going to happen to us.

"Kool," Dave said, "you're in breach of your parole restrictions, and so are your buddies. It's to the hospital for all of you, under tight guard, then to jail, awaiting your hearing."

The rest of the evening, Tiff sat on the couch, talking and scratching Chance's ear.

"I can see how protective she is of you. You didn't say anything, and she knew what to do. I think I should come back tomorrow night and cook your supper again. I can see how painful your arm is," she said, still twiddling Chances ear.

"Well, tonight's supper was awesome and only if you insist. I don't want to put you under any pressure now."

I thanked her again at the door and said that I would be looking forward to seeing her tomorrow night. I needed rest and headed for bed. Tomorrow's debriefing could be very tiring for me.

Up early the next morning, I showered with a plastic bag around my arm, then shaved, then I decided to take my arm out of its sling. Ten minutes later it was obvious I had made a big mistake. It felt like Tiff had hit me again.

At ten, McClung, in his police cruiser pulled into my driveway. Smartly dressed, with his gun slung on his hip, he knocked on my door. Chance was trying to wag her tail both ways at the same time.

"Morning, McClung," I said, as Chance nudged me out of the way.

"Morning, I hope you've been taking good care of my dog."

"Sure have, gave her a little exercise last night; gnawing, you know!"

"So, I read, those guys will never learn. They have all been transferred to state holding cells until their arraignment. Man, was Kool mad!"

"Are his two buddies' members of the same gang?"

"Affiliates, we raided their homes last night and found more drugs and weapons," McClung said, with a look of concern on his face.

I shut and locked the door leaving Chance behind to guard the house.

As I entered the restaurant, I noticed an upper balcony with one-way glass. We were ushered through the kitchen then up a curving bank of stairs where we entered one of the rooms by a back door.

"Morning, Rider, McClung." Tony said, "Glad to see you made it, Rider. Arm still sore?"

"Very painful," I said, looking around the room.

"Anyone follow us?" McClung asked.

"Just this fellow walking in now, he is definitely looking for someone."

He was large, larger than me, looked extremely fit, arms like hams with a pound of ink splashed over his body. He had a bald head, short trimmed beard and wearing reflective glasses, even though it was reasonably dark in the restaurant. His jeans were being held up by a massive belt and fancy buckle, leather boots and a head that was too small for his body. There was a chain hanging from his belt to his pocket, and at the end of the chain neither watch nor whistle were attached. I studied him for a minute taking in all his moves and trying to form a picture of his weaknesses, of which I could find none.

"Who is he, Tony?"

"Gus. That's Gus," Tony said. "The member we missed the other night. He was conveniently out of town. He's the one that's after you."

"Well guys, let's make this meeting twofold," I said. "I'm going down to meet this Gus fellow."

"Not advisable," McClung said. "When a favor is owed, it can be delivered anywhere. He knows that he will go to jail for what he does to you, and that's acceptable to him. If he falters, he will never see the inside of a jail or anywhere else, so you have to be very, very careful."

"Here's what I want you two to do," I said, and told Tony and McClung the plan. When I was done, I said, "I'm going down." Tony went in first, then five minutes later, I walked in as if looking for someone. Out of the corner of my eye I detected a sudden but slight movement by Gus. I headed over his way not making any show of recognition, and as I walked by Gus's seat, I made a sudden move that had me seated across from Gus, before he knew it.

"Keep your hands on the table or something nasty may happen," I said.

"Get out of here, dickhead" Gus said, moving his hands to the edge of the table where either a knife or gun were hidden.

"Not advisable," I said, brandishing a mean slim line knife that I pulled out of my sling.

"What the friggin' hell do you want, armpit? I don't even know you," Gus spat out.

"Just so you are aware," I said, smiling at him, "the gentleman sitting behind you has his Glock trained on you, and he tends to be a little trigger happy, and I'm not in his line of fire."

Not knowing what was happening or who I was, he was totally confused.

"I'm told that you were conveniently out of town for the raid on the clubhouse the other night. Got a little tip off, did you, Gus?" I said, watching his hands.

"So, what's it to you?"

"Well, all your buddies locked away for a long time, or soon will be, and we're just wondering what your plans are for the future?"

He just sat there looking at me, wondering where this was going.

"Well, let me tell you this, Gus. Just so you know who you're looking for, my name's Rider, and I hear you are looking for me."

Gus's hands shot off the table faster than I thought possible but stopped short when he heard the Glock behind him click. He returned his hands very slowly to the table. "You're dead meat, man!"

"And why would you say that?" I asked. "I found you— you didn't find me."

He just sat there studying me wondering how all this came about.

"If you injure me you know that you will go to jail for a long, long time. The police are watching you, and I'm watching you, so don't make any stupid moves, at least that we can see."

My knife was in plain view as a waitress warily approached our table and asked if we would like to order. "Yes, one coffee and make it strong. My friend here needs it." I smiled at Gus as I left through the front door, and returned back upstairs, through an outside back entrance. We watched Gus for some time, as he played with his coffee cup not drinking any. Looking constantly between his watch and the door, Gus made up his mind that whoever he was supposed to be meeting was not going to show up. Just as he got up to leave, in walked someone he knew. Gus returned to his seat, and as the person walked by, he slid a piece of paper across the table, in front of Gus.

I was out the door in a flash and so was McClung. We both ran through the front door and up to Gus's table, as McClung drew his revolver.

"Hands in the air," McClung yelled. "You're under arrest for bribing a police officer. Let's see the note."

As Gus's hand came up to try to swallow the note, the blow to his nose did enough damage to discourage any further movement. The note fell to the table and as I reached for it, I accidentally spilled Gus's coffee on his lap.

"Sorry, Gus, I didn't mean to make it look that bad," I said, with a smile on my face. Gus was beside himself, now he had wet pants or at least that's how it looked. McClung had called for backup, the patrons were temporarily evacuated, Gus was handcuffed, and I began reading the note.

Kill the girl, then Rider.

It will make it easier.

I felt sick.

As Gus was led to a waiting police car with his hands behind his back, I was able to distract the cop long enough to plant a blow on Gus's chin, breaking his jaw. Gus went down like a sack of potatoes, while I casually looked the other way. McClung materialized with Gus's contact—the one who had dropped the note on the table—also cuffed. They were put in separate vehicles.

"Rider," McClung said. "For obvious reasons I can't stay, but when you're ready to go home, call and I'll have someone pick you up."

"Thanks, McClung."

I returned back upstairs to find Tony with a smug look on his face.

"Did him a right-one didn't you?" Tony said.

"You didn't read the note."

"No. What did it say?"

"Kill the girl, and then kill Rider, it will make things easier."

Tony brought me up to date on the bust—drug busts that is—and sealed their findings. The FBI was still interrogating the gang members. The temporary cells had been emptied as most members had been shipped out of town. The holding cells they had been in were now full of the drugs and firearms, found on the different premises. The clubhouse had been searched, and the stick I had found on the couch was holding all Tiff's business transactions. Over forty houses were searched, finding drugs, firearms, and even some illegal immigrants in one house.

I caught a cab and returned home only to find my front door unlocked and Chance gone. I still couldn't even think of riding, so I locked up and walked the three blocks to Julie's house. At first there was no answer, then the door slowly opened, and I whistled for Chance. She came running.

"Good girl," I said, patting her. "Guard," I said, pointing at Julie.

Chance looked at me with a sideways glance than started growling at Julie.

"What are you doing, Rider?" Julie asked, a worried look on her face. "I didn't do anything except take Chance and she came willingly."

"She won't come again," I said, as I walked away down her sidewalk. With Chance beside me, I turned around. "And I'm changing my locks."

I returned home. I was tired and sore and needed rest. I fed Chance, locked the doors, and headed for the couch. Not long after a ringing woke me up.

"Hi Rider, it's Tiff. Okay to come over and cook supper?"

"By all means, Tiff. Give a knock first"

"Be there in ten minutes."

A different day, a different hairdo, a different outfit, but the same immaculate make-up, same swing to her hips, same smile, and—I hoped—the same cooking.

"Hi Tiff," I said, with a slight shortness of breath. Chance was trying to get through the door and, at the same time, was forcing Tiff against me.

"Oh sorry," she said, gaining her composure and stepping back allowing air to circulate between us.

"Not a problem," I said.

"Just never know when you're going to be forced against a guy," she said, grinning.

"Gus and two of his friends were at my place today," she said, shaking a little. "They just burst in yelling where is Tiffany, where is she! My workers were petrified till they left, and then they phoned the police."

"Well, when the police catch up with them, they're going to be put away for a long time."

I left Tiff to cook supper alone in the kitchen as I knew I'd only get in her way. We ate supper on the back porch with Tiff asking questions about my day. It was another splendid meal and pleasant time together. After cleaning up, Tiff announced that she had to leave but would return at the same time tomorrow. I wasn't looking forward to her leaving so suddenly but escorted her to the door and bid her goodnight.

The next morning, I caught a cab to get some groceries, and had the cab drive past Tiff's house on the way back. Parked in her driveway—although pretty much hidden—I saw a bike that I recognized.

—

"Okay Tiff," Parker said. "Tonight, is your last chance, can you do it, or do I tell Kool you failed?"

"No, no," she said, looking down. "I can do it, Parker."

"That's good because this is it. If you don't do it tonight, the boys will come after me, and if that happens, I will come after you."

"It'll be done. Now get out of my home, and out of my sight. And don't be so stupid as to bring your bike around here again. In fact, just keep the heck away from me altogether."

He grabbed her by the arm and swung her back. "I might just take you into the back room right now, you stupid little bitch."

Tiff brought her hand up to slap him a good one, but he was fast and grabbed her hand.

"Easy there little one. You don't want to make me mad now, do you?"

Pulling her head back and putting his hand on her throat, Tiff started gagging for air.

"You're hurting me," she squealed, through clenched teeth.

—

As I was walking up Tiff's sidewalk, I sensed something was wrong. I stopped short and listened. Looking at Chance whose head was turned sideways, I definitely knew something was wrong. "Let's go girl."

We ran up the stairs and heard Tiff first moaning, then yelling, as she struggled to survive.

"Go, Chance!"

Chance got the guy, and I got the girl. Chance had Parker pinned on the floor, Parker was fighting for his life, as Chance made sure he'd remember this memorable meeting.

I left Chance at the attack and pulled Tiff up. She clung to me like super glue. Shaking and sobbing, she kept saying she was sorry.

"I'm so sorry, Rider. I'm so sorry. I was going to tell you tonight, I really was," she kept saying.

I looked down at this 110-pound beauty and couldn't figure out what she was talking about, then a thought flashed in my mind.

"Tiff, I'm going to let you go for a moment. I want you to go dial 911 and then come right back." Tiff kept clinging to me and wouldn't let go. I tried to push her away. "Let go, Tiff, and go dial 911." She ran away and I called, Chance off.

Parker was a mess, the carpet was a mess, Tiff's clothes were a mess. And Tiff was a mess.

Running back into the room, she yelled in an agitated voice. "They're coming, and when I mentioned rape, the operator said they'd be here really soon. Oh gosh, Rider, I'm so scared of him."

Three police cruisers arrived at the same time and four officers approached the house, with their guns drawn.

Chance was still snapping and snarling at the guy on the floor, as he wriggled in pain, swimming in his own blood.

"I'm coming out, with my hands up," I yelled, exiting the front door very carefully with four guns trained on me. Not wanting to make any sudden moves which could trigger their reactions I moved very slowly.

"Rider," constable Dave called, "we were told it was a rape call."

"It is," I said, "he is inside with Chance guarding. He was strangling Tiff when I walked in. His name is Parker, and that's all I can tell you; the rest will have to come from Tiff."

Dave turned to the other officers. "He's clean, guys. Perp's inside. Wait till Rider has called the dog off, before approaching."

With their guns drawn again, all four entered the house behind me to find Tiff kicking the be jeepers out of Parker—who was moving less and less with each kick.

"Stop it, Tiff." I took her arm and pulled her away.

"Chance, come here, girl," I said, looking at the pitiful mess left squirming on the floor.

The paramedics arrived just in time as Parker had almost expired with the damage Chance had delivered—and to a lesser extent, the beating from Tiff. The paramedics were working feverishly to stabilize Parker so they could get him to the hospital.

"Wow, Rider, I thought the last one you dealt with was bad. You're sure keeping the plastic surgeons busy?" Dave said, as they wheeled Parker out the door, to the waiting ambulance.

"We've got everything we need," Dave said, "but Tiff will need to come down first thing tomorrow morning and talk to us. I can guarantee you that this one will not be getting out on bail."

Tiff returned in one of her custom-made outfits, and she looked great. Short pale pink skirt, cream colored blouse with light green flipflops, big smile, styled hair and makeup to a T.

"Sit down, Tiff," I said, looking like the world had just landed on my shoulders.

"I figured why that biker was here, but I want to hear your side of the story."

"I don't know where to start," she said.

"At the beginning," I said, rather sarcastically.

"Okay, I needed money to expand my business, and I ran into Kool as you know. He gave me a very low interest rate, loan with low payments. I agreed, and I was over at the club to sign the contract, the night you showed up."

"How much money, Tiff?" I asked.

"One hundred and fifty thousand for new machinery, larger staff, larger inventory, and a small addition to my house. Just before you walked in, he offered all this to me free, no strings attached, if I would give someone a pill. It was just a pill and he didn't say who, why, when or how. All he said was that after I had done it, he would rip up my contract."

"Did you really think he would rip up your contract?" I said, with a smirk on my face. "He may have ripped up the contract, but you would have been his, and others, for a long, long time."

"Well I had never thought of that," she said, starting to shake.

"Parker was here to make sure I gave you the pill tonight. He threatened me. I see what you mean, Rider."

"On the way to the hospital," I said, "I think you had better think about what you were going to do to me tonight. Would it have been murder, Tiff? I'm sorry, I really liked you, but I'm going to leave here, and I don't want to see you again."

As I got up, Tiff came running toward me, sobbing.

"I wasn't going to do it Rider. I was going to ask for your help."

"Why didn't you then? Why didn't you on the first night you came to my house and cooked dinner?"

"I… I… well, I was thinking how I was going to tell you."

"Sorry, Tiff," I said. "This friendship is over!"

I left with the same sadness I had felt when Angela had died in the jungle.

Chance and I walked home together. We both needed the fresh air.

CHAPTER

This is the way it worked. Into town. Do a job, then move on.

After my wife died, I left my SEAL team to work solo for the government. I didn't feel that I could protect my SEAL buddies as well as I would like, so chose to go undercover.

I sat down with a cold beer, Chance at my feet, no girlfriend, arm still aching, hungry, tired, and thoroughly pissed off. I thought all the times people had come knocking at my door, some good, some bad. How in the jungle, I had defied death many times, sometimes by luck, and other times by my training, and the only person who knew where I was and was looking out for me was Tony. I jumped up, found my phone, sent a message, made a phone call, called a cab, and with Chance, headed for the restaurant that would give me exposure inside and concealment outside.

I arrived an hour early and put Chance a few doors down from the restaurant—on the same side of the street, with a red ribbon tied around her neck. The ribbon made her stand out so I could see her at a glance. I then went across the street and planted myself on the sidewalk. With a can containing a few coins in front of me, with my injured arm hidden in the large coat I was wearing, I sat and waited.

Shades on, head down, eyes up fully alert, I was watching and waiting. It didn't take long before my suspicions were confirmed. Two agents—or outside workers—came strolling down the street. One large and very agile the other shorter and slimmer, with eyes darting and taking in everything he saw. At first, they noticed Chance but paid her no attention, thinking the owner was inside shopping. Then they glanced my way but were not interested in a colored doped-up beggar sleeping with a can in front of him.

They both walked into the restaurant and reappeared a few minutes later. The rush hour hadn't started, so very few people were in the restaurant, and I wasn't one of them. I kept my head down and eyes up as they had a chat, discussing where to position themselves. The slim guy was on the phone, and soon another guy appeared. While gesturing and pointing, they determined that I hadn't arrived yet, and had better get themselves positioned.

The smaller guy crossed the street, dodging the traffic while horns honked, and fingers were raised. When he reached the sidewalk, he headed toward me at a fast pace. With my head down and my eyes up, I watched as he closed, looking for the ideal place to position himself—somewhere he could see the restaurant but not be observed. Apparently, I had that spot.

"Move along, mister. This spot is spoken for."

He was towering over me with his shoe threatening to kick me, so I slowly started the process of getting up looking like a tired and stiff person, who really didn't want to move. I couldn't see the others across the street because of the sudden influx of traffic, so I decided this was my chance.

As I slowly stood facing my opponent, I swung my leg right up between his then with a chop to the neck he was rendered useless for quite some time. He lay at my feet in a heap.

The location I had chosen was outside a closed down candy shop, with a large indented entrance. Kicking the door open, I dragged him in with one hand. Then I searched him and cuffed him hand and foot to the nearest post. Then I exited and took my original position outside just as the traffic cleared.

I couldn't see the other two, but it wasn't long before they gave up their hiding spots, no doubt wondering what had happened to their leader. Looking up and down the street, then at me, with no clues, they were at a loss. Finally, the last guy to appear pointed at me and decided that maybe I had seen their leader.

He was more cautious crossing the street but still nearly got clipped by a bus, which was changing lanes to let passengers off. As he approached, a throng of people got off the bus that had stopped fifty feet past where I was sitting. As the passengers dispersed, a line of traffic built up behind the still stationary bus, giving me another few moments of cover.

This guy wasn't too sure about the bum sleeping on the street and didn't want to get close in case bugs jumped off me onto him. He waited till all the passengers had passed.

"Did you see a slim looking guy walk past here?"

I kept my head down but my eyes up.

"I'm talking to you, mister. Did you see a slim guy walk past here a few minutes ago?"

"Yeah, yeah," I mumbled. "one just got off the bus."

"Before that," he said, taking a step closer, but not close enough.

"What you say, man?"

"Before the bus came, did you see a slim guy, in jeans and a blue jacket walk by?"

"How much?" I said, head down eyes up.

"What?"

"How much," I pointed to my tin.

"I'm not giving you sweet dick," he said, walking into the danger zone.

The traffic had just started moving and was following the bus at a slow pace. I missed with the chop to the neck but the blow below the belt put him out. Having planted him next to his friend, and done a quick search, I cuffed him to a post.

I returned outside, stooping low to conceal my height and turned around as if doing up my fly after just relieving myself. I returned to my original position, head down eyes up.

The third guy across the street was eyeing me up, wondering if I had anything to do with the disappearance of his friends, but decided to wait a few moments before coming over to ask after them. With no phone calls being answered, he was absolutely at a loss as to where they were. His only option was to come over and ask, as I was the only living thing he could see on my side of the street. The traffic had stopped giving him an opportunity to cross, but he just kept looking.

I whistled for Chance who was beside me in a flash. I took the red ribbon off Chance's neck and put it in my pocket. The goon looked back at me, then back where Chance had been sitting, and then back at me, no red ribbon, same dog.

Now he was confused, but not confused enough to not cross the street without his hand in his pocket, holding his gun. As he neared, he withdrew his gun and pointed it at my head.

"See two guys walking around here?" he said.

I didn't answer because I was sleeping.

"I'm talking to you, mister."

I still gave no answer.

The kick never materialized. Chance was on him like a flash.

"Chance," I called.

Chance stopped and sat growling while pedestrians looked on giving us a wide berth. "Undercover work, folks," I said. "Police dog at work. Move along, please." I stood and took off the coat and what I was wearing beneath meant I looked a lot more professional now.

They slowly dispersed. I handcuffed the guy as if I were a cop and patted him down. The crowd moved away, and I was able to get him into the candy store, where I cuffed him up also.

"Are there any others, or should I put the dog on you again?"

"I'm not telling you anything, asshole."

"Chance," I said, and she was at his legs until he started screaming for me to drag her off. "Chance," I said again. And she stepped back. "Okay, now speak to me or you get more of the same."

"Some guy hired us to stand by and come into the restaurant when he called. He wanted us to remove you from the restaurant, then make sure you were never seen again."

"Know why this guy wanted to do a thing like that?"

I got no response, so I planted a karate chop on his neck rendering him useless.

I removed my disguise, crossed the street with Chance, and entered the restaurant to await my future.

The smile on Tony's face when he walked in twenty minutes later full of confidence was overwhelming.

"Afternoon."

"Afternoon, Rider, long time no see."

"Sure is! Two full days."

"Get your orders to leave town?"

"Thinking about it," I said.

"What do you mean, thinking about it?"

"Well, I'm not sure I'm going anywhere," I said. "Frankly I'm confused." I had a smile on my face now. "Tell me this, will you, Tony?" How did the gang members know I was home every time they came to my house? Who twice sent in enemy helicopters to get me, while I was in the jungle? How did the drug manufacturers know I was coming and have time to train Chance? And who was behind getting Tiff and Julie involved plus Gus and Parker?

He nodded as though taking me seriously. "Well, Rider, I wish I could tell you. We have folks trying to figure it out as we speak."

"Very interesting, Tony," I said, looking him in the eye. "But you and I both know who it is."

Tony hesitated, playing with his napkin; the hesitation was far too long for someone in Tony's position.

"Oh hey, hang on—you don't think it was me, do you? Why would I do something like double-crossing my own man? No, it was someone else, and we're working hard on it."

"Money," I said, shaking my head. "You did it for money."

"Get serious, Rider. You're way off in left field here."

"Don't think so, my friend. I know for certain that it was you."

"I'm curious what you think you have but—"

He pretended to get a text on his phone. "Dammit, hang on. I have to answer this," he said and got up. The phone in my pocket started vibrating, I didn't answer it. "Give me a minute, will you, Rider? This is important."

"Sure, I have to hit the can anyway."

By the time I was in the bathroom he had phoned. I answered. "Yeah."

"Come in and get him!"

"Okay," I answered.

I went back to the table and sat across from Tony, with my Glock handy if needed.

"Problems, Tony?" I asked, sitting down.

"What? No, just something time sensitive." He looked down at his phone.

So, we sat and waited. Tony started fidgeting and looking at the door.

"Is something bothering you, Tony?"

"No, no, some things take time," he said, still fidgeting.

"If you're waiting for the three thugs you hired to take me out, the only place you're going to see them is in jail with you." I smiled at him.

Tony's face fell.

I nodded to my backup sitting across the restaurant, and he called McClung.

Tony started to get up and thought better of it when he saw McClung and three other officers wandering in. Surrounding Tony, they told him he was under arrest, searched him and read him his rights. Then they nodded at me and went and sat at an adjoining table to give me a little one on one time with my handler.

"Okay Tony," I said looking him in the eye. "Spill the beans. At least let me know why you did it?"

Tony looked bewildered. I sat and waited. "First of all," Tony blurted out, "I didn't realize that you were as good or as bright as you are. I thought things would have been much easier, but you fooled me. You fooled everyone. As you said, the money I was being paid, for inside information was going to give me an early retirement. Now it looks like I won't be needing it."

I watched and listened as Tony ever so slowly moved to the outside edge of his seat. Without warning, he was up, and headed for the door—or at least that's what he thought. My foot foiled his progress. Laying on the floor he was handcuffed then led out.

Chance and I left the restaurant as they were pushing a still bewildered Tony into the back seat of the cruiser.

My ride home was uneventful except for one stop because Chance was sick, and that's exactly how I felt. Opening my front door, I was confronted by Julie sitting on my couch, feet tucked under her, with a big smile on her face. Chance started to growl. I had forgotten to change the locks.

"I came by, and when I saw that you hadn't changed the locks, I figured I was welcome back, so here I am, Rider."

I opened my mouth to answer when the door buzzer rang. I turned around with Chance following and opened the front door.

"Hello stranger," Tiff said, looking down. "May I come in?"

I stepped aside without saying anything, and Tiff brushed by me to the full glare of Julie.

"Tiff this is Julie. Julie, Tiff." There was a moment of hesitation by both ladies. The two ladies who had double crossed me.

Julie stood up and very hesitantly shook Tiff's extended hand.

"Well," I said, "this is very interesting. I didn't realize that either one of you would have the gall to come back here tonight."

My Phone vibrated.

CHAPTER

There was a coded message

>name's lance. 10:00 pickup.
>I'll be present, too bad about Tony.

After a fantastic meal I said good bye to the ladies, packed as best I could leaving the heavier items for the movers, and left Galt hopefully never to return.

If you enjoyed this novel and would like to drop me a line or a review, please do so, I look forward to hearing from you. If you didn't, just wait till the next block buster comes out, I'm sure you will enjoy it.

If you would like to be in the running to have your first name representing one of the characters in my next novel, please submit it to the email below. I take no responsibility for the type of character your name will be representing.

doublecrossed2021@gmail.com